Cabañuelas

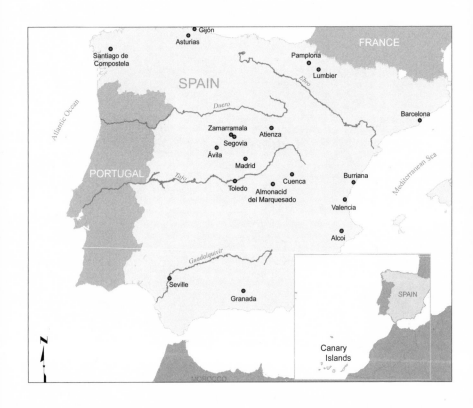

Cabañuelas

A Novel

Norma Elia Cantú

University of New Mexico Press • Albuquerque

ISBN 978-0-8263-6061-8 (paper)
ISBN 978-0-8263-6062-5 (e-book)

Library of Congress Cataloging-in-Publication data is on file with the Library of Congress.

Cover illustrations courtesy of Vecteezy.com
Designed by Felicia Cedillos
Composed in Centaur MT Std 11/14

To all who transcend borders, fronteras of all kinds on all levels,
to all nepantlerxs who love their borderlands, to Elsa,
sister and best friend, and to Elvia, whose love completes me.

Living on borders and in margins, keeping intact one's shifting and multiple identity and integrity, is like trying to swim in a new element, an "alien" element.

—GLORIA ANZALDÚA

Yo no soy bonita, ni lo quiero ser, porque las bonitas se echan a perder.

—CHILDHOOD HAND CLAPPING RHYME

. . . only the things I didn't do crackle after the blazing dies.

—NAOMI SHIHAB NYE

Contents

Part IV La Cruz de mayo

Part V Epilogue

Las Cabañuelas

Every January my father would figure out las Cabañuelas; he would note the predictions by observing what happened the first thirty-one days of a new year. Once, on my birthday on January 3—I must've been seven or eight—he taught me to tell how far away lightening had struck by counting the seconds between the lightening and the thunderclap. He also taught me about las Cabañuelas: Today—January 3—corresponds to March, so it is not so cold, but it's not warm. But will it rain? he asked, and then he proceeded without waiting for an answer, We'll wait until the twenty-second and then the thirty-first to find out the complete picture.

Confused, I asked for an explanation.

The first twelve days correspond to the months, and then the next twelve days correspond to the months in reverse. He wrote it down for me in Spanish:

1 y 24—Enero	5 y 20—Mayo	9 y 16—Septiembre
2 y 23—Febrero	6 y 19—Junio	10 y 15—Octubre
3 y 22—Marzo	7 y 18—Julio	11 y 14—Noviembre
4 y 21—Abril	8 y 17—Agosto	12 y 13—Diciembre

Entonces, from the twenty-fifth to the thirtieth, the days are divided into halves, so the morning of the twenty-fifth indicates January, the afternoon February, and so on. Then it all hinges on *one* day—the last day of January. Each hour stands for a month until you reach noon, and then the next twelve hours count the months again in reverse. So, you take what is happening on the third and on the twenty-second of January, plus what the morning of the twenty-sixth is like, and then 3:00 a.m. and 10:00 p.m. on the thirty-first. Observe it all in detail, and las Cabañuelas will tell you what kind of March it will be. ¿Me entiendes? ¿Sí?

¡Gracias!

A mis antepasados and the Creator who guide my life y a mi familia in all its complexity—I acknowledge and thank them all for their unconditional love and support. I especially thank Elvia E. Niebla and Elsa C. Ruiz for their love and for being there . . . here . . . everywhere. Doy gracias to the people throughout Spain who allowed me into their homes and hearts, who shared stories and histories of their beloved towns and fiestas, who offered friendship and companionship to a Tejana/Chicana who may not have known what to do with such generosity. Gracias also to the staff who labor at the Biblioteca Nacional in Madrid and the Fulbright-Hays Program; without their support I would not have been able to complete the research for this and other projects. My deepest gratitude to my fellow Fulbrighters, with whom I shared many adventures during our time in Madrid—Alan, Gina, Dwayne, Ivy, Robert, Sarah, and others. Thank you to Andrea Christina Wirsching for her magical map skills. I want to thank my distant cousin Henry Bisharat for access to my great grandmother's photo. Heartfelt gratitude to my current academic home, Trinity University for providing the time and space for me to finish the book, and to the amazing folks at the University of New Mexico Press: Elise McHugh, the copyeditors, the readers, the designers, and the entire editorial staff, whose work enriched and contributed to the birthing of this work of love. ¡Gracias!

Nena relishes every moment with her large, boisterous family. It's Christmas Eve in Laredo, Texas, and soon she will be leaving home to spend nine months in Spain. Nostalgic and anticipating her upcoming trip, she is already missing them all, missing this place, this land. Her home. The house on San Carlos Street that holds such love. Such sorrows.

The day begins with the usual hustle and bustle of the Christmas Eve tamalada, the family's tamal-making tradition that goes back in the family's history for generations. Nena wakes up to the sound of the neighbor's rooster, Ernesto, with his scraggly cock-a-doodle-doo or ki-ki-ri-ki—depending on whether it is Spanish or English. Nena smiles at the thought of old Ernesto being bilingual.

She wants to spend a few more minutes in bed under her thick colcha, the quilt Bueli and Mami made for her when she left for college. But. It's 5:00 a.m., and she must get up and get to the tortillería to get the dough for the tamales! Soon she's at the door of Tortillería la Fe, but already there's a line. Get there by five, Papi had advised, or they might run out; you'll have to wait, hacer cola. Giddy with the smell of corn, Nena waits patiently as people stream into the small tortillería. Twenty pounds, she orders, and the young man in charge asks, ¿Le ponemos las hojas? ¿El chile? What else, husks? No, she declines. Only the masa.

The night before, Papi had pulled out the old hand-operated molino to grind the meat that he and Mami had bought: "un trozo de carne pa' tamales." Beto the butcher knew exactly what that meant and asked, How many pounds of masa? Veinte, Mami answers expertly. Como 9 o 10 kilos, Papi says, enough for twenty pounds of dough. Beto doles out the trozo needed and wraps it in white butcher paper then hands it to Mami with a wink.

Nena comes home to find her sisters chatting away as they shred the meat using forks and knives; it's still too hot to handle with their hands. Mami has been up early to get it all set up for the three kinds of tamales—meat, chicken, and beans. First, she cooks the meat—pork and a little bit of beef—a guisado with rich spices. The chicken should be ready in no time, as it cooks along with the pot of beans on the stove. Mami prepares all the fillings: guisando the chicken with a rich tomatillo sauce—her special secret a spoonful of sugar added as she purees the salsa in the blender. She prepares the pork with two kinds of red chile—pasilla and de árbol—just enough to give it taste without making it too spicy. The beans, too, are cooking on the stove, prepared with cloves of garlic and strips of bacon for taste. Once they're cooked, Mami will fry and refry them, set them aside to cool.

Mami orchestrates the whole operation, assigns different people to different tasks. Most of the kids and young teens are "embarrando," spreading the masa on the corn husks. Tía Licha prepared the dough, kneading and testing it for readiness by dropping a bit the size of a pea into a glass of cold water. If it floats—and it does . . . the pearl size bit of masa plops down to the bottom but quickly bounces up to the top—it's ready. Let the spreading begin! The comadres, Mami's friends and neighbors, come to help. Mami goes to help them when they prepare their tamales. That's how it is. Reciprocal. Everyone helping one another.

Mami fills the hojas then folds each tamal carefully and with a loving thought pats it down and places it on a cookie sheet. Tía Licha, always in charge of the hojas, pours boiling water onto the husks that she has cleaned and placed in the big tin tub. She's carefully separated and trimmed the corn husks. Her job? To keep them moist and coming so those spreading the masa always have the best hojas ready.

Papi also lends a hand, laughing at a joke comadre 'Pifania is telling. Something about a rancher who wanted to marry off his son so he goes from ranch to ranch to find him a wife. At each place he asks to see the most beautiful young woman there. At one place that would be Pantaleona, but when the rancher commanded, Que venga la más bonita, Pantaleona's younger brother proudly replied, La más bonita ¡es Panta! So the rancher tells the son, Pícale al burro, and off they go on their way, the rancher missing his chance to marry his son to the most beautiful woman around, all because of the misunderstanding. The young kids don't get the joke, so Mamagrande patiently explains it to them. The apodo for Pantaleona is "Panta," but together "es Panta," which means "it is Panta," can sound like "espanta," or "she scares people."

As they are working on the tamales, Mamagrande starts a game where everyone has to say their favorite dicho: De tal palo tal astilla, she says and points to Nena's brother, Jesse, who is helping Papi. Mas vale pájaro en mano que ver un ciento volar, Nena's sister Dahlia contributes. I have a better one, says Esperanza. Más pronto cae un hablador que un cojo. They all laugh because Junior, Nena's cousin, is hobbling around with a sprained ankle. El que no habla, dios no lo oye, Papi says. And comadre 'Pifania pipes in: Cada quien pa' su cada cual. Wait, that's not a dicho, says Mamagrande—or is it? Sí, sí, they all agree it is. The kids can't contribute because they don't know the dichos, so the adults help them out. Cada cabeza es un mundo, Nena says, when it's her turn.

Mamagrande takes each single tamal from the cookie sheet and places it in the tamalera for steaming; she strategically arranges the tamales in a spiral around the tejolote, the pestle of the molcajete. Nena thinks of the Fibonacci design she learned about in her college math class. Mamagrande prays over the tamalera, the steamer where the tamales will cook. She prays again as she carefully places a heavy brick on top of the lid to keep the steam in the tightly sealed pot. While the tamales are cooking, everyone who has come to help goes off to get dressed for the party. Some will come back for the rosary, others will come for the party, and most will come back for dinner. Still others—las comadres— won't come tonight; they will gather with their own families for dinner.

It's the last Christmas of the decade, and what a decade it's been. The seventies! Perhaps it will be the last Christmas that they are all together like this in the kitchen making tamales, laughing, reminiscing. Telling jokes. Chismeando, gossiping about those who are not helping with the tamalada. The stories go on and on as everyone remembers Nena's tías and tíos, her cousins, in Monterrey, Chicago, Dallas, Houston. She still misses her brother, Tino, still remembers the last Christmas he spent with the family in 1966. Then he was off to boot camp and training and only came for Thanksgiving, not Christmas, in 1967 before he left for Vietnam. The 1968 Tet Offensive, a distant historical event hits Nena's family. Tino is gone. Will never be there with them for holidays, will never be there with them for what is to come. The joys of new babies, the sorrow of grandparents' deaths. So much joy and so much pain. No. Tino will not be around to experience all that is to come. He will be forever nineteen. Forever young, like Dylan sings.

Papi gathers everyone who has come by, all decked out in their Christmas Eve finery. They pray the rosary kneeling on pillows, using the rosary beads that Mami keeps in a ceramic box—an angel on the lid guarding its contents. Mamagrande starts the prayers, but Papi helps her along the way. Nena feels a knot at her throat as they conclude the rosary and Papi's sonorous voice begins the letainías. Nena loves the poetry of the lengthy litanies with the beautiful metaphors. He follows with a prayer to Mary, Por estos misterios santos, de que hemos hecho recuerdo, te pedimos, oh María . . . Finally Mami, in her sure and calm voice, begins Nena's favorite prayer to Mary: Dios te salve reina y madre, madre de misericordia, vida y dulzura y esperanza nuestra.

Then it's time for the youngest child to perform: undress the baby Jesus and lay him on a bed of colación, Nena's favorite Christmas candy, on the platter reserved for this very purpose. Everyone lines up to approach the child para adorar al niño dios and ask for a blessing. Kiss his hand, or his foot, or his forehead, Mami instructs the kids, and ask for a blessing. Can I make a wish? asks Xóchitl, Nena's youngest sister who is fifteen.

They move on to the kitchen for the meal. Everyone gathers around the table holding hands. Her father leads with the sign of the cross, then an Our Father and a Hail Mary, first in Spanish and then in English so the grandkids can join in. Then everyone goes around and expresses thanksgiving. When it's Nena's turn she chokes up and thanks everyone for their help while she's away. Xóchitl is shy, doesn't want to say anything: Finally, she murmurs a quick, Thank you God for helping me make the cheerleading squad this year. Papi ends the prayer by asking God for Nena's safe return. His voice cracks a bit, and Nena notes that he is teary eyed. So is Mami. Nena knows in her heart that they are thinking, as she is, of the last Christmas Tino spent with them around this very table. Tino. The brother who came home from Vietnam in a flag-draped coffin. Tino. She wants to reassure them. She's not going to war. She'll be back next year for the tamalada. Back for Christmas and the rosary and the dinner.

Everyone wants to know what she's doing in Spain, why is she going? To do my work, she explains, at the Biblioteca Nacional, to read about fiestas and plays—pastorelas, mojigangas—to analyze the similarities with our own fiestas in Laredo. It's going to be a book. Maybe a documentary.

That seems to satisfy them, but still they are afraid for her. Her sister Esperanza is excited and wants her to go although she is pregnant and will be giving birth in a couple of months and wishes her older sister would be home to share the joy.

Papi was worried she had been fired from her job at the university; he doesn't quite get it that she has applied and received a Fulbright to travel, to study in Spain; that the job is secure. He has consulted with the priest at San Luis Rey Church, Father Bernardino, who is from Spain. He reassures Papi, it's safe. She's going to be okay. Since Tino came back in a casket from Vietnam only twelve years ago, Papi has become more possessive, more wary of his children going off anywhere. He fears for his oldest child although she is no longer a child. But. She is not married. She is too independent. He fears that she will be hurt. That she might not want to come back home.

Right after dinner, before opening the gifts and before midnight mass, Mamagrande takes her aside. She has come from Monterrey to say good-bye. She whispers in her ear, Maybe I'll die while you are over there. Nena hugs her tight, smells her old lady smell, doesn't want to consider the possibility. Remember what you have learned. Hazle caso al corazón, but don't go falling in love, mi niña, you hear, ¿me entiendes? You come home! she says out loud and everyone laughs.

After misa de gallo at San Luis Rey Church, the usual Christmas Eve midnight mass, Nena reviews the day's events. Feelings of love and nostalgia invade her thoughts like the warm waters of the Gulf caress the shores, and she feels her whole being caressed by love. She basks in the memories that surround her like the glow of the Christmas tree lights. As she drifts off into a dream, she's comforted by the familiar sounds of night. On this special night, special and familiar sounds signal home: neighbors popping firecrackers, the neighbor's dog barking, Tejano music blaring from a neighbor's radio. Faded and distant sounds that penetrate and seep into her consciousness. A siren wails in the madrugada. Orion rules the skies. A distant star sparkles above all the others.

Part 1   Época de desamor

Fiestas de enero

*A*zucena Cantú, a.k.a. Nena, a folklorist studying fiestas, a student of life—after all, isn't life a series of fiestas?—sips her café con leche at the corner café, marvels at the urban hustle and bustle of the crowds on the busy Madrid street. It's Fiesta de Reyes in Madrid. But. "Saudade," Nena scribbles in her pocket calendar, her agenda as they call it here, with the cover image of a two-faced Janus looking backward and forward all at once. Drowning in an overwhelming sea of loneliness of homesickness she gasps for air, dates her entry: el día de los Reyes Magos. The day of the Epiphany, January 6, 1980. Feeling: Saudade.

She's alone. In Madrid. What else but saudade? Good to have a word for it, a Portuguese word for a yearning for what was left behind, for a feeling that has no word in English, "homesickness" not quite it, nor in Spanish, "añoranza" almost the same but not. Nena resolves to be strong y se aguanta. Grin and bear it, she tells herself, This too shall pass. Soon after she's immersed in her life in Madrid, it subsides somewhat, but the love for her land, for her home, will remain nestled in her heart, will not let her go. An umbilical cord tugs at her insides, tying her to that place where her grandmother and her mother buried her ombligo when she was but a few days old, when that dry piece of her, reddish brown with a gray tinge, fell off to be ritually buried, to forever call her back to her place in the universe, the place where she is most herself. Most grounded. Her place. Her home.

Throughout her stay, but especially during the first month, in January, she will remain homesick for the border, for her communities on the banks of the Rio Grande—Laredo and Nuevo Laredo. Yearning for the comings and goings of her home, filled with children and neighbors and family visiting from Chicago or Monterrey or just down the street. The love for that land, for that place, palpable and real. She is one with that land. No, she had chided herself one day as she worked in her mother's garden and felt the connection to the land, not just visceral but with conciencia, with full consciousness. No, I will not be a Scarlett O'Hara! It's more symbolic, this love I have. It's the love of el olor a tierra mojada when it rains; the new green of the mesquite and the yellow blossoms of the huisache in early spring; it's the love for a land few can understand. The love of rattlesnakes and horny toads, of red ants as big as roaches and roaches as big as giant moths; love for a sky filled with thousands of monarchs migrating south, a sky where the cenzontle, the woodpecker, and the hummingbird along with the egret and other migratory birds mingle and roost for the night on creek beds, tree branches, and telephone wires. You have to watch where you park or your car will be a mess in the morning! Yes, her homeland, a complicated land where the grackles' deafening cacophony ushers in nightfall, and the afternoon skies fill with puffy clouds that promise rain but seldom deliver.

Her South Texas home resides in her as she resides in it—they are one. She feels the river waters, the Rio Grande, the Rio Bravo coursing through her veins. The sweet scents emanating from her mother's treasured sweet-smelling garden, the huele de noche, el azahar on the orange and lemon trees, the jasmine and gardenia blossoms, each taking turns to sweeten the air; these are the scents that are ever with her. Nena feels a pull, an inexplicable tie to that land, that piece of earth, her beloved South Texas—and northern Mexico, too. Texas with its troubled history of political corruption, of despots ruling with iron hands, and of Texas Rangers lynching Mexicans. Of drugs and violence, but a land full of promise, too. A Mexico that is almost not Mexico. Norteño and fierce out so far, so different from the center. This land where two countries come together, a confluence of cultures, where two languages mingle into a unique Spanglish, Tex-Mex, where two ways of measuring the world coexist—pounds or kilos, miles or kilómetros, litros or gallons. Nena learned to measure the world not in school but in daily life growing up. It is the land of Sunday carne asadas in the backyard with friends and family: the women cooking in the kitchen, preparing the rice, the potato salad; the men drinking Coronas or Schlitz, or Modelo, or Lone Star, as they grill the cabrito or prepare the brisket. Sometimes women drinking, too; sometimes men cooking the rice, too. Tequila shots to celebrate birthdays or just because. The land where musics blend seamlessly, Tejano and rock and roll, punk and conjunto. The land of Tejano dances at the Civic Center on Friday nights and quinceañeras on Saturday nights. The land of a unique gift-giving culture with its regalitos for every and all occasions, or just because. The culture that protects and shelters. But also the culture that circumscribes and limits. How can she not love this land? How can she not hate this land? This land of her ancestors? This land of the future? How can she not love the cultural experiment that it is?

Nena bundles up in wintery Madrid, misses the warmth of home, of South Texas. She has been away from home before: first studying in a small, racist university town only a couple of hours away from Laredo, then to a university in still another racist town in the Midwest. Yet despite the obvious racism that reared its ugly head now and then, she finds friends and caring, loving people. Mentors and colleagues who understand her, who urge her to go on, to do her work. She is sure the same will happen here.

After a lifetime of being surrounded by people, of no privacy, of being the older sister, the good daughter, the good student, she is on her own. Even in the Midwest, family was there to support, to offer a warm home-cooked meal, a home to come home to if need be. Older now, she has learned to be herself, to be by herself. She is a whole ocean away from her land, her people. Alone.

In Madrid, she sits alone. Alone at a tiny table in the café that will become her refuge, her private space. She writes: What am I doing here? What draws me to this alien land, this land of conquerors, this land peopled by those I learned to hate when I heard the stories of their cruel ways, how they destroyed sacred books, defiled life, uprooted our customs? Customs they couldn't kill, couldn't erase.

She knows Madrid is her destiny; the dream nestled in her heart for decades has come to pass. She will learn about her roots, about the origin of so many of the fiestas she studies, about her culture. She looks out the window through the lace curtains at passersby, looks around at those in the café with her, and reconciles her doubts, her fears. It's all beginning to feel familiar; she begins to feel at home.

On the night of the Epiphany, she is out on the street watching the crowds gather in anticipation of the parade, the Cabalgata de los Reyes Magos. Everyone's bundled up against the brisk January winds; the children, wide-eyed, not sure of what's to come, hold an adult's hand to feel safe. The fiesta and the celebration send Nena reeling to the past, to the celebrations of Reyes on the border. How her family would travel to Monterrey from Laredo to be with her paternal grandparents. Her eyes flood with tears, remembering—Mamagrande with the aquamarine eyes, Papagrande with his hazel eyes like her father's, stately at exactly six feet tall, aunts, uncles, cousins, and more cousins. The shoes filled with chunks of coal . . . or with candy on this very day, el día de Reyes. If you were good all year long you got candy; if not, just chunks of coal. But no one ever got coal in that house on Washington Street in front of the Alameda. Monterrey, a city south of Laredo, in Mexico. It too is part of Nena's home. Her land. She misses her childhood. The past is a foreign country, someone once said. Perhaps, Nena thinks, it is so, but it's not forgotten. She can smell the leche quemada candy cooking in the big cazuelas in Mamagrande's kitchen. Every holiday they traveled south to Monterrey. Somehow Mami managed to ensure that they come bearing gifts—oranges and grapefruit from their trees, hand-knit caps, gloves, scarfs, and candy, caramelos. Nena loves the colación—Christmas candy—her Grandmother buys en el mercado. The sugar-coated anise seed colación so unlike the peppermint of the red-and-white-striped candy canes, the caramelos Nena's family brings from Laredo.

Nena's Mamagrande fills the living room with the nacimiento. Pesebre. Crèche. Belén. So many names for the same thing—the figures representing Jesus's birth. Tía Luz sets it up every year with the ancient delicate ceramic figurines—the holy family: Mary, Joseph, and the child. An angel and a star suspended above the manger. Several animals: a cow, a burro, and tiny chickens and ducks. The characters from the Pastorela: Bato and Gila and a hermit and the devils, all seven of them! Of course, the three Magi, los Reyes Magos, three kings, their mode of transportation a camel, an elephant, and a horse—the treasured figures passed down from one generation to the next. A tiny mirror is a pond and tiny fir trees rest on angel hair. A bright star atop the pesebre that Mamagrande inherited from her great grandmother, the daughter—or was it the granddaughter?—of the original immigrant from Spain, from Jerez de la Frontera, the ancestral home of Juan Manuel de Vargas, Mamagrande's great grandfather. The photograph of her great grandmother haunts Nena. María de Jesús Ynocencia Ayala Ábrego Garza. Who was she?

Now that she's in Spain, Nena is tempted to do research, go to Jerez, dig in the archives. But. She decides against it. Let others do that, she thinks. I must focus on the work at hand. A distant cousin has already found that their great-great grandfather, Juan Manuel de Vargas, arrived in Monterrey in the 1770s with the Spanish military. The handsome Spaniard soon married the daughter of the mayor of Monterrey in 1776—Nena was incredulous, thought her cousin was inventing ancestors in high places like so many Mexicans trying to find connections to Spain. But then she saw the documents and was convinced. She had to accept that one of her earliest ancestors was a military man, a man of violence who no doubt perpetrated hateful acts against the native people, against his enemies. But Juan Manuel, Nena imagines, was also a romantic. So, when he met the well-placed young woman of eyes so blue they reminded him of the summer sky in Jerez, he knew they were

destined to be together. How they met is a mystery, but Nena imagines they met as young people of the time met, through mutual family friends, or at a dance en el casino in Monterrey, or perhaps at church. No matter how, what matters is that they met, and the rest is history. Nena's history.

Mamagrande's mother, María de Jesús, the story goes, was practical and ambitious. She married José María Ayala Garza, and among their ten children was María Guadalupe, Nena's grandmother. Mamagrande, who is the link to Nena's roots in northern Mexico. But. Her maternal line is another story. The story of a border family full of foreigners and Indians, Coahuiltecan no doubt. Her ancestors generations back have lived and died on this land that is now south Texas and northern Mexico. Maurilio, her maternal grandfather, worked for the railroad. His people were from Monclova. He was certainly Indian, but no one ever talks about it. No one claims their Indian roots. Instead everyone refers to their Spanish roots.

Nena's father tells stories about Mamagrande's siblings, among them María Antonia Vargas Ayala and her three brothers, Manuel, José María, and Regino. During the Mexican Revolution Papi's ancestors supported pro-revolutionary president Francisco I. Madero. Tío Manuel, especially, intrigues Nena, because the story goes he ran a Spiritist religious printing press. He was President Madero's spiritual advisor and served as chief of police in Mexico City during Madero's presidency. Was it his son who became a priest? Nena wonders. Regino eventually became mayor of San Nicolás de los Garza near Monterrey. Both of mamagrande's brothers died tragic deaths, according to family stories: Regino died in a duel in 1927, and a union member murdered José María in 1940. Nena's father tells these stories and is proud but conflicted as he is a union man. He remembers the event and how his father made his sons swear not to get involved in the violence. Papagrande was a pacifist and preached peace at all costs, even when his eldest son, Gonzalo, was killed in a brawl at a village dance, a case of mistaken identity, everyone claims. But. Papi witnessed the murder, saw his brother take his last breath. He lets his moustache grow from that day forward in honor of his older brother.

Mamagrande. Named María Guadalupe to honor our Lady who reigns over all Mexicans. She inherits no one's name; she is the first to be named Guadalupe in the Vargas Ayala line. But Mamagrande inherits her great grandmother's blue eyes, and at fifteen with her father's blessing marries Vicente N. Cantú, the twenty-five-year-old third son of a landed family.

Vicente, whose lineage is not as clear. Was he Cantó and changed it to Cantú? Nena knows it makes no difference as they are variants. But. The other story is that he invented a middle name and used "N" for "None" as a joke. Was he really a descendant of the military man, Carlos Cantú? The capitán whose family hailed from Italy originally. Who came to the Americas by way of Islas Canarias. Was he from the tiny medieval town, Cantú, in northern Italy? Was his a Jewish family ousted during the dark times when so many fled, so many died?

Nena's father is one of seven who survive; seven more siblings die either as infants or tragically: Alicia dies of love; Luz, killed by a stray bullet; Gonzalo, killed by mistake at a dance brawl. Four others die as infants, all buried at the panteón in Nuevo Laredo.

In the photo at their fiftieth wedding anniversary, las bodas de oro, their seven children—Rogelio, Vicente, Carmen, Jesús, Lydia, Florentino, and María de la Luz—surround them. Papagrande is stately; Mamagrande wears a golden diadem with seven gold leafs—one for each of her children—and a black mantilla over her white hair. She's only sixty-five. So much pain! Sorrow! Did she ever know joy? Surely she did, as most women do. Nena imagines Mamagrande smiling as she cradles a newborn infant in her arms. She imagines Mamagrande praying for her children as they go off into the world.

In Nena's memory Mamagrande is always in mourning. She rules the kitchen like a queen her empire. No one else cooks in her kitchen. She waves a cooking spoon, a rolling pin, a knife, like a scepter. She wears a blue apron that she herself has sewn, trimmed with dark-blue rickrack and piping. She sits in a rocking chair as she crochets and knits while watching telenovelas. Nena and her cousins, playing jacks or jumping rope just outside, can hear the TV turned up high because Mamagrande can't hear but won't wear a hearing aid. Hard to imagine that tiny old wrinkled woman as the young fifteen-year-old bride in the photograph that hangs in the living room. Hard to imagine her singing a lullaby to a child in Anáhuac at the family parcela. Hard to imagine the pain as deep as the oceans, las penas, the pain of losing loved ones—children, parents, siblings. Hard to imagine.

Reyes Magos

*I*n Madrid, in this land of kings with its own share of magicians, Nena stands amid the crowds in the cold, watches the parade, marvels at the Cabalgata de los Reyes Magos with three gentlemen, caballeros of the elite, who are the three kings riding camels atop flatbed trucks. Decked out for the parade, they shower the crowd with caramelos. Caramelos that she knows to call gomas, chiclosos, dulces, hard candy, taffy, but never the caramelos she knows so well, the red-and-white-striped candy canes of Christmas. It is the day of the Epiphany, and her eyes tear with the cold, or is she catching something? Or is it that she misses her home? The three kings, the magi, magicians who knew the mysteries of the universe, of a child born to bring peace. She misses the rosca de reyes, the sweet bread with the tiny doll baked right in it. Who will be the lucky one to find it this year? Who will host the party on February 2, the candlemass feast? El día de la candelaria. Who will "levantar al niño," raise the child Jesus decked out in a new outfit and sit him on his tiny wooden chair, a throne? Who will put out the buñuelos and the champurrado for neighbors and friends to enjoy?

January in Madrid. Christmas season over, but still shoppers crowd the department stores, el Corte Inglés, Cortefiel. Must take advantage of linen sales at the lencería stores, trying to clear out inventory, exquisite linens embroidered and edged in lace and made by nuns shut away in

convents or old women dressed in black, shut away in small rural Spanish towns. Must get the latest shoe fashions at shoe stores already displaying spring styles. The bookstores are teeming with people. It's after the holidays—Día de Reyes signals the end of the long Christmas holiday, the most important commercial season, even here—maybe especially here—in this most Catholic of countries.

In no time the Christmas season is gone and the magic along with it. Los Reyes and their gifts will return next year. Olentzero will return to Navarra and País Vasco. Nena runs into the legend in one of her readings on Christmas traditions. The figure of the carbonero remains a mystery—is it pre-Christian? So much to learn! So much to research!

Roomies

𝒩ena settles into the apartment in Madrid, a "piso," she learns to call it. Glad it's worked out with Veronica, a.k.a. Ronnie, and Giovanna as roommates. Ronnie, a Norteamericana from Michigan, is the epitome of a Midwesterner—blonde, petite, with eggshell-smooth skin. She's a scholar working on old medieval texts at the Biblioteca Nacional. Giovanna, from California, is tall and angular, her hair a modified afro, soft blonde curls framing her lively face. Is she Italian? Irish? Nena guesses Italian because of her name. Her area is Golden Age theater. Sylvia, who returned to the States at the end of the fall semester. The Fulbright office in Madrid connected Nena with them. Works out perfectly, Ronnie said when Nena called from Texas. Sylvia leaves in December, and you arrive in January.

Easily, smoothly, Nena settles into the piso, the apartment on calle Rodríguez San Pedro near Metro San Bernardo, in a staid, old Madrid neighborhood. The landlady, señora Barreneche, an empty nester, has converted part of the family's piso into an apartment to rent to students from the States and make some cash to supplement her widow's pension; she lives in the piso next door and fancies herself a surrogate mother to the Norteamericanas. Can't quite get it that Nena, a brown woman, is also a Norteamericana and insists she must be from South America. Señora Berreneche marvels at Nena's command of both English and Spanish.

Soy de Texas, Nena clarifies, teaches her a bit of history. Los Estados Unidos won the war with Mexico and took over more than half of Mexico's territory. Mexico was part of Spain; Texas was also part of Spain at one time. Por eso, we speak Spanish.

That first month in Madrid, Nena fills her pocket calendar, her agenda, with citas—movies, dinners, copas with friends, and trips. It is January, her birth month. A true Capricorn, she plans it all out. Researching the rituals, the religious dramas. At the Biblioteca Nacional Nena reads the oldest play written in vernacular Spanish, a mere fragment of a play that reenacts the visit by Gaspar, Melchor, y Balthazar—the three magi—Los tres reyes! No mention of one being black, and yet he is always depicted as such, as an African riding an elephant, bearing gifts for the Christ child. Myrrh. Incense. Gold. Gifts that signal wealth, gifts fit for a king. It's exactly what she is looking for—evidence that the traditions in Laredo are rooted in Spanish as well as indigenous practices. And here it is, the same elements from la Pastorela—the old shepherd's play still performed in the barrios of Laredo by common everyday people as an act of faith. But there is no Indio in this version. Still. The roots lie in this fragment of text, this cultural artifact. But this is only part of the work she is to do in Spain. She suspects she has many lessons to learn, many lessons to teach. That's what scholars do. Research. Teach. Learn. Serendipitously, the work appears, and you follow it sometimes blindly to the project that emerges. Trust. She must learn to trust. Se hace camino al andar, wrote Machado. That is what she must do, trust that the path will open before her.

Nena continues the work, not quite sure what that work is, where it will lead, but certain that this—the reading, the writing, the digging in the archives—this is what she must do. This work. She thinks of her teaching and how this work may surface in her lectures, how her students will benefit from her experience in the archives. For now, she is content to take notes, to write in her journal, and to read and read and read. That is the work.

Soon, too soon, by the end of January in fact, the enterprise has changed direction. Her planned course of study is derailed. She realizes that she wants more freedom, that she no longer wants to be limited to analyzing the archives on the fiestas of Spain and finding correlations to the ones in south Texas. But that is what got her the Fulbright: her proposed project, to read what is in the Biblioteca Nacional about the ancient religious fiestas and the contemporary expressions. She is going in a different direction and is concerned about the project. Nena's research plans change. She shares her concerns with Giovanna and Ronnie. They understand. But. Not quite. They are focused on documents. Manuscripts. Can't imagine Nena's research. Fieldwork that will gather data on the fiestas; she must go out and visit the towns and participate in the fiestas. That is what her work becomes—fiesta fieldwork. But.

Every Sunday, Nena reads in *El País* a weekly listing of the fiestas all over Spain commemorating a community's heritage, a legacy—a patron saint's day, or secular celebrations for a town's bygone glory. She had expected to travel no farther than to and from the library, where she could read and write, but soon the fiestas all over Spain beckon, daring her to venture out into the España profunda, the Spain that lies beyond the bullfights and flamenco of the travel brochures, asking that she immerse herself in the small-town life of a Spain that is being transformed before her very eyes. Post-Franco Spain takes her along a different path, compelling her to attend the fiestas, to know them viscerally and not just intellectually. To drink the wine and eat the special foods— paella in Valencia, tarta de Santiago, mazapán in Toledo, montaditos, tapas. She must live it, not just read about it in the library. She will travel to towns and villages, enjoy the immersion into the cultural event as she photographs the spectacle, talks to the people who retain their ancient traditional dances, who sing traditional songs, and who don traditional dress. Her calendar fills. A full agenda every weekend.

Having roommates is a new thing. Nena has never lived with veritable strangers. But she is happy to have their company. Their views on what is going on in the world. Their advice. Glad that she can drag Ronnie to a movie or ask Giovanna to go for a walk at her favorite park, el Retiro. They get along well and support each other. It's okay to take a day off, they tell Giovanna when she has severe cramps. Don't worry about it. Stay home. Nena fixes her a chamomille tea the way her mother would fix it for her.

It's okay, Nena. We understand, Ronnie says when Nena apologizes for staying up all hours. She is a night owl, they joke, and they are early birds. They apologize for getting up so early, waking her up when she's just gone to bed. Soon they fall into a routine. Roomies, Giovanna declares they are. Nena likes the sound of it. Roomies. We are like sisters. Almost.

During the week, Nena sits at a desk in the Biblioteca Nacional, the library of her dreams, near the stately post office building on the roundabout with the fountain of Cibeles, majestic and regal. She walks along Recoletos, the wide boulevard that leads to el Prado. She fantasizes— sees herself in the nineteenth century hanging out with writers and scholars; they too worked in this library. Met for a drink at Café Gijón. Emilia Pardo Bazán and Galdós, arm in arm, walk down the Gran Vía. Or maybe not—the scandal would've been too great! Pardo Bazán was a folklorist too. She worked among her people, did her fieldwork in Galicia. Nena yearns to find out more. Yearns to travel to Galicia. She's read Caro Baroja's research on Galician folklore and feels drawn. Many years later Nena will travel to A Coruña to visit Pardo Bazán's home-turned-museum and dig into her archives. But. For now, all she can do is imagine and invent a life for her, for them. Imagine and dream.

Morning Ritual

*M*ost mornings, Nena sets out at eight o'clock from her piso. If she's feeling lazy she takes the old-style elevator down to the ground floor, otherwise she walks down the five flights of stairs. The porter greets her in his Galician-accented Castellano, Buenos días. Starched white shirt and hand-knit wool sweater—he must own several identical ones in various shades of blue. Nena imagines his wife or his sister sitting at home knitting. On her way to the metro, she stops at the café across the street from her apartment building. The café has become her refuge, her place to welcome the day. She has come to know the menu, to love the fresh churros, deep-fried twists of flour, dipped like biscotti into a large cup of sweetened café con leche. That and *El País*, the complimentary newspaper for patrons of the café, and she's set to start her morning. Alone and quiet, she reads the paper; all part of the process of waking up. She misses her hometown paper with the local gossip column and the obituaries and the Garfield comic strips. *El País*. Spain's equivalent of the *New York Times*, more liberal and progressive than *ABC* with its conservative bent. The waiters know her; they comfortably cuss and exchange easy banter with the customers and with each other—¡Joder, no seas cagapalo! ¡Coño! She tunes them out, comfortable in her status as outsider. It is mostly middle-aged men on their way to work who stop for their cortado; the older ones chase it with a tiny glass of anís.

Some mornings, when she's late, breakfast will collapse into a brunch; instead of churros, she has a bocadillo de tortilla española, the potato and egg concoction with garlic and salt, fried in olive oil, served in a French bread bun, a bolillo, the word Nena knows for gringos, not bread. The bocadillo de tortilla is not the mariachis of her mornings in Laredo, although the ingredients are the same, save the olive oil. Mariachis. Burritos. Taquitos. Breakfast tacos. All the same. A flour tortilla filled with potatoes and egg, or better still chorizo and egg. Nena remembers working in the CP&L utilities office back in Laredo in the '60s. She has a special place in her heart for Carlos and Gordo, the janitors—or, as they joked, the facilities engineers. Every day, dressed in their blue jumpsuits, they would take orders and go to the nearby panadería el Águila to buy bolillos filled with papa con huevo or chorizo con huevo. Nena and her coworkers—Araceli, Buddy, Aminta—devoured the breakfast delicacy during morning coffee breaks. Strange that the Spanish have not discovered this exquisite combination; with their excellent chorizos and bolillos, it would be a hit. Still. The bocadillo de tortilla española comes close enough and will do as a late breakfast that will serve for lunch.

Some mornings she dawdles by the gypsy selling flowers, admiring them all—red roses, yellow gladiolas, exotic calla lilies, birds-of-paradise. Hopes she will have nardos, the tube roses that are her favorite flower. The gypsy calls her *maja* and *chata* and offers her a bunch of red carnations for a pittance. She accepts the offer. In her hands the carnations explode the drab, gray winter day away with red, passionate bursts. On such days when the gypsy succeeds and makes a sale, Nena dashes upstairs to place them in a vase. Later, a red burst centered on the dining room table will welcome her home. The red livens up the piso as the sound of castanets pierces the heart; the piso is transformed, the staid piso she shares with her roommates, wallpapered with velvet-embossed moss green crying out for the red of the carnations. It's the red of Chinese good luck, of trumpets blaring. The red of her mother's roses, the red of fields carpeted with wild poppies that she will admire from a train window on her way to Granada. Granada, where her heart aches at the plaintive song of the cantaores at the Peña de Platería. She goes with Mario, a bullfighter who is just beginning and has hopes of being the next el Cordobés, the legendary bullfighter who has just returned to the ring from retirement. But.

Raros e incunables

Weekday mornings Nena takes the metro with thousands of madrileños going to work. She arrives at the Biblioteca Nacional at nine o'clock to find fellow researchers waiting for the ujieres, the ushers, to open the doors. Soon after, she's at her usual spot, en la sala de raros e incunables, smack in the middle—the middle desk of the middle row—waiting for the books to arrive, the manuscripts and first editions from the eighteenth century. Or earlier. She works at the sala de raros, the rare books reading room at the Biblioteca. Raros. That is what the scholars who pore over rare manuscripts are, she thinks: raros. Rare birds whose work keeps them inside, stooped over manuscripts, deciphering writings of long ago, looking for clues, for keys to unlock secrets. Among the ones working this spring in Madrid, Nena meets Sean, the tall Australian with the blue eyes, eyes so blue they remind Nena of the prized marbles Tino played with. In a strange-sounding English he tells her a family story of how his Irish family fled Ireland and ended up in Australia. Rose, a small, petite woman who is preparing an edition of Calderón de la Barca's *La vida es sueño*, seeks Nena out and shares her dilemma: she has not found a good hairdresser to trim her short locks in Madrid. Not a problem, Nena volunteers, I can trim your hair; I studied in Monterrey, and I brought my special scissors with me. Steven, the scholar of nineteenth-century Spanish whose mother is from Costa Rica and has an Anglo name because of his gringo father, befriends Nena and joins her and her roommates on outings around Madrid. They all agree that he makes the greatest discovery: an unpublished Galdós novel! ¡Se sacó la lotería! And Nena's roommates: Ronnie, a medievalist collating all editions of not one but two texts by Fray Luis de León; and Giovanna, the Golden Age scholar of theatrical works who seeks clues in the plays of earlier ages. These are her friends, her colleagues. Nena feels at home with them. She too is an odd bird in this world of scholars who spend a lifetime looking at old manuscripts, their minds and hearts in their work. Her goal? To find written records of the fiestas and the celebrations from her homeland; traditions that have traveled across time and space and that have melded with indigenous traditions. She finds allusions here and there, performances of certain plays recorded in church ledgers that allude to the cost of costumes for the Christmas play or the Corpus Christi procession.

The librarians, the workers—also raros—act as they always have. Must be leftovers from the nineteenth century, Nena and her friends joke in the cafeteria over a copita de vino during their afternoon breaks. Raros. But. Sometimes, sometimes a manuscript cannot be found in the stacks, and the librarian with the blue dust jacket comes back empty-handed. No explanation, just a shrug, no está. Thousands of books from collections wait patiently to be catalogued, for this is the time before digitized manuscripts. It is still the time of yellowing index cards handwritten by librarians and neatly filed in wooden drawers before card catalogs become obsolete. Nena imagines the archivists who are long gone and whose existence persists on the tiny, elegant script carefully and masterfully cataloguing the holdings of this or that scholar's library. El Duque or el Marqués, or simply a wealthy man's personal library bequeathed and brought in and added to the stacks. Nena notes that there are no women's archives in the collection.

Boxes upon boxes of the still-to-be catalogued items lie asleep in the inner depths where outsiders are not allowed. It is the domain of the clerks who take the request slip—carbon paper between pink, blue, and yellow, baby colors, she thinks. They retrieve the requested items and bring them back . . . or not. Not Found. The simple reason, no explanation given, none expected. Nena often finds a dead end, no manuscript for a citation she has uncovered in an old catalog or a mention in an old manuscript. Nena learns to be patient. No room for frustration. No room for disappointment. When she hits the jackpot and finds a whole play or a ledger with the entire fiesta documented, she celebrates. Shares her joy with the others—Ronnie, Giovanna, Rose, Sean, and Steven. They do the same when they have found a jewel in the pages of an old archive.

The day she uncovers the pastorela performed in the nineteenth century with a clearly Marxist bent, she is thrilled. The devils are the capitalists, of course. Examining *Teatro antiguo español hasta mediados del siglo XVIII: comedias manuscritas anónimas,* Tomo 5, Nena finds the handwritten scripts of a shepherd's play that resonates with the pastorela still performed on Christmas Eve in a neighbor's backyard in Nena's barrio. Her discovery brings tears of joy, and she feels as if she has found a long-buried treasure.

This is the work. The recovery, the past connecting with the present through the literature of the folk. Only a scholar would be thrilled with such mundane and seemingly meaningless discoveries. Once a Chicano social scientist chided Nena for studying such things, for digging in the Laredo archives at St. Mary's University in San Antonio. What does that do for our people? For la Causa? Nena could only respond with a poem—

You ask: What does an archive hold for us?
What does it do for us? Does it feed the hungry?
Succor those who suffer?
How does it advance our cause?
Our past lives in the archive
Dormant. Exposes violence.
Like códices with depictions of Spanish conquistadores
Slitting the throats of Aztec warriors,

Silent witnesses to a never-ending slaughter,
The archive awaits our work to unearth our history, our truth
—the good, the bad, the beautiful and ugly truths.
The stories feed our imagination,
Our sense of self: we are a people with a history!
Words may not heal a bleeding wound, or offer a salve for a painful
     joint,
But they offer surcease from the suffering of a historical
Record that is a boot at our neck, an erasure that is a knife in our
     heart.
Our history, our literature, our dances, and our rituals
Testimonio of our human experience—all of it lives in the archives
Almacenados, hidden away, stashed away.
Recover it and we recover our truth.
Our bodies carry an archive of suffering, of pain
To decipher, to heal this body
Of one, of multitudes,
Study the archive. Be an archeologist
Unearth all truths.

Happy Birthday

*I*n Madrid that cold January, Nena relishes the cozy warmth of the piso. It's her birthday, and she is called early in the morning by Señora Berreneche to come to the phone. Nena sleepily answers, recognizes Papi's voice. Thinks it may be an emergency, but no, they just want to wish her a happy birthday. Mami and Papi: Muchos días de estos, ¡que la pases bonito! ¡Feliz cumpleaños! Her baby sister, Xóchitl, who is no longer a baby, whispers, Happy birthday, Nena. Her sister Azalia, too: Happy birthday, sis. They have stayed up—it's barely 1:00 a.m. in Laredo, 7:00 in Madrid; Papi timed it just right so they can talk to her. All day their voices stay in her heart.

Riding the Metro, on the way to the library, Nena remembers her last birthday. She had traveled to visit her friends Raúl and Martha who live in DC and Sandra who's visiting from California. No te agüites, Martha had cajoled, we'll have a blast. C'mon! And so they did. They celebrate at a Spanish restaurant near Dupont Circle. The meal, exquisite. She talks of her plans to apply for the Fulbright to realize a cherished dream of traveling to Spain. They are supportive and encouraging. Do it, Martha says. ¿Por qué no? asks Raúl. Órale, Sandra pipes in. Nena loves being in DC with her friends. As they drink glass after glass of sangría, their memories flow: the time that Chela, their mutual friend who had moved to New Mexico, was home for the George Washington's Birthday fiesta and they went across the river into Nuevo Laredo, then tried to cross with some mangoes, knowing full well that they were breaking the law. They laugh remembering Martha's strong, No, sir! when the customs agent asked, Do you have anything to declare? And again, after he sternly asked, Do you have any mangoes? No, sir, Martha insisted. Martha is telling the story so she dramatizes her role.

Nena pitches in: I almost had a panic attack—uniforms do that to me. I don't do well con las autoridades. I think it's from a previous life.

Or from this one, Raúl says—after all, the border's scary.

Nena adds, Remember how strong the smell was? I am sure the agent could smell the mangoes even though Chela had carefully stashed them in the trunk with the Mexican rug and the boxes of galletas marías.

We all chipped in to pay the two hundred dollar multa, and we chalked it up to experience, Martha remembers. What's a small fine paid to have that shiny memory to cement their bond?

So many adventures, Nena exclaims. She reminds them of the many times they got stopped for speeding north on IH 35 heading to San Antonio for a weekend of shopping and going to a concert—was it Tom Jones? No, it could've been when we went to see *Last Tango in Paris*, or maybe a Broadway play. Or Tina Turner.

No sé, but it sure was fun!

It's their karma, they joke, to be together, to celebrate and to commiserate. They toast Nena's birthday. Nena: To good friends! Raúl: To our future! Sandra: To the birthday girl! Martha: To the many birthdays we've shared!

Not so many, Raúl chimes in. We're not that old!

No, but we're all grown up, Martha asserts. And it's been many birthdays we've celebrated. To many more, she jubilantly raises her glass. Clink. Clink. Clink. Like a wind chime, tinkling in the breeze, Nena observes.

We are so lucky! I have my job in DC and so do you, Raúl. And Nena will soon be off to Spain on her Fulbright, all settled in with her university position, a scholar and an artist! You do still paint, no?

Rarely. No hay tiempo, there's just no time, and it's not for sure I'll go to Spain, Nena answers.

Pos claro que sí, you'll see . . . Lástima, I love your portraits! Martha continues: I think we've done pretty good for kids from Laredo. Remember Olivia de la O? She's now a professor, too—teaches English, I think. And Randy, the one who was in community college with us? He's now a CEO. And only thirty-five! Even that guy who jumped out of a window at Christen Junior High, remember? He's back and is a big shot at the bank.

I love Laredo, Nena exclaims. Love the people. Love the place. It's special. Unlike any other. So glad I was able to come home to work; the teaching position is exactly what I want to be doing.

Ay no, Raúl says. I do love some of the people. My family, of course. But. No. I'll never go back there. Raúl is unforgiving. Hates the close-mindedness of that town on the border.

That's why I left for Houston, he says. The gossip and the judging of everything. I got fed up. That town can be toxic for a gay man. Or deadly!

They all agree, it is backward and not safe if you're gay. But they also agree that they were sheltered growing up in Laredo. How the culture is so oppressive and supportive at the same time. We were fortunate growing up where everyone knows you, everyone watches out for you, the whole barrio—family and friends—the entire community always there, protective and caring, Martha says.

Or not, Raúl chimes in.

And we did have some great teachers, Nena points out. Martha agrees. Remember la Sorrel? And Miss Lindheim?

Some of them were racists, Raúl adds. They thought we weren't smart because we spoke Spanish. ¡Pendejos!

Nena agrees and says, Still, despite the internalized racism, the low expectations, some of us made it. She reminds them of how they resisted and made it.

Yes, we were always there for each other, Martha says.

We *are*, Raúl asserts. ¡Siempre!

Nena remembers that gray DC day and how they walked to the Vietnam
wall and she shed a quiet tear. No matter how many times she has seen
her brother's name on that block of granite, it's always the same. The
tears and the feeling of drowning overpowers her. Vámonos, Raúl had
said, and they walked away. Sitting on a park bench, Martha commands,
Here, take our picture. They pose for the photo sitting on a bench, and
Nena snaps the photo through her tears.

El trajín

*I*n January, all stores—the small and the big—lure consumers with end-of-season sales as winter lingers. Señoras wear their furs, and not just for the Sunday-morning classical music concerts at the national theater, Ópera metro stop. Nena saves her pesetas (for it is the time before the Euro) to make sure she can afford at least one concert a month. Free lectures at the Ateneo. Free concerts by budding musicians who are sometimes more accomplished than the tired, almost-famous ones. Nena wants to do it all, attend concerts, operas, plays—affordable at student prices.

But this too shall pass. This month of waiting. The weekend's classical music concert, music dark and somber, stays with her as she follows the routine of quotidian tasks. Mozart, Mendelssohn, Strauss, Wagner. Nena learns these musics yet never feels completely at home. Jazz, Conjunto, and her beloved Tejano—those are home, the musics that linger in her mind. She plays the cassettes—Sunny and the Sunliners, Flaco Jiménez, René y René—to abate the deep saudade that hits hard on weekends after she talks to her family. She, Steve, Ronnie, and sometimes Giovanna along with other Norteamericanos go to dinner on Sunday and then walk to the telefónica to place long-distance phone calls at the locutorio. Home is only a call away. Late Sunday evening she knows everyone is at home visiting as they barbecue. A carne asada. The event as well as the food—carne asada. The phone calls bring joys and sorrows. But this too shall pass. This time of waiting. This homesickness. The saudade never totally abates, but it is made tolerable because she is doing the work that she dreamed of back in Laredo, a respite from her job at the university, where the teaching and grading never stop. She never has time for her painting or her poetry, although she makes time for community service: the literacy classes she teaches at the colonias, along with her students; the public humanities events at the city library that bring in Chicana and Chicano writers; the refugee assistance center through Amnesty International that helps the Central American immigrants flowing in through Laredo. The trajín in Laredo is different from the trajín in Madrid, but just as all encompassing, all consuming. The tasks of living.

El trajineo, the Spanish call it, the daily struggle to live, to buy groceries, to cook, to wash and clean and work, to make a living, to pay the rent, to pay the bills, to buy the necessities of living. ¡Qué trajín! She learns to moan against the never-ending task of living. Along with others, the banker as well as the waiter, who seem to be all men; along with the nurse and the teacher, who seem to be all women. Spanish society—just as at home—remains trapped in glass ceilings and wooden floors that won't budge until twenty-five years later, but only slightly. Back and forth to the library, back and forth to the work site, back and forth to the market, back and forth to the weekly tertulia with her friends. January was a long month, a month of getting used to life in Madrid, getting used to a big city, the rhythm so different from her academic schedule or the pace of life at home on the border. Time. Space. Rhythm. All different. But soon she settles into the routine. Into the certainty of tomorrow, of nothing-ever-changes, nothing-ever-happens. Until one day in February.

Febrero loco . . .

*N*ena reads about fiestas far and wide all over the peninsula that is
Spain—up in the mountain villages and down in Andalucía and
the urban centers as well. Soon she's overwhelmed with so many February fiestas—secular and religious—and finds solace in her friends:
her roommates and others who urge her to pursue her work. At the
library, everyone is curious. On Thursdays they ask, Are you traveling
this weekend? And on Mondays, What did you find? ¿Cómo te fue?
How are you doing with the work?

For a long time banned, Carnaval is back with a bang and is the
big February fiesta. Nena plans to stay and observe it in Madrid. Carnaval. A fiesta that will kick off the doldrums of a wet and gray winter. She schedules it on her agenda, along with other February fiestas,
smaller local ones, fiestas en los pueblos—saints' days and community fiestas where a patron saint is honored and sung to, held aloft,
and paraded up and down the narrow, cobbled streets, or secular fiestas where old battles are relived. In all, the same spirit of celebration,
of jubilee, of abandon reigns. Almost everyone gets drunk, and there's
joy and rejoicing as folks come from far and near, come home for the
fiesta del pueblo, in Almonacid, Alicante, Alcoy, Almagro, and some
that don't start with the distinctive Arabic "Al" like Belmonte or
Zamarramala.

At one of the fiestas, Nena asks one of the old women sitting to the side in an old metal chair, watching the procession, How is life in your village?

Peering over her rimless glasses she answers, La vida es dura como la tierra en los pueblos de la Mancha, tan dura como la tierra donde uno la vive. Nena feels overwhelmed. Such parallels! Yes, life is as hard as the land where one lives it in the towns in la Mancha. But also in the towns in Texas or Colorado. Or as hard as the factory floor where her mother's cousins work up in Gary, Indiana. As hard as the cotton fields where she and her family labored under a hot sun. As hard as the smelter where her father works. Life is hard for the poor.

The woman taps her cane on the hard surface of her courtyard, whispers, The ground remembers the feet that have walked upon it. Nena muses how after centuries of being trod upon it is packed hard as cement. Nena wonders how many have set foot on this very piece of land. This pedacito de tierra that was their home. She remembers the sun-baked yard in her home back in Laredo.

The woman peers through gray-green hazel eyes with obvious cataracts, wears a black kerchief over white hair. She's in traditional luto, wearing black down to the cotton stockings and worn leather shoes. She invites Nena to stay for dinner. You will find, she says in a distinct Castellano, that in all of Spain, in la Mancha or Galicia or Andalucía or Cataluña, life is hard, hard as this land. Hard for those who work the land, for those who must work day in and day out to make sure the olive crop is harvested, that the fishing boat has enough nets, that the bakery has enough yeast. Dura. La vida es dura. Hard.

La Endiablada y Nuestra Señora de las Candelas in Almonacid

*W*omen are everywhere, but at the fiesta on February 2 and 3, it is the men who rule, who perform the parlamento, who dance. It is a fiesta full of devils, la Endiablada in Almonacid del Marquesado. Nena observed many similarities between this ancient dance and the matachines in Laredo. The religious dance group celebrates the Holy Cross only a few feet from the border, from the Rio Grande, by dancing every May 3 and December 12 to honor the Holy Cross and the Virgen de Guadalupe, respectively. She finds joy and celebration in Almonacid. Sí que se dio gusto. Such joy to see the similarities and the differences!

Nena relishes the experience. But. She remains oblivious to her future. Still to come into her life: Paco. He's in her future, her destino. He is in Almonacid for his birthday. But. They don't meet; they remain strangers to each other.

Lorenzo and Paco have been friends for a long time, since they were en la mili and were stationed in Segovia—a friendship forged during their time serving as soldiers right after high school. Lorenzo teaches anthropology en la Complutense, revealing to Spanish students their heritage, the treasures in their own villages, their own backyards.

When Lorenzo calls that morning to invite him, Paco agrees to go. Why not, nothing else to do that Sunday. Why not drive with some young people to a small remote town in the province of Cuenca to taste the food, to experience the fiesta, see the endiablada, the parlamento, and the juegos? Not too far from Madrid. May prove to be just the thing to chase away the winter doldrums. Besides, it's his birthday!

Lorenzo and his entourage of students and his friend Paco come looking at the fiesta in Almonacid for vestiges of pre-Roman rituals older than Christian or Roman fiestas. Lorenzo traces the origins of the cowbells the dancers wear, the devotion to San Blas, the town's patron saint to a pre-Christian era.

A young woman, Rocío, his coworker's daughter, is in the group—what a coincidence! She thinks he's handsome, older, more mature. Not like her classmates, who only know about playing games. Youngsters who have not read her favorite authors. And don't want to read them. Paco is her father's friend. But so what? She's old enough to know what she wants. Her mother became her mother at her age, at eighteen, although everyone said Spanish women didn't bear children until they were older—those were different times. Life in Spain in the mid-60s is a foreign country to Rocío in 1980. She refuses to be like her mother. It's 1980! No motherhood for me, ever. Such blasphemy! She admires Paco's wit, his smarts—so worldly. And he speaks so well, sounds like he's quoting a book, she thinks. She is sure he flirts with her. Immersed in the fiesta, they talk. En la Endiablada, he explains, the devils are the sins that run wild. San Blas, the saint calms them down. He says, You're like the saint, I'm the devil. They laugh.

Nena arrives alone from Madrid in a bus full of others coming to Almonacid for the fiesta, like her, but for them it's a homecoming; they come bearing memories of fiestas past, of their childhood en el pueblo. Soon she is not alone, makes friends among the revelers. She meets a young woman, Pilar, a student who introduces her to a couple of local historians who have written the story of the Endiablada and are making a video of the celebration this year. What a fiesta! The singing and the

dancing. And the parlamentos in the church. The dancers wear huge
cowbells strung along the waist with leather belts. Must weigh a ton!
They jump and spin like diablos, dance in the church, and then one of
them reads el parlamento to San Blas. It's his feast day, and they parade
him through the streets, blessing the roads and the people who come to
see, to pray, to witness the fiesta one more year.

Paco, who is her future, has come to celebrate his birthday in this
strange little town with the strange custom. Watching the procession,
they stand on opposite sides of the narrow street. They don't see each
other, don't know each other yet so don't exist for each other. Oblivious. So the flute and the drum don't mean anything yet to them. The
music is muted. And she records it all with her heavy tape recorder,
takes photos with her Pentax, a gift from a friend who bought himself
a newer model.

   She just wants to know what it's about. For her work. For compari-
son's sake, she tells Pilar's friend, who has the professional equipment.

She interviews an elder who speaks to her of the past: Antes era mejor, todo más auténtico. Nena tries to explain that it's normal for things to change, that authenticity is a construct. But. He will have none of it.

She chats with one of the men who's dressed as a diablo in bright-print cotton. He is wearing a star. She explains, We have the pastorela, our shepherd's play at Christmas; it also has seven devils. Sometimes they are the same seven deadly sins; it too has changed. The man sits on a ledge, his cow bells behind him.

Oh, sí, pero no, he answers. Esto es distinto. This is different, and he explains, The devils at Christmas are trying to keep shepherds from worshipping. These devils are worshipping San Blas himself. They have been vanquished. It's the custom. Es la tradición. We don't know much more.

Soon Nena is tasting "rosquillos" and "rosquillas" festival food, eating what everyone eats on this feast day. She drinks it all with her whole being, the blessings and the parlamentos and the procession with the saint held aloft on the shoulders of those who have vowed to sacrifice, held up high for all to see, for all to adore, to inspire and comfort those who need inspiration and comforting. It is Candlemass, el dia de la Candelaria, and Nuestra Señora de las Candelas is also celebrated, but San Blas is the main character.

Nena remembers the fiesta in Tlacotalpan, a small town on the Papaloapan River in Mexico where the Virgen so like this one is taken in procession through the town and down the river with canoes loaded with flowers preceding and following hers.

Nena writes in her agenda in tiny script: a fiesta is a fiesta—the food, the drink, the prayers, the procession—somewhat different but not so different from the ones back home in South Texas, or in Mexico.

In Almonacid, among so many people, she is homesick when she sees friends gathered in bars. That now-familiar feeling surfaces again, an ache for home. Saudade. An ache for her friends. Her family. Suddenly it's her last night in the States that comes to mind. She had stopped in

Washington to visit her friends, cherished friends—Martha and Raúl who have jobs in DC. They are united again: the three musketeers! First they have drinks in Martha's apartment. Dom Perignon and caviar on tiny crackers. Then they walk to a nearby restaurant for dinner. Nena, who rarely eats meat, enjoys the sirloin steak. The baked Alaska. Walking home, she leans over and shares with Martha: I feel like a character in a movie. Martha responds, Must be the string quartet on the corner—ambient music, feels like a soundtrack to a movie.

Nena wipes away a tear, remembering. The crowd in Almanocid has thinned as everyone has gone into the church. Nena walks into the crowded church. Feels a strange premonition again. This all will change soon, the piper and the drummer who play the sones, the tunes, and the dancers in their brightly colored traditional dress will not do so for long. Or will they? She must document, record what is happening, for it will surely change. She who hates crowds has immersed herself in this one and knows she cannot stay away from the fiestas she is reading about in the library.

In Madrid she delved into the archives and found the origins of the Endiablada, found the history of how the saint came to Almonacid. Not unlike other stories, this one brings with it a bit of tension and is rooted in the rivalry between neighboring towns. Reading the archival texts, Nena found sources that date back centuries about the history of conquering groups in Spain. The most logical root seems to be the Celtic, and then the superimposition of Roman and Christian elements that seem to exist for all "devil rituals" including the shepherds' plays, the pastorelas, with the seven devils that battle and are vanquished by the archangel Michael. Ultimately, Nena deduces it is about good and evil, the eternal conflict. Quetzalcóatl and Tezcatlipoca in Aztec mythology. This celebration, the Endiablada de Almonacid, collapses two fiestas, Candelaria and San Blas—not surprising as they occur on the same day of the liturgical calendar, February 2. The Jewish roots of the Candelaria feast are transformed into the Catholic celebration, and this doesn't surprise her; Mary was Jewish, so of course she honored the tradition of staying home for forty days. La Cuarentena. Nena remembers the forty-day postpartum period that her mother observed after each birth, the bindings with cotton muslin and the strict dietary restrictions.

Inside the church the devils of la Endiablada, los diablos, dance decked out in outlandish clownish garb, wearing cencerros, noisemakers—large copper cowbells—strung around their bodies. They don elaborate red mitres on their heads. They are protecting Mary as she brings her child to the temple for the first time without the shame that must've accompanied the unusual birth.

San Blas? Well, that is another matter. Nena discovers an old text that cites the first celebration in Almonacid in his honor. It's from the seventeenth century. The two neighboring towns vying for possession of the image, Almonacid del Marquesado and Puebla de Almenara, both claim the saint that had been found buried by a shepherd in the fields between the two towns. But the saint would not budge even when the people from Almenara brought their strongest ox to pull it home. The Almonacid contingent only had a few weak mules, but the strong ox gently trotted over to the group from Almonacid, and so the message was clear: the saint chose to remain in Almonacid. The shepherds joyously rang the church bells—as they do now during the fiesta—to signal their jubilation. The diablos are proud of their cowbells, their loud and deafening sound. Some of the men dance with sticks, but this year there are hardly any interested in that much more subdued and low-key expression, so women will take it over lest it disappear altogether. The Palilleras, so named because they dance with palos, large sticks, are led by an alcaldesa as they dance throughout the town during the fiesta. When Nena is visiting there's a small band of men who still dance. They remind Nena of sword dances, and their names are reminiscent of the matachines sones. The maypole dance, called "el cordón," is similar to "la trenza," and the "paloteo" reminds Nena of the way the matachines use the stylized bow and arrow as noisemakers. They also dance "la culebra," very similar to the entrelazado of the matachines, a son where the dancers weave in and out of formations.

Nena observes the events and wonders about the "baño del santo." She approaches a diablo, a participant dressed in a wild yellow, red, green, and purple cotton print holding his headdress—an elaborate construction with natural flowers sticking up and the images of San Blas and Our Lady of Candelaria glued to the sides. Leather straps strung wih jingle bells hold up his cencerros, the cowbells. The man is about fifty and is obviously having a hard time keeping up with the younger dancers; he is taking a break from the dancing and gladly engages Nena in conversation. He explains that it is symbolic of the way they washed the saint when they unearthed the statue out in the field and brought him to the church. But why bathe him with anís? That he cannot answer. It's always been done like that, he concludes. When Nena's back in Madrid she digs in the archives some more and

finds that in some cases it is brandy that is mentioned. Still it remains a mystery. Perhaps it is the alcohol. Perhaps a priest way back thought it was a good idea.

Inevitably the tradition will change. On the last day of the fiesta, after the mass concluding the fiesta, somber men recite poems or dichos for both Candelaria and San Blas. Everyone cheers when one of them pokes fun at a politician or inserts a joke into the dicho. Nena, aware that she is witnessing a tradition that is in flux, thinks that this may be the very last time that men oversee the dichos. As fewer and fewer men participate, and as women want a larger role in the fiesta, they will be the ones parading around town dancing, and they will be the ones reciting the dichos. But that won't happen for a few years. For now, Nena lets the fiesta's energy engulf her, and she is one with the townspeople as they go about celebrating their saint. A young boy dressed as a danzante climbs the ledge, and Nena snaps the picture.

It's February, and Nena consults her Cabañuelas notes. She's not surprised that on January 2 it had been cold and rainy. But it had been breezy, not rainy, on the fourteenth of January, so the rain won't last all day, or all month. And it doesn't. It is sunny that afternoon when she boards the train to go back to Madrid. It is sunny and cold when she arrives in Segovia only a few days later. The whole month will be crazy and unpredictable.

Santa Águeda in Zamarramala

$\mathcal{B}$ack in Madrid for a couple of days, Nena works in the library rounding up information for her next field trip, her next fiesta. On Thursday she's off again, on the train from Madrid to Segovia on her way to that quaint little town, Zamarramala. Nena once again feels that strange electric feeling. Her skin, a receptor, a warning. She feels a premonition that things are about to change. Nena had read all about the patron saint, Santa Águeda, of the small village near Segovia. She found various versions of the story of the fifth-century martyr from Sicily whose breasts were cut off because she would not renounce her Christian faith. Although Nena couldn't find a link to any such fiesta in Texas or in Mexico, she was intrigued by the connection to a military feat: Zamarramala's women helped their men take over the castle, the mighty fortress, the Alcázar in nearby Segovia, from the Arab soldiers. She read about their leader, the most beautiful woman of the town, who was also martyred in similar fashion: her breasts were cut off! So, Santa Águeda carries her breasts on a platter and is decked out in elaborate jewel-encrusted garments. Since the eleventh century, or perhaps in 1227—it's unclear when the tradition began—what is certain is that for centuries the town has honored Santa Águeda and their ancestors, the courageous women who helped their men take over the Alcázar. Nena expected to find a procession, a special meal, and other elements, but other revelations were coming her way. Perhaps drawn by the incongruity of a celebration for and by women in a most patriarchal and sexist environment, Nena chooses Zamarramala, where women take over the town once a year.

Nena arrives early on Saturday in Zamarramala by bus from Segovia, where she spent the previous night at an hostal. As part of the centuries-old fiesta, the women take over the town for a day, at a time when hardly any women run for office, when there are hardly any women bosses anywhere, except at home. Jejejeje. The men joke and laugh. Even the feminist ones who know better. And in that town, as they had since 1227 or thereabouts, women take over for a day; later it will be two days. In 1980 two sisters reign as alcaldesas, as mayors of the town. They receive the symbol from the alcalde in Segovia and officially rule over their town. The Pregón that starts off the festivities ends with a poem that reminds the young women to honor their mothers, their ancestors' heroic deed—the reason the fiesta exists:

> ¡Niña de Zamarramala,
> Recuerda a tu anciana madre
> Que no descansó bailando
> Hasta conquistar el Alcázar!
> ¡Ay, niña de Zamarramala,
> No te olvides de tu madre!

Nena translates the song but is not quite happy with it, for even the very first word gives her trouble: "niña" could be "daughter" or "little girl" or "girlchild."

> Daughter of Zamarramala,
> Remember your ancient mother
> who did not rest dancing
> until the Alcázar fell.

Oh, daughter of Zamarramala,
Don't forget your mother.

The poem is a reference to or perhaps the reason for the inclusion in the fiesta of young women and little girls who, all decked out in their finery, celebrate. A heavy burden, a charge to keep the tradition alive, a tradition that honors foremothers who saved the day back in the thirteenth century.

The menfolk dance and honor them all, the women of the town. Young men swing huge banners in a flag dance that awes and inspires everyone. They swirl and flap flags bigger than them. The sound of the flapping adds to the music of the fife and drum corps. The crowds applaud the dancers and their artistry with the flags.

The procession is solemn, with a fife and drum group leading the way. The sculpture of Santa Águeda is carried by women. Shouts of "¡Viva Santa Águeda!" greet the saint along the procession route. It's Santa Águeda, she of the martyr complex who remained a virgin, even after life in a brothel, she who has saved the day for so many, the truly milagrosa, miracle worker—as many who pray to her attest. She is the patroness of women who are breastfeeding or who have mastectomies due to breast cancer; she seems to adapt to the times, indeed! It is an old fiesta, an old story made current. Santa Águeda, not as famous as Lucía, with her eyes on a platter. Agatha holds her breasts, bloody and puffed up like cupcakes on a tray. Symbols of her sacrifice, her martyrdom. The infidels came but she wouldn't budge, wouldn't succumb, and she paid for it with her life. It's a long story a woman tells Nena: La pobre de la Santa con su martirio, the saint's martyrdom. In her glory, she died for God.

In this town the women remember and celebrate. All pray to Santa Águeda, and a priest blesses the breads shaped like her breasts that will be part of the special meal. In this town they dress in traditional costume from head to toe: a white embroidered shawl, a manto or mantilla framing the face. A kind of mitre called a montera holds the mantilla in place—elaborately decorated with jewels and a wool pompom and held

with twelve buttonlike silver ornaments called "apostles," no doubt because there are twelve. They wear a black velvet short-sleeved vest, called a "jubón," open at the neckline to show the white embroidered blouse. The white lace apron wraps around the waist over a long black skirt that swirls during the dance. The women, or Águedas, wear this traditional dress made even fancier for the occasion. The Águedas don the proper attire, resplendent with the gold jewels that have been passed down for generations—heavy necklaces and earrings and bracelets dangle as they dance. The traditional dress reminds them of the past, of their heritage, a signifier of what it means to be from Zamarramala. For almost eight centuries on her feast day in February, Zamarramala, near the city of Segovia, celebrates Santa Águeda and the townswomen who played a crucial role in a military action. Two alcaldesas reign over the fiesta. Everyone rejoices.

The ritual burning of the pelele, a man in effigy, is part of the fiesta, an obvious reference to the desire to end the machismo that reigns in these lands. Nena thinks of the burning of the zozobra in New Mexico.

Although at another time and for another occasion, vestiges of similarity remain. She notes another similarity: within the mixed audience at the events that happen over two days, segregation is strictly enforced. Only men perform the flag display; only men play during the procession—a fife and drum corps. Only women dance el baile de las Alcaldesas, nothing but a simple jota, and only women burn the pelele.

Only women dance while the men play the sones with drum and flute. Nena befriends an older woman and her daughter—both are dressed in traditional dress for the occasion. They introduce her to the two alcaldesas, and Nena congratulates them, explains what she is doing. She photographs them as they walk, dance, and lead the way to the church.

The alcaldesas invite Nena to join them in the private meal. All the town's married women—whether dressed as Águedas or not—go into a large room that could be the church hall or the town's meeting place. The only man allowed for the ceremonial lunch is the church priest, who after all wears a skirt.

Nena stays quiet and eats the chorizo stew she's offered and the pastel, traditional sweet cake, and drinks the local wine. She's an intruder at the private fiesta with the women. But she still belongs; after all, isn't she a woman? But. She's not married, and this is only for married women in town who have earned their place at the celebration, who are to be fed by the men. Her newfound friends allay her concerns and tell her she's been invited by the Alcaldesas so she belongs. Y punto. Nena looks like a local, but taller, wears jeans and a white cotton shirt. The photos show a smiling priest surrounded by the townswomen. But Nena is not in the photo, because she is taking the photo with her trusty Pentax.

Yes, Nena feels special. Como ellas. Como todas. She wonders if she will ever be married. If she will ever pass on her traditions, her treasures to a beloved daughter. Nena is certain that traditions such as the Águedas of Zamarramala in this medieval village will survive if only because of its recently granted status as a UNESCO Heritage Site. These mothers will pass it on to their daughters, of that there is no doubt. They will bequeath their gold jewelry to their daughters and their granddaughters: earrings, bracelets, necklaces, especially the gold cross. They will place the white mantos on their heads, wear the montera like a crown.

Part II   La fuerza del destino

La fuerza del destino

*I*n early February, at the appointed time on the appointed date, it happens. But. It's Ronnie's birthday and the roomies are celebrating, but Nena chooses not to celebrate with them. Ronnie understands. Instead Nena heads to a jazz concert. Nena notes in her journal that the Cabañuelas have predicted accurately. Surprises. Unexpected happenings. Crazy February. Febrero loco . . .

She goes alone to meet her fate. Not a tragic fate, not a terrible fate, but a fate nonetheless. El destino. En esta época de desamor, when the lover left behind in the States is but a shadow, an emotional aftertaste. He has written a letter that remains lost in the trajín. He has written of his great love, but she will never read his words, his declaration of love. The letters lost like so many others. Nena feels herself falling out of love, swiftly, like a dream fading into nothingness with the bright light of day. El desamor. She feels the pain and knows that that era has passed in the story that is her life. An era full of expectation, of potential, of walking hand in hand with the beloved on quiet winter evenings, the crunch of snow underfoot. All past. That time of graduate school when love is in the background, not at center stage, a diversion, a subplot in an intense narrative, not the main plot. She has moved on—her job, her life in Texas. Just like she knew when she left south Texas that the time had come to change, to leave her friends and family, to move on to study far away. Now she feels that

Madrid is as alien as Nebraska. Time goes on. She is in another time, another place. Otra etapa de desamor. A loveless stage.

But. The overlap is palpable. A turn of phrase or a certain gesture, a shrug, reminds her of home. Of how even if the language is different it is the same. She yearns to be home among familiar foods and people, customs so ingrained in her that she doesn't even see them. Like the automatic response to her name, Mande. Or the quick "salud" when someone sneezes. Nena yearns for what she's left behind and cherishes what she carries with her.

This is the month. Es el mes. This is the day. El día. Her destiny, her path, has led her here. To this theater—Alcázar, Alameda, something with an A—Alcalá Palace, that's it! A theater, turned movie house, turned concert hall for this special night. Dizzy Gillespie is playing.

As soon as she spied the giant signs on walls and street corners all over Madrid announcing the upcoming concert, she began asking friends to go with her. But no one took her up on the invitation. Her friends had good reasons: It's good, but it's expensive. It's great, but I have too much work to do. I wish I could, but I already have plans. I don't like jazz. Most will join Ronnie for her birthday dinner. En fin. She is alone. Better to do something alone than miss out, Mami advised once when Nena was not going to go to a party because her best friend was grounded. She can't understand why Ronnie doesn't change the date of the dinner. Ronnie doesn't understand. What's so important about Dizzy Gillespie? she asks. She had gone to a Billy Joel concert, and she didn't ask anyone to go with her. She just went. That was Ronnie.

But. Nena is determined. Expects the music to send her home, to remind her of familiar arms cradling her. She didn't really understand jazz until graduate school, when she listens, really listens. At a jazz concert in Omaha, only there at the insistence of that loverfriend, she allows herself to listen. Truly listen. She has learned to love this music so foreign to her ears. Blues and jazz. She thinks of the Zoo Blues Bar in Lincoln, Nebraska, Friday night outings where she learned to drink tequila and beer. The long-lost arms that cradled her have been left behind. But like all loves, that love changed her, left her with something more durable, more permanent, more lasting: a love of jazz and blues. You have to develop a taste for it; it's not for everyone, he had whispered in her ear. Jazz is of the soul. That's what the jazz man said; his soul one with hers. You can't really dance to it, although she always wants to. Wants to let her body move and flow with the sounds, to stretch her arms and stand on tiptoe and just collapse as the trumpet rises and falls. The sounds of the trumpet—melancholy, lonesome—tugging at her heartstrings, bringing her closer to her appointment with fate. Like that old short story read in English 101, "Appointment in Samara," where an encounter with death cannot be avoided. But. She doesn't really know; it's just a feeling, a deep feeling of anticipation.

Nena, fleeing an encounter with one fate, runs head into another. She didn't see it coming. She has said no to the group going out for copas and dinner on a Saturday night to celebrate Ronnie's birthday; she said no to her friend from the tertulia, María José, who invites her to a movie at the filmoteca—the filmmaker will be there. No, thanks, I'd rather hear Dizzy, she said, and then had to explain who Dizzy was.

Among all the people streaming into the theater in groups or in couples, Nena feels alone. She is alone. But she's glad she came. Nena arrives alone. Buys the ticket at the window marked "taquilla." Just one? the teller asks. Yes. She buys her ticket when all that's left are the expensive seats in the orchestra section. All the cheap tickets sold out. She finds her seat, row K, seat 33. Good center seat, she thinks. Prepares to hear the familiar message of the music. She settles into her seat, listening to the sounds around her, some friends visiting, a couple of octogenarians in front of her. How wonderful to be with someone when you are eighty! Just last week at the filmoteca where she went alone to watch *Salt of the Earth* a happy couple had asked why she was alone. Blatantly, just like that getting into her business the way people did at home in South Texas. So norteño! In northern Mexico, people do the same. That's norteño, people say, attributing the practice of telling people, total strangers, what you think—that color looks good on you, or you shouldn't wear yellow, it makes you look dead—to those of the north, from Nuevo León, from Tamaulipas. And here Madrileños are doing it! Telling her she should find a partner, can't be alone in Madrid! She keeps finding similarities between this foreign place and her beloved land. Not just in the fiestas she is studying but in everyday words spoken at random. Like when she heard a little boy shouting to another to trip their companion, Métele la zancadilla! Just like her little brother would shout.

In the pre-show low roar of the crowd, she hears someone behind her exclaim, Es un fenómeno, este tío, just terrific. Nena smiles, thinks to herself, I know, and his music is mine. I own it with my soul. Just as the opening act is about to start, Paco walks in, sits to her left. He's complaining about the ticket price. He is immediately questioning her. Who is she? Intrigued that she is alone at a jazz concert and paying such steep prices. She only nods at first but answers his questions politely, doesn't want to appear rude. Standoffish. Then the lights dim and a local group, Hot Jazz Madrid, begins playing. Decent. But not what everyone is waiting for. The anticipation builds as everyone waits for the legend to appear. The opening group ends. Some of their fans in the audience hoot and holler, ask for an encore, but they decline. As they leave the stage, other musicians are coming on, setting up. Quickly, as if gliding in, the heavy, dazzling figure appears on stage: Dizzy. They are playing a tune Nena recognizes as it turns into "Night in Tunisia." He continues flowing into light banter, jokes about "Salt Peanuts," tells a story about President Carter who, being a peanut farmer, is also a good sport. But the music! The music! So alive, so strong, so in her heart it won't let her sit for long. Nena jumps up with the crowd and stomps her feet and swings her body. Her whole soul is wrapped up in the notes. She sheds a tear or two, moved by the plaintive sounds, by the crowds' emotions. Paco is watching, but she doesn't know, doesn't care. But.

Intermission. We'll be back, Dizzy promises. Paco leaves to reunite with friends, invites her, but she declines, stays meditating in her seat. Savoring the moment. Reaches into her purse, searching for her agenda, and can't find it. She left it at home, so she writes on a metro ticket stub, notes the titles of songs she knows by heart—in tiny cryptic code she lists the songs. Around her, the audience members are stunned and ecstatic all at once: ¡Es fenomenal, el tío! Noche de recuerdos. Memorable.

That's how it starts. At a jazz concert one day in February en el Alcalá Palace. With Dizzy.

Madrid, Madrid, Madrid...

1980. Carnaval. The fiesta signals a return to normalcy. Carnaval has come, and the dancing in the streets is unleashed for the first time since the dark times of the dictatorship. Nena learns that when people speak of la Guerra it's not the Second World War as it is for her parents' generation, nor the First for her grandparents, nor even Vietnam as it is for her generation at home. La Guerra is always the one that hits home. And here it isn't any of these; it is the Civil War, la Guerra Civil Española, someone corrects her. She of course knows of García Lorca, the gay poet executed in Granada. She knows of those like Hemingway who came to help the Republican cause and failed. But there's so much more! So much more to learn, to understand.

But. Franco is gone. He is dead and gone, as they used to say on that TV show back home—was it Rowan and Martin's *Laugh In*? Or was it *Saturday Night Live*? But. His shadow lingers in the attitudes, the expectations. Nena often hears the elders—Señora Barreneche, the butcher, the bank teller, or the old man who is the porter—yearn for the good old days of no homeless, no youth out drinking, smoking till all hours of the night, no girls wearing tight jeans. They yearn for the golden past of decency and safety. But. She hears no such sentiments from her friends at the tertulia or the library; they remember the beatings, and the early '70s, the victims in Vitoria, the trips to France to watch the latest movies. And to London for safe abortions. Of course, the poor never had access. They stayed and suffered. And the gypsies were persecuted as always. And here it is 1980. Franco is gone. He is dead and gone. And the festival spirit invades Madrid: Mardi Gras. ¡La Movida!

The new socialist mayor of Madrid, a writer, an intellectual, but also a political force, Tierno Galván is all in favor of fiestas. But. Still no masks allowed for Carnaval. Unless it's an antifaz. So Nena dons a midnight-blue one, jokes that she feels like the Lone Ranger, el Llanero Solitario. Paco smiles, and the smile turns into a soft laugh as he says, Tienes ojos de mora, Moorish eyes, they're beautiful. She feels a warmth spread all over her body and blushes beneath the half mask. He wears a moss-green antifaz. She notices his eyes are green . . . or hazel. Borrados, they call such a color at home. They have been out a few times, but this is the first real date, as it were. Not just meeting at a café in the evening between work and dinner.

It's Carnaval, and impromptu dancing erupts everywhere. Paco and Nena dance in the streets of Madrid and in a quiet neighborhood pla-zuela. The Agustín Lara song "Madrid, Madrid, Madrid" blares over the loudspeaker. The neighborhood near the Rastro fills with music, el barrio entero se llena de música. Light bulbs, bombillas cristalinas, brighten the glowing circle. Nena notices a young woman standing to one side watching them. Paco and Nena dance round and round. Nena's feet barely touch the ground. The young woman is crying. Nena notices, wonders what's wrong, and whispers it in Paco's ear, and he turns and tightens his hold on her. Must be la época de desamor, he whispers. The season of non-love. And indeed, to the side a couple steals a kiss as they dance by, and the young woman devours the couple with her eyes. Yes, it is obvious. There is love, but there is pain, too. Desamor. I've been there. Am I in the same época? Nena wonders.

And then another young woman, younger and darker than the weep-ing one, what the Spanish would call morena but in Texas would be called aperlada, approaches. Paco and Nena are walking away from the crowd, and she stands in front of them. He introduces the two women. Rocío is her name. Nena and the young woman greet and kiss each other on each cheek, as is the custom. Paco and Rocío greet, too, kisses on the cheek. He calmly asks for her father. He is well, she says. Then they walk away, hasta luego, adiós, adiós, hasta luego, adiós. He explains, She's a coworker's daughter; he's been ill. What a coincidence to run into her here. But Nena senses there's more he is not saying. She's just a child, no more than seventeen, maybe as young as fifteen. Too young for him, she ponders. Nena feels ancient next to her. The young woman Rocío goes her way, as Nena and Paco hold hands walking through the nearby barrio, stopping for a glass of rojo, deep red wine, at a bar.

At first Nena didn't like the taste of wine. But she's learned to love the fruity, dry taste. They are in a bar, the floor strewn with sawdust. The bartender keeps tabs with chalk on the bar in front of them. She loves the ambiente—the smell of humans but also of frying food and strong perfume, all mingled into the smell of the bar. The sounds of people talking, laughing, loud and cheery, the sevillanas playing on the jukebox—the noise, even the noise of the pinball machine that someone is playing—and the tastes, so many new ones, some familiar ones: cheeses, olives, fried tapas, and all kinds of seafood.

They are enjoying the evening, their company. But all the time Nena is thinking of Rocío and how she looked at Paco. Decides to ask him about it. ¿Cómo conoces a Rocío? She asks in between sipping wine and comments about the sevillanas playing on the jukebox.

He answers, She's the daughter of a coworker.

Pero hay algo más ¿no? Nena asks.

Bueno. Sí. We met a couple of weeks ago on my birthday in fact. Did I tell you I am an Aquarian?

Nena senses that he is trying to change the subject. And decides to not pursue the subject. But as soon as she consciously decides to drop it, he says, She's been calling me. I guess I flirted a bit when we met and she is smitten. But it's nothing serious. She's just a kid. She'll get over it. Además, her father, is a good friend. She could be my daughter!

Nena is pleased he decided to tell her. Asks, Really? How old are you? How old do you think I am? he asks teasingly. And Nena responds, also in jest: Oh, maybe close to seventy. And they both burst into laughter. Half of that, he whispers in her ear. And you? Or should I not ask? Nena stops, looks into his eyes. I just turned thirty, she says. I never lie about my age. Or about anything, really.

Bar hopping, they eat and drink at different bars, eating things she doesn't recognize, things too expensive for her budget. Calamares, boquerones, pescaditos fritos al estilo andaluz. Paco loves the tiny fried fish, reminds him of the times he lived in Andalucía. How popular they are in Málaga, Torremolinos, Denia. All along the coast you can find them, he informs her. The crunchy, salty delicacy melts in her mouth. He also introduces her to some Asturian delicacy from his homeland . . . laughing, he launches into a rendition of the himno Asturiano:

Asturias, patria querida,
Asturias de mis amores;
¡quién estuviera en Asturias
en todas las ocasiones!

Nena smiles and, tasting, asks, What is it?

He misunderstands and answers that it is the himno Asturiano that his father used to sing. Paco continues singing the second verse and puts a pretend flower in her hair as he sings . . . y dársela a mi morena que la ponga en el balcón.

Nena wants to know it all: the foods, the stories, the music. She yearns for more information about it all, not just enough to decipher the politics of this time of transition, but about the economy, the social mores as they change and shift. But tonight it's food and drink. She shies away from the squid in its ink. Calamares en su tinta, so fresh! he says, and she believes him but won't try the dish. Trusts him, but not totally. Why? She trusts him enough to share that she has no one in Madrid, just friends. No family. When he walked her home with his friend that first night after the Dizzy Gillespie concert, he marveled at how adept she was at riding the metro late at night. She had just met him so she was careful; she led him to believe there was a family waiting for her. Of course, it was not a total lie, not a full lie—there was a family waiting, the landlady, Señora Berreneche, who treated her like a daughter, and her roommates, Giovanna and Ronnie.

That night, Nena writes in her journal in the third person:

Noche de Carnaval, Paco and Nena se van de copas—from bar to bar, drinking wine, vino tinto that she has quickly learned to love, cheaper than coffee. They dance and talk and get closer. They are in Madrid en Noche de Carnaval. Noche mágica. Magical!

She writes:

Agustín Lara's song plays over and over: Madrid. Madrid. Madrid. Pedazo de la tierra en que nací. Paco claims Lara wrote all those songs, even "Granada," without ever visiting Spain. Imagine!

She also writes that she has learned that Madrileños are called cats, yes, gatos. And the women wear chulapa dresses for fiestas. But not for Carnaval. Paco said, They'll wear their dresses for San Isidro in May, you'll see.

Why cats? Nena asks. Paco tells her the story of how in the eleventh century, when the Moors ruled Madrid, the troops of King Alfonso VI—Christian of course—under cover of night because they wanted to surprise the Moros, approached one of the gates of the walls. But they couldn't manage to climb until one of the soldiers used his dagger to climb the outer wall.

But how? Nena asks.

¿Qué se yo? Seguro, he inserted his dagger, or maybe he was a rock climber . . . but he managed to get into the fortified tower and raise the

Christian flag. Because he was so quiet and agile, like a cat, the others started calling him "Gato." In fact, the story goes, the others wanted to honor him, so they all took on the nickname. And since then, madrileños are called gatos.

Nena thinks he's pulling her leg and responds to the tale: No te creo. I haven't heard anyone called that. And Paco laughs his tinkling laughter and won't own up, won't tell her if it is true or if he made it up.

At least he's not a gypsy, Martha, her friend from home, tells her when Nena calls to wish her a happy birthday and she shares the news that she's seeing someone she met at a concert who is becoming more than just a friend.

With your ways, nomás eso faltaba. Just watch that he's not a gypsy, or an Andaluz—they are the worst, enamorados and sinvergüenzas.

How would you know? Nena asks and admonishes, Don't be such a racist! She reassures her, No, he's from Asturias. Still, Martha worries that Paco is a philanderer, a shameless cad!

What does he do?

He works for a publisher in the book design unit. He's a graphic artist, Nena explains.

Martha cautions, Just be careful, you never know. He may just want to lure you into his bed.

Nena laughs and retorts, But that's all men, not just the Spanish. Look at the Chicanos with their womanizing. Mujeriegos, that is why the word persists. Nena muses on how the old suffix, long dead, persists in that word. Por algo.

Non, je ne regrette rien

*N*oche de Carnaval. After dancing in the streets, after bar hopping, Nena and Paco go to his apartment on the quiet street, Marquez de Zafra, to listen to music and have a last copita and talk. He plays opera arias for her. Smoothly, with a wistful look, he offers her more than friendship.

No, she answers. I'll go home soon, and it will hurt too much.

So? That's life, así es la vida. It may hurt, but at least you've enjoyed life. It's life. No regrets. As Edith Piaf sings, "Non, je ne regrette rien." And he hums the tune.

It's the omen that she didn't know she'd been waiting for. It's one of her favorite quotes. One of her favorite Piaf songs. No regrets. She hears with her mind's ear Piaf's throaty voice singing the song, Non, je ne regrette rien.

Perhaps, she answers. But not tonight. Not like this. Perhaps our friendship will be more than just a friendship. But not now. Someday, quizás.

Another song seeps into her mind . . . quizás, quizás, quizás. Perhaps. As if on cue, he hums the song in her ear. Perhaps, perhaps, perhaps. She knows but is still hesitant. Quizás.

Then one Saturday night it happens, after a movie, a delicious dinner he has cooked for her—croquetas de salmon, paté on tiny crackers, and the plato fuerte, fish with a cream sauce, and even a delicious flan he made from scratch. They play Scrabble in Spanish and end up kissing and hugging . . . eventually he guides her to his bed. The chenille bedspread a soft caress. They share intimacies. Sweet talk and reminisce about their childhood. He brings out a box of photos and introduces her to his parents, tells stories of how his father was killed in the aftermath of the War. How up in Asturias the resistance was so strong the reprisals were even harsher. How his mother was left alone with two children to care for—Paco and his sister. Never remarried. Took in laundry to make ends meet. How he had served his military service stationed in Segovia, hating the Franco dictatorship but unable to do anything but go along and not escape to France or Italy like some of his college friends had done. His dreams of being an artist thwarted. He moved to Andalucía for a spell, then to Barcelona, and now Madrid. In Barcelona he was settled and had a relationship with a catalana that he thought was forever; she didn't. So, he moved to Madrid, ended up a graphic artist for a publisher designing book covers. Freelancing and helping his friends with magazine design. Así es la vida, he concludes.

Nena shares with him stories of her land, of her family. How they would pick cotton during the summer months, and how her father was stricken with crippling arthritis and could no longer work but still did odd jobs for neighbors and friends. How he had worked at a smelter, where the hard work sucked the life out of him. How he would come home exhausted after back-to-back shifts and collapse and sleep for hours. She tells him of her love of that land, of that family, of the two towns on the border between Mexico and Texas, how she misses them, how she misses her life there, how she wonders how her students are doing at the university, how her siblings are surviving.

She confesses, I must return to do the work there. At the university. And with my family, too. Be there for my parents and my siblings. As the oldest I have a responsibility. I must go back. He reaches for her and holds her tight.

I know, he says. Pero, you might change your mind.

63

They cuddle, and the sweet lovemaking happens naturally, as if it were a given all along. They sleep in each other's arms. Dream of a life together that might never be.

Maybe in an alternate reality, she tells him over coffee and churros the next morning. Our intimacy, our love, will remain. Maybe. Quizás.

She doesn't tell Paco about the lover back in Nebraska, but she has broken up with him. Nena never mentions her life in that cold Midwestern town. The long-distance romance. The feeling is one of emptiness. A hollow space remains in her heart, and she must admit to herself that Paco is filling that void, that vacuum. He has managed to get under her skin, into her heart. He plays jazz LPs for her. Full operas, too. They go for long walks in the city. Drive to nearby towns.

Her roommates are worried. What if she pulls out and leaves them without her share of the rent! But she assures them she would never do that. Besides, she says, I only stay with him on weekends, anyway. This piso is still home.

Home is where the heart is, Ronnie teases her one afternoon when they come home from the Biblioteca and find a letter from her father and she bursts into tears reading it. Details about the niece who was born over there, across an ocean in a hospital on the border where many children come to see the light, where the mothers give them light. Her sister in her pain remembers the sister friend so far away as she gives light to her daughter. February 18 and it's seven hours earlier in Spain. Nena won't know of her arrival until later; she is awakened the next day when Señora Berreneche, who thinks she is like a mother to her, knocks on the door and calls Nena to the phone. Across the miles the thin wire carries the message. It's Papi's voice. Strong and proud, telling her the news, a granddaughter is born. I'll write with details, he says. The beloved sister, Esperanza, has given birth to a daughter. Rejoice!

Now a letter, with a kind regaño. Why has she not written? One letter in early January and a couple of postcards, and nothing more! Nena is torn. Tells Ronnie, I must find the time to write a long letter. Let them know what I am doing. What my life is like. They worry.

But Ronnie is unsympathetic. Her own life drama unfolds, taking unexpected turns. She has received a love letter from an elderly man, a friend of the family in Michigan, and she is unsure what to do, what to say. She is not interested but doesn't want to hurt the kind man or her parents, who probably would be happy if she accepted him. Alas, life is complicated, even for those who appear to have it all and more than anything who appear to have it all under control.

February has come and gone. All is as predicted. Unpredictable. Las Cabañuelas set it up—that second day in January the weather changed from gray and rainy to sunny and bright, and at 2:00 a.m. on the thirty-first, Nena had been out with friends and feeling lost in the big city. It was for her a month of discovery, of finding friends, of finding her way around the Biblioteca, that beloved library that had become her second home, and of traveling. She was spending her stipend on books and on travel, but it was the right thing to do. She was certain. But the yearning for home remained ever present. The work was exciting and fulfilling, yes. But. A month of going from desamor to a love that stirs her heart. Yes, las Cabañuelas predicted it all. Febrero loco . . .

. . . Marzo otro poco

It's March and time to travel south to record fiestas, spring rituals. Paco is driving Nena to the tertulia. He was going to work for a bit in the office and would pick her up later.

February is my birthday, you know. Sí, Nena whispers, Febrero loco . . .

Y marzo otro poco, Paco completes the saying. Así es. Wonder where that comes from?

The weather, Nena answers. It's crazy how it can change, that's why las Cabañuelas work.

Las Cabañuelas. What's that?

Nena explains, It's what happens in January that tells you what will happen the rest of the year.

A ver, a ver, ¿cómo es eso? Son brujerías, ¿o qué?

No, it's a way of finding out what is going to happen. My dad told me all about it when I was a kid. Aún recuerdo. He made a point of teaching us about the stars, the constellations and such. Cosas que solo los del campo saben, you know, because he was of the earth. Always loved growing things—corn, squash, tomatoes, y hasta sandía, juicy watermelons! And the Cabañuelas is how he would know what the weather would be like. And in February and March, it was crazy! Bien loco.

He seems satisfied with her explanation, and Nena thinks about the old ways, the old knowledge that helped people survive. Wish there were

Cabañuelas for figuring out what's going to happen to relationships, she says aloud.

Not possible, Paco says. Relationships are even more unpredictable than the weather! Febrero loco, marzo otro poco, ¿y tú y yo? Even crazier!

In February she had stayed close to Madrid, gone to the fiestas that were popular and that she felt safe attending. But Nena has been finding references and articles in the old volumes in the Biblioteca about fiestas that also exist in Mexico that she wants to explore. Moros y cristianos, Holy Week reenactments, and the feast of Saint Joseph. Saint James. Saint John. Those are the ones she chooses. Popular ones and not just the touristy ones. Those similar to those at home. Often those not too far from Madrid. She chooses Alcoy in Alicante for Moros y cristianos, Cuenca in la Mancha for Semana Santa, Atienza for the Caballada, Caravaca de la Cruz for the Caballos del Vino. Valencia for las fallas, the feast of San José Labrador, March 19. Sant Josép as they say in Valenciano. Yes, spring will be busy. Later in the summer, A Coruña for San Juan in June and Santiago de Compostela in July.

When she shares her list with Paco, he seems disinterested. Jokes that she's still dwelling in the past, the fiestas won't survive. No le importan a nadie, no one cares anymore. ¿San José? Paco asks, Is that the festival when one goes to the river to bathe?

Nena smiles as she answers, No, that's San Juan—June, the twenty-fourth, it's celebrated everywhere, but I have chosen to go to A Coruña for that one. Want to join me?

No one goes to the river in Madrid, he tells her. El Tajo. No, you don't want to go there.

That's true, Nena agrees. Some of the old ways are no longer followed. Although in Texas some may still cut their hair so it grows back plentiful, shiny, and with curl, but not too much curl. But in A Coruña they celebrate a lo grande. Still have the old traditions. It's one of their major fiestas. But that's not till the summer; it will be San Juan in June.

How about July? she asks. Want to come with me to Santiago? I won't be walking the pilgrimage, not this time! Maybe some day, pero not now.

That night, they are in bed, and she is preparing him for what is to come.

I will be gone quite a bit from here on in, she explains. I must travel to these fiestas. ¿Me acompañas?

He declines her invitation. No puedo. I can't just leave. We have major deadlines in the spring. But. I can meet up with you cada y cuando, occasionally, if you like. And you can write me long romantic letters from all those places . . . I would like that.

Of course, I'd like that too—still, you can join me. He avoids answering. A ver qué pasa. I can also write letters and postcards, she responds. We'll see.

Valencia's Falles y Ninots

$\mathcal{A}$t the tertulia in Madrid, Nena meets mostly writers and poets and some visitors and guests who come, curious to find out what it's all about. Some become good friends: María José, Nelson, Manolo, and Tomás. Literature lovers, writers, thinkers, poets. She hits it off right away with several of them. Manolo is sweet and caring, and he shares his poetry with her. She is aware of his marital problems, so Nena expects him to launch into a sad story of how his wife doesn't understand him, or some such. But. He tells her he wants to talk, so she agrees to meet him on her way to the Biblioteca so they can talk, and they meet one morning for coffee. Turns out Sofía has left him for a woman and he is embarrassed, ashamed, doesn't want others to know but suspects the gossip is thick and heavy about the affair. Nena knows because Nelson told her. Wonders why Manolo has not said anything to her.

Oh, I see, Nena says when he confesses how lost he is without Sofía, his wife. How he can't believe he had not seen it coming. She asks, And what do you want from me?

Absolutely nothing. Nada. Just friendship. I'm hurting. Estoy herido. No puedo más. I just needed to talk. That's all.

Nena hurts to see Manolo crying as he tells her how he found out about the affair, how Sofía didn't deny anything when he confronted her. He's sad and hurt, reminds her of a puppy with his tail between his legs. Nena's heart breaks to see him suffer. But. She wants to hear Sofía's side of it. What happened? How did she end up with a woman after ten years of marriage with Manolo? She'll never know. Sofía doesn't come to the tertulias, doesn't really like poetry or his friends. But. Nena feels a kinship with her. But. What can Nena do to ease Manolo's pain? And just like that she knows: take him with her to Valencia!

Ya sé, let's go to Valencia. Las fallas will burn away all sosoria. Is that the word?

No sé. Soy de Galicia, he confesses. And tells her about that magical land of duendes and witches.

But you know what they are, no? ¿Las fallas?

'Ombre, claro. It's when they build elaborate and beautiful structures and then burn them all on el Día de San José.

Yes, she confirms. Ephemeral art at its best.

Later that week, Manolo invites Nena to play hooky from her work at the Biblioteca and drive out to Toledo, to that beautiful walled city in la Mancha for lunch at an expensive restaurant in the casco viejo. She had Toledo on her list—wants to go for the feast of Corpus Christi in June. Nena feels mischievous. Feels free. In his red car—can't figure out what it is, must be Italian, she thinks—he plays a cassette, a music Nena loves, Millodoiro; strange celtic new-agey music fills the car. Flute, bagpipe, violin, all together in a delight for the ear. The songs stay in her head for days. Over lunch Manolo tells her he's giving up. He'll be moving soon; already gave notice at work. He's got family in León, or maybe he'll go to Bilbao. Or perhaps back to A Coruña. He can't decide. But he must leave. Can't bear Madrid with all the memories, his ex around every corner. He will continue working on his poetry and get a job with some law firm. Maybe he will start a press to print books in Gallego now that they can. It won't be easy, but he simply must do it. It's been quite a blow, he confesses, I am lost.

Well, las fallas will heal it all, Nena promises. You'll see.

Nena and Manolo leave Madrid, arrive in Valencia, eat paella valenciana

twice a day and it is never the same. They enjoy the bunyols de carabassa that remind Nena of empanadas de calabaza. The music is everywhere in the streets of that city by the Mediterranean. In Valencia that year, the theme for the fallas is Disneyland. But. The falleros don't all agree. They are creative and the neighborhood sets are scenes from various events and characters, not all from Disney. A giant King Tut pyramid and various children's structures are all set to be lit on the nit de foc. So incongruous, Nena thinks as they walk through the neighborhoods and see the beautiful structures. Nena is fascinated by one that has strange blue figures—pitufos! A couple of elaborate blue Smurfs. Nena can't tell if it's one competing in the children's category.

Another one with a strong political message intrigues her: a politician—obviously the prime minister—is surrounded by protestors carrying placards against and for NATO. These relatively smaller ones in the various neighborhoods hardly prepare Nena for the enormous castle, the centerpiece in front of the Ayuntamiento. As befits the star of the celebration, the falleros have erected the most elaborate and beautiful Falla in front of city hall. During the day, a procession of young women and girls dressed and coifed as traditional Valencianas bring flower offerings. Delivered and positioned on a trellis set along the wall of the cathedral, the flowers won't be burnt. Nena photographs the young women and girls in procession.

For the fallas, or falles as Nena learns to call them in Valenciano, the fires are set simultaneously on the nit de foc, the eve of St. Joseph's feast day. The smaller ones first, then the main one at city hall. People stand under the fireworks, the sound so deep and loud that their hearts are bursting. People crowd in, pushing and shoving, wanting to get a better view. Nena smiles to see little girls and boys on their fathers' shoulders, wide-eyed and afraid and secure all at once. A fiesta unlike any other.

The falleros have been working for months and have stayed up all night working so that the structures are all set up to be mounted right after the processions on the sixteenth of March. On the nineteenth, la nit de foc, they will burn. The children's structures first, then the main ones at major intersections in the various barrios—each comissió fall-era, also called a casal faller, is responsible for its own structure.

All the beautiful ephemeral artwork will go up in flames, all that work!

There's political ones and sarcastic ones and even scatological ones that remind Nena of the piñatas that often appear in fiestas in Laredo.

Several years later Nena will remember these elaborate structures as she sees the Ronald Reagan piñata that Don Cipriano, one of the piñateros from Laredo, will build for the Smithsonian Festival of American Folklife. That artwork is equally ephemeral. The many hours of work to create something beautiful, it all ends in broken pieces and the defeat of all that is evil.

Finally, around one in the morning, the main falla at the ayuntamiento, the one everyone has been waiting for, is lit. But first the mascletà, fireworks so loud and spectacular Nena thinks she will lose her hearing. The fireworks rain overhead, and the distant moon hangs in the sky like the eye of God watching it all. Manolo holds her hand. But Nena feels nothing. The smell of the pólvora is so strong she feels nauseous, just the way she did when her friend's father shot into the night air one New Year's Eve in Laredo. Gunpowder makes me sick, she tells Manolo.

But being there amid the throngs is another dream come true. The entire town has falles burning through the night, la nit del foc. Nena had not imagined all this even after reading and researching the tradition. The lowly ritual that began centuries ago when the carpenters' guilds celebrated their patron saint, Saint Joseph, by burning their leftover wood, wood that was not good for furniture or buildings, or maybe even some good wood that they would sacrifice to the saint as a gesture of gratitude for favors granted, prayers answered.

Nena stays in Valencia and Manolo goes back to Madrid. He will talk to Sofía. Make it right. Forgive and forget, Nena has advised. Be friends. Be happy that she's happy. Then, if you leave, you leave with a happy heart.

I'll try, he says. And, I am leaving.

Nena asks, Why not just get a divorce?

No way, he responds. It's not easy. Still illegal in Spain.

But.

Nena writes a letter:

Dearest Paco,
I wish you could be here to experience the fallas. I feel right at home in Valencia. Went into a bar, and I swear I thought I saw my uncles! My father's brothers. Tall, big-eared and big-nosed! I got some good interviews. Some good photos. I can't imagine being here and not being a researcher, a scholar trying to theorize these traditions, looking at the fiesta as a cultural event that reveals more than meets the eye ¿Qué crees? I can't wait to discuss it all with you. This one is not really a religious fiesta. Although it celebrates San Josep, the root, I believe, is in some pre-Christian fire ceremony. I think I will go to another town to talk to people away from Valencia. I'll send another letter from there, ¿vale?

Abrazos, besos, y el cariño de siempre,
xoxoxo
Nena

Although Nena is glad she experienced Valencia's fallas, the exhilaration, the energy, she feels let down. Several people she talks to encourage her to go outside of the capital to the real fallas. So, she must go somewhere else. She asks around, and everyone agrees she should visit either Villa-franca del Cid or Burriana. She decides on Burriana. Several people suggest that las fallas are more authentic in the villages, and she decides to go into places where many still speak Valenciano even after years of Franco's attempt at making everyone speak Castellano, where the fallas may indeed be purer, less commercial, less about egos and posturing. But. She finds Burriana is not quite as big as Valencia nor as small as some of the villages. By the time she gets there, the fiesta is over, and most people are back to their daily routine. Not much interested in talking about the fallas now that the festival is over.

Still, she finds some folks who will tell her their stories as they are in the process of cleaning up, of making it all right after the fiesta. The bar owner tells her how his sister is one of the main organizers and arranges for Nena to talk to Montserrat, who proceeds to tell Nena all about the ways the townspeople wait all year long to burn what they don't want. It started in 1928 when we got our very own falles, Montserrat proclaims proudly. Her grandfather was involved in the early years, and so the family has kept it up.

Nena's trip to Valencia was a resounding success. She collected great interviews and visited two locations—one urban and the other rural. Great for contrast and to match up with festivals in the States, where the difference between rural and urban is also marked by degree of wealth and depth of religiosity. Although the fiestas in honor of San José took on a totally different character in the Americas, they remained rooted in the European ones that were in turn rooted in pre-Christian spring festivals. In Peru, Bolivia, Ecuador, and, of course, in Mexico, the patron saint is honored in similar ways with religious and secular observances—processions, dancing, drinking, bullfights, and special foods.

On the train back to Madrid, Nena writes in her agenda, which is now full of field notes and has morphed into more of a journal than a fieldwork log. Entries that begin with notes on the Falles y Ninots soon turn to Paco and her fears of getting too involved, fears of what will happen, fears of having to leave Paco. Her stay in Madrid is as finite as the burning of the hoguera, of the fallas that will result in ashes that the street-cleaning crews will whisk away; all will return to what was. It will look as before. Until next year.

She also writes about what Manolo confides in her as a friend: his fears that Sofía was a lesbian all along and his worries that he might never heal; he wonders if his heart will ever love again. Why couldn't he see it? What was wrong with him? He asks Nena.

Nothing, she answers. Nothing's wrong. It was just your destiny and Sofía's destiny. Every relationship is unique, and growth happens no matter what. You must forgive. And as she says this se muerde la lengua, she bites her tongue, as they say, because she knows she must forgive, too. But what is there to forgive? She sends words, that is all she has, postcards and letters . . . daily journal-length letters detailing the events, the fiestas, the customs, the meals, but never mentions the man she's with. After all, he's just a friend and not a lover. Nothing to tell, not really. So why not mention him? She could. But.

El Retiro

*B*ack in Madrid she calls Paco, who comes to pick her up at the Chamartín train station. Hugs her and won't let go. I've missed you. He wants to take her to his place, but she insists that she must go to her piso. Her roomies are waiting for her to settle the month's bills. She's been gone and must take care of that and other stuff. He agrees and, as he drops her off, tells her to be ready on Saturday for a special outing.

The next morning a rainbow greets her as she steps out of the building. Overnight rains came and cleaned it all. Spring surprises Nena. On Saturdays and some evenings, Paco and she take long walks to enjoy the crisp spring air. One afternoon her friend María José comes by the Biblioteca to take her away. At the Parque del Retiro they walk and talk. María José, who teaches Portuguese for Berlitz, has a relationship—está "liada"—with Erik, one of her students who comes to Madrid on business from the Netherlands. His company wants to send him to Portugal as well. He's so tall, she coos . . . and he is so loving. Not like her ex-husband, who never bought her flowers, never gave her a compliment. Always after her about cleaning the bathroom. Isn't it funny how such things can make one fall out of love? María José wants to talk about Erik. He has asked her to marry him, go to Portugal with him. She's debating with herself.

What do I do, Nena?

You're asking me? I can't give you advice. I don't know what to do myself. Should I stay in Spain? Go back to Texas? Go back to Nebraska? No, mujer, I am not the person to tell you what to do.

I'll ask my mother, then. She left my father, you know. I was only ten when we moved here from Portugal.

Months later, when Nena is leaving, going back home, they say good-bye at the airport that summer day: María José, who teaches her to make tortilla Española, who is herself a foreigner, an immigrant, coming from Portugal as a child with her mother and grandmother. As Nena is about to board the plane that will take her back to Texas, María José will take off her earrings, de migajón de pan, tiny hand-painted roses made of bread dough, and put them in Nena's hand. So you won't forget me or our friendship. And they kiss both cheeks, a hug seals the promise.

Spring Fever

One afternoon in late March, Nena and María José stroll leisurely in el Retiro. María José has decided not to follow Erik but to stay home. She's staying, and that's that. He can come visit her; she can visit him. It can work. Yes, Nena advises, it can work. Shares her story of her graduate school love and how they made it work long distance. Shares with her the way she has let go of that chapter in her life; a love that has faded like a polaroid snapshot left out in the sun. But, it's different, Nena reassures her. Maybe in the fall, you can reconsider.

It's spring, and the park is full of flowers—lirios, margaritas, and some she doesn't recognize. The swans glide peacefully en el lago, and the sweet-scented air soothes the tears that come to Nena's eyes as she tells María José about jazz and opera concerts and how she's resisting—will not fall in love. Still has feelings for the other love that is quickly fading like a poorly developed photo fades with time. Nena likes the metaphor. She confides in her friend. But like photos, it will never totally fade from my life, it's part of who I am. I will never forget. Not ever.

Fast friends sharing experiences, Nena shares stories of other loves. Those back home who betrayed her. Who never said I love you. Who idolized her. All who told her that no one would ever love her the way they did. Why do they all say that? asks María José. Could it be that once we love we feel no one has ever loved that way? Perhaps no one has.

In fact, no one has. Each relationship is unique, teaches unique lessons. So, no. No one has loved you the same way. No one ever will. Still.

Nena shares with her friend how she's jotted down what lessons she is learning from her relationship with Paco. In her journal she's written, He is solid. Makes me feel grounded. Once someone told me that the sign of whether you love someone is if you feel butterflies in your stomach and you are not even hungry. Well, that's not happening. So maybe I'm not in love; maybe it's just infatuation. Maybe it's just the attention—he came along at the right time. When that couple had just chided me for being without a partner in Madrid. I set it up! The universe was merely complying with my request, my intention. Pero, then what happens? I do sometimes feel the butterflies—a strange sense of foreboding. As if something is about to happen.

Still. Nena's no fool! She will not let her guard down and remains engaged but distant. Resists his holding her hand in public. Cannot allow herself to be with him constantly. Limits their visits, their outings. But with time she forgets. She allows the forgetting. A letting go. And she returns to that warm feeling. On weekdays it's easier to have him pick her up at the library, go to dinner, and then go to his place. And on weekends when she is not traveling, she stays over and they go on outings, enjoy each other's company. Enjoy just being together, quietly reading or working together in his piso, cozy, as if they'd been together for years.

She tells María José, It must be spring fever. Why else do I feel this way? They link arms, laugh, and walk by the pond where two swans squawk, apparently having an argument. Nena and her friend laugh even harder. She laughs so hard tears stream down her cheeks.

Chinese Test

*A*t a bar near Recoletos, the fresh calamares dipped in a light batter and deep fried remind Nena of the onion rings at the Glass Kitchen in Laredo, but the taste surprises her. She sips a glass of tinto; they are having tapas before dinner. It's been a warm day. Paco picked her up at the Biblioteca, and they took a cab to the bar to meet Luis. Paco left his car at the office. Didn't want to mess with traffic and parking at the bar. Luis never shows, so they decide to go to dinner. As they walk out of the bar, Nena puts on her jean jacket; the late March evening has turned chilly.

He suggests a Chinese restaurant that's way over near Plaza España. We can take a metro, he says. Be there in no time.

Nena agrees, Chinese would be terrific, and besides it's near a red-line metro stop, her line, so she'll be near her piso and he can keep going on the metro to the office to pick up the car. She tells him that and he smiles—you're always planning, anticipating. So? Nena retorts. No, nada, it's just an observation. Love that about you.

Vale, she responds. The term as familiar now as "okay."

In the metro they stand in the somewhat-full car. Close, holding on to the chrome bar, he looks at her and she feels tingly all over. She tries to distract herself by observing the passengers: Four young teens, punk haircuts and pseudo-gothic getup, talk loud and dirty. A matronly red-haired woman wearing too much blue eyeshadow disapproves, holds her purse tightly against her chest. An old man wearing a toupee pretends to read a newspaper, but Nena can tell he is listening to the kids. A Central American couple, speaking in a distinctly Salvadorean Spanish, talk about their children. And various and sundry tired workers go home for the evening, immersed in their own inner dialogue. And then it's their stop. Plaza España.

They rush out with the crowd and walk to the Restaurante Chino Gran Dragón.

Near the entrance a sign warns against blocking the driveway: No Aparcar en la Rampa. Nena smiles at how here in Madrid there is a sign with the very language that would find purists back home in a tizzy. Aparcar is so similar to parkear, which is what they say in south Texas. The purists insist on estacionar. And rampa, obviously a cognate for ramp, would render the speaker a pocho, or pocha, someone who knows more English than Spanish and whose Spanglish is a disgrace to the mother tongue. Háblame en cristiano, Nena's father always insists when she or her siblings lapse into Spanglish or English at home.

She and Paco have had the discussion about language, and Nena was adamant, explained that there is no perfect language, no wrong language either. Patiently explained why she speaks both English and Spanish and how it is for border dwellers like herself to use both to create a new form of communication. In Laredo they call it Tex-Mex, but more and more she's been hearing "Spanglish" used to refer to that particular language she and others like her use, happily and smoothly blending both English and Spanish. He tells her he is fascinated and loves it that she lapses into that language with him. Still, he often asks what a word means, or a phrase. One day, without thinking, as she was trying to get him to push a button on the recorder, she instructed, Púshale el botón. He turned to her with a wide grin and said, Te entendí, ya hablo Tex-Mex!

As they walk in, the tiny bells hung on the door ring and Nena is surprised at how similar the interior is to a Chinese restaurant in Lincoln—red velvet wallpaper, a fish tank greeting the diners, and an altar with a happy Buddha and a few offerings. The Oriental Kitchen in Laredo only has a semblance of Chinese décor—the Happy Buddah next to the cash register, and a giant fan with Chinese characters gracing the wall. The food is predictable fare, but you can ask for jalapeños with your egg rolls and there's Mexican candy—dulce de calabaza—for dessert. But here Nena finds the menu challenging. Some things she knows. Rollitos de primavera is easy: spring rolls. But what is Familia feliz or árroz tres delicias? The menu is printed in Spanish and Chinese.

Trust me, Paco says. I'll order for us.

When the food comes she is amazed at how in just a few weeks he knows her likes and dislikes. He's ordered the perfect meal: the rolls, a rice dish, and beef and chicken dishes. He asked for Chinese spinach that's not even on the menu! They share it all. Laugh as they read their Chinese astrological signs and try to figure out if indeed they fit the characteristics.

He explains that the Franco government allowed Peter Yang, the owner, to set up the restaurant, first in Barcelona and later in Madrid, because he used to be a priest in Shanghai. Franco allowed him to set up his restaurants in Spain at a time when few foreigners could do business in Spain. Immersed in discussion about the politics and the way Franco controlled everything, even who could open a restaurant, they don't notice, but suddenly there's a woman at their table saludando, Hola, ¿qué tal Paco, qué hay? He rises to greet her and the other woman who is now approaching.

He introduces them: Rosi, Mili . . . Nena, una amiga. And they greet. Nena senses that they are inspecting her, feels like a bicho raro, a rare animal under their scrutiny. The women move on and sit at a nearby table, and Paco explains that they are his coworkers Rosa María and Milagros— friends who have worked with him for over eight years. She feels that she is under Rosi's critical eye; she can't relax. They finish their meal, and as they are leaving they say good-night to Rosi and Mili.

Nena suddenly understands: he planned it all, it was a set up. He was showing her off. And she is both pleased and disappointed. Did she pass the test?

Walking. Talking.
Reading. Sewing.

*R*ainy, Saturday morning in March. Nena and Paco take a long walk, stop to window-shop, to read titles in bookstore windows. They compare views of what books mean or meant to them. I read *Gone with the Wind* three times, she says. Tells him the story of how at sixteen she thought it was a wonderful romantic story; at twenty-one she realized it was a historical novel; but at thirty she hated it as the sexist trash that it is.

He smiles. I have not read it. Saw the movie—liked the history. But. I read *Pedro Páramo*, he proclaims proudly.

Nena considers that he is trying hard by bringing up a Mexican classic.

Historical novels, love them, he says.

I'm not into that, she admits.

They are different as can be. Favorite titles revealing so much. The French and the Russian writers up there for both. He likes Galdós; she, Pardo Bazán.

I want to read some contemporary Spanish writers, she says. Women writers preferably.

I can get you some that are just out. The press where I work puts them out, you know. Let me find some titles for you. Okay? Rosa Montero, you'll like her.

They opt to walk instead of taking the metro, and as they near her piso, they end up at a phone booth near the metro entrance.

See, here is where I call you from, she confesses.

Really? Near here, a couple of blocks over, lives a friend of mine, he says.

She fingers the coins in her pocket. The coins. Pesetas. Spent on phone calls. No móviles then. No cell phones to interrupt and to bring people together and so far apart. It is a time before cell phones. Everyone is reading in the metro. Magazines, books, even books of poetry!

It's as if holding a book is also a sign of status. Everyone smokes cigarettes, carries them like a complement to being well dressed, having good taste. Cigarettes are part of one's attire. There are no No Smoking signs, no smoke-free places anywhere. Her aversion is clear, and yet no one seems to notice that she is coughing or that her eyes are watery. Nena is grateful that Paco is a non-smoker.

No, never have been a smoker, he tells her when she asks. ¿Y tú?

Tampoco, I never started. Promised my father I wouldn't if he quit. And he did so I didn't.

Women feel liberated with their cigarettes; feel glamorous wearing tight, straight-legged Lois jeans and spike-high heels, cigarette in hand. Nena is tempted but resists the allure. She promised her father she would never smoke if he quit—both she and Tino promised—and she has never smoked cigarettes. But. The shoes are an even stronger force, and she almost succumbs, trying on several pairs in a shoe store on Gran Vía. She resists the urge to indulge her penchant for shoes—shoes, everywhere and in all kinds of colors and styles, from alpargatas to elegant boots and pumps. But. She sticks to her Birkenstocks. Ugly shod thin feet, sooty from the street. When it gets cold, she resorts to her brown leather penny loafers bought at a bargain because no one wears them here; she brought some heavy boots she's had since she lived in Nebraska but has no use for them here; it's never that cold. The heavy sweaters remain stashed in her closet, taking up room.

The reading is therapy. Barb, her friend from Lincoln, sends a care package: *Rubyfruit Jungle* by Rita Mae Brown and some poetry books by local poets. She devours them and fears she may be lagging behind, not keeping up with what is being published. But. At the same time, reading, any reading, eases the saudade. What else can she do?

To mitigate her homesickness, Nena comes up with a plan. She'll start sewing. She likes good fabrics, likes to sew although she has not done so in ages. Her mother, an accomplished seamstress, taught her how to sew the old way, making her own pattern. Nena loves to pick fabric and cut the pattern with measurements, not the Simplicity or McCall patterns that would never fit her thin frame just right. Once she has decided, she goes to the fabric section housed in the basement of the department store she has come to love, for in it she can find anything from a fancy pen to fabric for sewing—El Corte Inglés. She buys a pale-green plaid cotton. She then cuts and stitches a blouse by hand. She buys various colors of thread and embroiders a string of flowers along the neckline. She will wear the top when the weather is warmer. Just creating it makes her feel at home. Her roomies are impressed. Ronnie asks, How do you find the time?

It's my therapy, she answers. I just have to do it.

Her mother asks her to find crochet patterns, her father asks for chess books. She scours bookstores and finds some at el Rastro, the largest flea market imaginable. She often visits el Rastro on Saturdays and Sundays with Ronnie, scouring the vendors' stalls for fun and unique wares. The vendors set up in their usual places week after week, so she gets to know them. She visits the one with the antique toys regularly. Chats about this and that and snaps photos of the dolls. Silent witnesses to the chaos around them.

On one of their outings, Nena buys a Guatemalan huipil at the Rastro. Remedios, the gypsy who has the vintage clothes stall, calls her over. Nena has gotten to know her. She bought a shawl from her a couple of weeks earlier. The vendor has no idea what the piece of garment is exactly. She got the huipil as part of a pallet of used

clothing she bought from another vendor. Clothes sold by weight. Remedios can salvage almost anything—clean it up, mend it, iron it, and sell it at the Rastro. Nena barters some, and as she does she imagines the story the huipil must hold in its woven threads. How did a Guatemalan huipil end up here? Amid the trash there are treasures. The huipil is one. She also finds dolls, new ones with shiny, bright dresses and yellow yarn hair. She's thrilled to find chess books for her father—she buys them one at a time and sends them to her father in installments. So much to wade through!

Alas, she cannot find crochet patterns in books for her mother. But she finds finely crafted doillies that she buys for her to copy. As in life, the treasures abound, remain hidden until you learn where to look. And as in life they appear when you least expect it.

Friday Ritual

*O*ne Friday afternoon when she's not traveling, Nena walks from the Biblioteca to Paco's place under a light spring drizzle, enjoying the humidity, feeling her hair curl. She even splashes in a puddle, careless and carefree, like a schoolgirl. She thinks back to the puddles she and her siblings liked to splash in playing out on San Carlos Street on those rare rainy days in September.

She called Paco and they decided to have Chinese from the restaurant down the street from his building. He has already picked up the boxes with her favorite sweet and sour shrimp and fried rice. She arrives, takes off her sandals, and she's massaging her tired feet when Paco offers, Let me wash your feet.

Are you kidding?

But he's not, and he does. Venga, he instructs, and they squeeze into the small bathroom with the pale-yellow walls, the color of sand. She feels pampered as he sits her down on the bathtub's edge, rolls her jean legs up, and puts her feet in the warm running water. He lovingly caresses and kisses her feet.

Now your hair. Venga. Your hair is so long, I love your long, curly hair.

No, she protests, the food is getting cold.

But he will not be deterred. We can heat it up later, he says.

He proceeds to wash her hair in the tiny sink. They laugh as he whistles a tune while he shampoos her hair with Herbal Essence. As he massages her scalp she feels pampered and loved. She feels at home.

Come, it's your turn, she says. And now it's his turn to object, but he finally succumbs to her pleas to let her wash his hair.

Me encanta como hueles, just love your scent, he says as he snuggles into her hair, drying it with the deep-purple towel.

¿A qué? Herbal Essence? She laughs and uses the same towel to dry his hair.

No, your scent. I'm not sure what it reminds me of. Cinnamon and anise. Also mint . . . altogether. It makes me drunk. Your essence. Your you. Your very own smell. It makes me drunk, he whispers.

She teases, Interesting that you who don't drink are drunk!

Right, I don't drink alcohol, but I drink you, your scents. Why don't you believe I'm crazy for you? Only for you. No one will ever love you the way I do. Forever.

Nena chastises him, although her heart is all aflutter. Stop it. No digas tonterías. You know I'll leave soon, so don't come around with that now.

So, what if you leave? You are always talking about living in the present, as the Buddhists tell us to do. Well, for now, you are here in my arms and in my mind. Forever.

He looks into her eyes.

Nena denies him his feelings: I don't believe you. Eso de forever is a line men use to lure women, puro invento de los hombres para ligarse a las mujeres.

He insists, Don't be stubborn. Believe me. Creémelo. You are imprinted in my brain and in my heart forever.

She questions him, ¿A poco? Really? And thinks, No. I can't allow this to go any farther. He is a gachupín! She had not realized it before, but the conflict is real for her. It's visceral. The hated Spanish who conquered her ancestors, how can she? Is she a Malinche? Her grandmother's words haunt her: Don't fall in love, mi niña. Am I falling in love? I can't. I won't. But.

He persists, Forever. Te digo que sí . . . flaca. He uses the term of endearment that she doesn't appreciate. As he kisses her.

To her surprise, Nena kisses him back. She was not expecting that. Her head full of contradictions and conflict, she changes the mood and says, Let's eat, as she leads him by the hand to the kitchen. I love Chinese, she exclaims.

Wonderful, it's still warm, Paco observes and snuggles close to her as they sit at the tiny table in his kitchen. Her fortune cookie reads: Your travels will be your teacher.

His: Your smile will tell you what makes you feel good.

He wants her to spend the night, but she wants to go back to her apartment. I'll take the metro if you don't want to drive me. I have things to do for tomorrow.

He drives her home and before getting out of the car parks in front of the apartment building. He holds her hand. Tell me how you feel. I keep telling you I am crazy about you, que estoy enamorándome, even if I don't want to because I know you are leaving. But I can't help it. Así es. So. How do you feel?

Nena feels trapped. What can she answer? Her heart is melting, so she knows she too has strong feelings and is being cautious, not wanting to hurt. Heeding her grandmother's admonition. I can't, she whispers. I can't. Not yet. Maybe never.

He repeats, How do you feel?

Nena teases, I feel squeaky clean! I love that you are so loving. No one had washed my feet before, at least not since I was a child—I'm sure my mother or my grandmother, Bueli, washed my feet when I was a kid. She knows she's talking too much and too fast, trying to divert his attention.

He reaches over and kisses her. She is one with the universe, her soul is one with his. But she remains aware that the doorman is probably watching them. That Señora Berreneche is probably peeking through the curtains, also watching. She pulls away and gets out.

He follows her to the doorway and says, Okay. Okay. Vale. Vale. I understand. No te asustes, don't be afraid.

She doesn't call him on Saturday or Sunday. Stays in and works on trasncriptions of the interviews. Writes letters home. Goes to mass at a nearby church, just because. Goes to a movie at the filmoteca by Plaza España. Alone. He has no way of calling, and she knows it. When she is at the movies on Sunday afternoon, he comes by and leaves a note with the doorman. It's cryptic. Short and sweet. Llámame.

So she walks to the corner to call from the public phone. He answers and they talk, make plans for next week. It's going to be a busy week, she says. I am really busy.

Yes, so am I, he says. Pero, ¿podemos quedar para comer? ¿Voy por ti mañana?

No. Mejor el miércoles, pick me up at the tertulia on Wednesday.

On Monday at the library over a cup of coffee, during their morning break, Nena shares her dilemma with Ronnie, confides that she may have gone too far and there's no turning back. Don't worry, Ronnie advises, you are leaving y se acabó. All will end as it must, you'll see. On Wednesday he picks her up, and they have a quiet dinner at one of their favorite restaurants on the Gran Vía. They talk about their week, chat about his friend Lorenzo, who is going to Chile to do research on fiestas. She tells him about María José and her dilemma. They avoid talking about their fears, their feelings. Safer that way.

Public Displays

*O*n Friday they go to a farewell party for Lorenzo and Camila at their place. Nena doesn't know this group of friends, mostly coworkers of Paco's and a few faculty members, Lorenzo's colleagues, but she enjoys herself talking politics—some are bad-mouthing Adolfo Suárez and praising Felipe González, others are defending him and the way he's handled the transition—and talking about literature and the latest spiff at the way the ministros were selected. No women. Nena is in her element talking politics and literature. Although she is often at a loss and can't quite follow all the political alliances. She knows the PSOE and the PCE—obvious, Partido Socialista Obrero Español and Partido Comunista Español—but the other acronyms and parties are difficult to keep in perspective. Too much.

Paco has a bit of wine and soon is feeling sick. Nena feels a headache coming on, so they leave. Go back to his apartment to relax and listen to music. Healing music, he claims—Vivaldi's "Four Seasons." It will help, he promises, and her headache subsides.

The next morning, a lazy Saturday morning, they take a long, leisurely bath, feel scrubbed clean as if they'd been to a baño árabe, the kind of Arabic baths where you emerge as if renewed, like the one Nena went to in Fez where the bathers scrub you down as they go on with their conversations, as if they were scrubbing down a pet or a child. Never mind who you are, what you do, in their expert hands you are a body to be washed, and they do their job well. Nena and Paco emerge that Saturday walking hand in hand. Nena allows the PDA, a public display of affection, that she normally shuns. Of course, it could be private display of affection. Holding hands is inoffensive, feels right. But there are some gestures she will not tolerate. In fact, their first argument was over exactly that.

¿Es que te avergüenzas de ir conmigo? he asks, wounded, thinking she is embarrassed to be seen with him as she removes his arm from around her shoulders. He is slightly taller at five foot nine, and it felt so natural to drape his arm around her shoulders as they walked.

No, Nena shoots back, it's not that, I just don't like the way men do that, no me gusta cómo los hombres le ponen el brazo sobre el hombro a las mujeres al andar, as if proclaiming to the world, ¡Es mía! She's mine. All mine.

Paco is curious, perplexed, asks, Pero, why would you think that? It's not about ownership of the woman; it's about showing your feelings publicly, like shouting to the world, I love her and she loves me, and I am the luckiest man in the world.

And Nena insists, Pues no sé, for me it means the other, the ownership, a sign of the patriarchy.

He stops walking and looks at her. I knew it! You and your feminist ideas are at the root . . . Or is it your prudish ways? The same ones that taught you to say *mande*? I have to warn you, stop saying it or someone will believe you and order you around. So she almost shouts but instead whispers back, But not you, right?

And he resumes walking, his hands in his pockets. No, not me. I am falling in love, and I am at *your* beck and call. Order me. Mándame y obedezco. He looks into her eyes, and she looks away. ¿Qué, flaca?

And don't call me that.

Why not? It's a term of endearment. Like when I call you *chata* or *moza*. Or *chicanita*.

Estás loco de veras, she accuses him. Loony! They are not the same. She cringes and is aware that she's picking a fight. She doesn't mind that like all Spaniards he seems to use terms of endearment like *chata* or *cariño* freely. And a couple of times he has called her *chicanita*—she found that endearing, although she doesn't like diminutives and hates being called Nenita. But. *Flaca* elicited a similar reaction. Perhaps it's a reminder of kids teasing her for being skinny. She remembers a line from a poem she wrote when she was in high school: "You can never be thin enough, they say, but I know better."

She knows the pain of taunts, of teasing. *Esqueleto rumbero*, the kids would tease, and hot tears would roll down her cheeks. *Palillo* and *pinche flaquinche*—they'd hurl the words.

Sticks and stones hurt but so can words.

Her reverie is interrupted as she hears Paco pleading, Please understand, we are one, I am yours. You are mine.

She stops. See what I mean? No one owns anyone. Not you me, nor I you. It's against what I feel and believe. No one can ever utter those words and remain respectful of the other person. Ray Charles sang, You don't own me . . . y así es.

And they continue walking, and now she is holding his hand. And he says, Pues yo sí. I respect and admire and love and adore you . . . and I claim you, eres mía. Solo mía. And I am yours. Take me, I'm yours . . . isn't that what the song says?

Now she is confused and perplexed; the feelings she's been keeping at bay rush forward, and she is swallowed by it all, and tears come to her eyes as she says, Songs are songs. Only that. Like my Papagrande's dichos, there's always one to refute the other.

That night on his brass bed, as they snuggle close and fall asleep under the chenille bedspread that reminds her of the one at home when she was a child, she thinks, No, no one owns another. But it sure feels like being owned, this thing called love, or lust, or whatever it is. And she knows that this too might pass as it has in the past, as it has for that other gentle man who loved jazz and taught her to listen. She taught him to feel, he said.

Paco whispers, Where would you like to go tomorrow for our paseo de domingo? I know you love our Sunday outings.

And she answers dreamily, I do. If it doesn't rain, let's go to Segovia, and we can take my friends.

¿Las Norteamericanas?

Yeah, why not? They've been wanting to go.

Won't they be offended?

Claro que no, why would they be offended?

No sé. Because of how I talk or how I look or how I dress.

Nena smiles. That's sweet that you think they would find fault. They adore you, she reassures him.

Segovia

*N*ena, Ronnie, and Giovanna squeeze into Paco's apple-green Seat and fly toward the aqueduct city. It's not raining when they drive away from the city; the weather is clear, and Nena begs Paco to stop the car so she can take pictures of a field of amapolas, the red poppies bright against the blue sky.

Then suddenly the sky turns gray, and a light drizzle begins to fall. Nena jokes that she can feel her hair frizzing up. And she can—it feels like it is defying Segovia's gray gloom with its wispy, tight curls. They arrive and the rain stops. They stroll along ancient streets. At one point Paco stops and exclaims, ¡Alucinante! This restaurant was here when I was stationed here. They're in front of a tiny restaurant by the military compound.

You were in the military? Giovanna asks innocently.

Yes, I served. We all did. We had to. They had killed my father, but I still had to come. I traveled from Gijón, my hometown in Asturias. Lorenzo, you've met him—he points to Nena with his chin—and another friend Pepe, and I. We had been together since elementary school. My mother, 'ombre, casi se muere. She was devastated. But I was eighteen, and he had been dead for more than fifteen years.

Did he die in the war? Giovanna asks.

No, years later. The killings didn't stop when the war ended. Paco pauses as if remembering. Have you heard of the Red Terror? Well, the

casualties of the White Terror were even greater. A deep silence falls like a shadow as all of them feel his sorrow, palpable and heavy like the gray clouds overhead.

Paco continues, I hardly remember him. I knew nothing of the details of his death, but I knew how hard it was for my mother. I hated them, all those military men full of their power. Gillipollas. Excuse my French, as you say, he apologizes to her friends. Hope I didn't offend.

Ronnie answers too quickly, Of course not. Nena senses that they are judging him.

She is embarrassed but not much. Wants them to like him but also wants him to be himself, to allow his anger at the military and at the men who ruled with an iron fist after the war and even now. Los militares. Los politicos.

They stop in front of a store, and Nena takes a picture of the window display: dolls in traditional dress. ¡Qué majas! Ronnie exclaims.

What memories! he muses as they walk the streets in Segovia near the aqueduct.

Good ones? asks Giovanna.

Yes, some of them. We would go out on the town . . . and I fell in love. She was blonde with velvet eyes, like in the Agustin Lara song, eyes the color of jacaranda en flor.

I thought you said they were blue, Nena adds, remembering a story about one of his girlfriends.

No, velvet. Or maybe they were blue. Or green. It's been a long time.

Did you love her? Ronnie asks.

Of course, with the love an eighteen-year-old can feel.

Turning to Nena he says, Not like I love you. We were just kids. What do we know of love at eighteen? Nothing, eh? It's just hormones gone wild.

The Roman aqueduct duly impresses them, and Paco leads the way up as he tells them of the Roman presence in Spain. If you go to Córdoba you'll see a statue to Seneca. He was born there! And all over Spain the Roman ruins lie dormant, unexcavated, except for a few sites, he

explains. In Andalucía, well in Sevilla, to be more exact, the Roman theater is perhaps the best preserved. And in León you can see the Roman wall. In many villages the Roman bridges still stand. They were built to last, Paco says with a grin.

In front of the cathedral three women, gypsies, accost them, follow them, showing them crocheted and embroidered tablecloths, napkins, peddling their wares. One is more brazen and comes up to Nena and offers a sprig of rosemary and says, I'll read your palm, tell your fortune. Nena smiles but shakes her head no. Paco intervenes, No. No. No. Ale, vamos. And he shoos them away. Nena can't figure out if she's relieved or upset that he did that. They were only doing what they do to make a living. There was no need to use such a tone. Paco senses her discomfort and says to the group, You just have to talk like that, otherwise they will follow you until they make a sale. Or tell you silly predictions, take all your money. It's a scam.

At the cathedral Nena lights a candle for her new niece—may she be forever blessed—and for her parents—may they be healthy and live long. They walk to a restaurant Paco claims is more authentic than the popular Mesón de Cándido, where all tourists go for the local delicacy, chochinillo asado. This one is far better, Paco explains. And when they get there, the waiter knows Paco and seats them immediately although there is a line. The food is indeed delicious, and Nena makes an effort and has a bit of the chochinillo, putting aside her aversion to pork. For dessert, flan. Homemade! Reminds Nena of María José, who makes the smoothest and creamiest flan Nena has ever tasted.

The traffic is horrendous as they drive back—this always happens on Sundays coming back into town, Paco explains. He invites them all up to his piso for drinks. The traffic will lessen in about an hour, then he'll drive them back to their piso. In his apartment he turns on the stereo system and has them listen to six versions of the same aria.

Giovanna discusses the music with him. Nena feels left out. Despite her efforts to educate herself on classical music, she feels inadequate, musically illiterate. Unless it's Tejano or conjunto she doesn't dare discuss music with anyone. She's an expert on the music of northern Mexico, los Alegres de Terán, Chelo Silva, and local groups like Sunny and the Sunliners, Little Joe y la familia, who used to come to Lincoln to play at the Radisson Hotel for Mexican dances. She also loves the music her parents love, boleros and rancheras from the movies—Tito Puente, Pedro Infante, Antonio Aguilar, Tito Guisar, Toña la Negra, Javier Solís, and a young Armando Manzanero. She also knows her generation's music: Leo Dan, José José, and others. Of course, nueva trova, the political music of the Americas, Lucerito, Mercedes Sosa, Silvio Rodríguez. She has discovered Triana and loves the sound of flamenco rock. But Paco will have none of it. It's not pure, he argues. He offers them wine, and a lively conversation ensues about the benefits of drinking a glass of wine every day.

It's almost midnight when Paco drives them all back to their piso on Rodríguez San Pedro. That night Nena is listening to the radio and bursts into tears when the announcer switches from the classic jazz pieces he's been playing to play "Una furtiva lachrima" from Donizetti's *The Elixir of Love*. The music is touching her the way listening to Valerio Longoria, or Bonnie Raitt, or Willie Nelson, or Sunny, or even Linda Ronstadt or Joni Mitchell touches her. And she thinks, I guess this is my music after all.

Asturias y Tejas

Nena and Paco relished discussing their differences and similarities. We're continents apart, he jokes. Although they agree, they also disagree. They enjoy discussing politics, social class, of course, and gender differences and comparing their childhood memories, stories of growing up in Asturias or Tejas. She holds firm to her disdain of the colonizers; he understands but tries to argue that it was a long time ago—almost five hundred years ago!

One afternoon, after walking for what seemed hours, they are sitting at a park bench en el Retiro near the fountain when Nena tells him how once she had danced with a black man at a party and her friend's brother came up and told the guy to beat it. The black man was stationed at the air base in Laredo, and the local guys always had problems with the local women dating these foreigners. The racism was palpable.

She talks slowly and pensively, reminiscing and reflecting on the incident. How she couldn't believe it. Her own brother wouldn't have done that. Then she tells him of another incident. Once, almost on a dare, she had a date with an Anglo who was a nurse at the air base hospital. It was so bizarre. Her coworker Araceli set it up. Nena met him at a parking lot because for some reason she didn't want her family to know. She went with him on his motorcycle to his trailer, where he lived alone as so many of the air-base guys did. They had dinner, smoked a joint, and then listened to the Who. He had a terrific stereo system he'd gotten in Japan when he was on R and R from Vietnam; it was reel to reel and the sound was terrific. *Tommy* rang out as if live. She was thrilled. The music was so alive. And then he took her back to her blue station wagon, the Blue Lady parked at a grocery store parking lot, and she went home. Not even a good-night kiss. The next day, her coworkers Tati and Araceli quizzed her. They wanted to know everything, but there was little to tell. They didn't believe her. And when he called later that day she decided to end whatever it was that never started and told him not to call again. It was so strange being with someone with whom she couldn't even speak in Spanish, and he was so young, and she was a bit scared—what if she fell in love? No. Better end it. As she told Paco the story, she shared that she often wondered why she was always avoiding, always on the defensive. Always seeking a way out.

That's just who I am, she concluded her story. Paco had been listening attentively. He had initiated the conversation, asking her to tell him about race conflicts in the States. But he had not been ready for her personal stories of being a mestiza, of dating, of being herself.

Confessing to Paco felt right—it felt as if he'd understand and not judge her, and it would give him information so he wouldn't expect anything from her. No commitments. No promises. That night as they were going to bed he pulled out a box of photos to show her. His father's picture, his mother's, and his own baby pictures and photos taken when he was in Segovia en la Mili. There was a young blonde girl. Is this the girlfriend from Segovia? Nena asks.

No, es Katherine, es inglesa.

The young woman is wearing a sweater, una rebeca, and Nena asks, for now she can ask anything and not feel ridiculous, Why is it called a rebeca?

He looks at her quizzically. It's from a movie. The protagonist was named Rebecca; she wore a sweater like this one. What do you call it?

Suéter. Or in English cardigan, sweater. What was the movie?

De Alfred Hitchcock, la película es *Rebeca*, like the protagonist.

He explains, It's also called a jersey, pronounced "hersay" because it comes from Jersey in England.

And he asks, ¿Y porqué los americanos dicen elevator y los ingleses lift? And she knows the answer. Nena asks, Why do they say vaqueros or Tejanos for blue jeans?

I don't know, probably also because of the movies, he laughs. Do you know?

And she doesn't know the answer. Asks, Why do they say Americanos and not Norteamericanos?

He answers, Because they think there is no other world outside of their own. They forget everything. Short-term memory. They even forget that they are immigrants. Of course, not the Indians, the Native Americans. But all the others, every single person in your country is an immigrant or descended from immigrants.

She points out that it's the same in Spain. Many don't know world geography. She tells him of the old man in Almonacid who asked where she was from, and when she said Tejas he asked, ¿Y eso está en Cuba? She tried to explain that, no, it was part of the United States, but he insisted, Pues sí, allá en Cuba, ¿no? He wouldn't let her have the last word; with his toothless grin and cataract eyes he was certain of his knowledge. His old wooden cane hitting the ground with authority.

And Paco answers, Esos gillipollas, they'll die off soon. They're what we have left of Franco's regime when textbooks were a joke. For sure that man never even went to school. And if he did he bought into all the fascist propaganda.

It's the same everywhere, Nena responds. Those who have gone to school may at least know that they don't know everything, but it's sad to see so many just buy into the system and not even recognize their own colonization. The schools teach nothing of our history as a colonized people. That's why I want to go back. To teach about who we are, what we have endured.

Are you sure? You'll wilt and die if you go back.

Nena smiles and doesn't answer. She asks, How did we get to this from looking at a photo?

He lovingly holds the photos. The photos strewn on the chenille bed-spread speak of his past. Each photo tells a story. He pulls out one of him and his sister as kids. She's older. The sister, Paloma, still in the small town in Asturias. She's married now, and with three children she needs all the help she can get. His mother cares for the children when Paloma goes to work at the dairy farm where her husband also works.

Nena talks of a photo that reminds her of this one, a photo of her younger brother, Tino, on his second birthday.

How he cried and cried at the photographer's until she sat next to him and held his hand. Nena feels the sadness surface as it always does when she thinks of her brother. In the photo, they look to the side. Papi must be dangling his keys, or whistling, or clapping his hands to get their attention.

¿Qué pasa? Paco asks, sensing her sadness.

She shares the story of how one Monday morning in February, death came to their door, how her father reacted in anger and sorrow. Her mother wailing in pain—their cries and open weeping scaring the younger children, pulling the neighbors to that house on San Carlos Street; like metal attracted to a magnet they came and kept coming until the day his body arrived in a flag-draped coffin. Tino looked so peaceful, as if he were asleep. She cries quietly as she retells how she made phone calls, notified family and friends. How she called her boss at the office and then called her father's boss, too. She tells him stories of her father, of how hard he's worked all his life. Shares with him her fears for his health. They talk about family. Sharing their dreams. Secrets of childhoods spent under the watchful eyes of parents who care for and love them.

Their intimacy deepens with each shared story of joy or of sorrow. They are constructing a narrative full of their lives, a retelling of a story that's already happened.

The cloud that hangs over them is palpable to Nena: the future. What will happen come the summer? How will they end up? Where? Amor de lejos . . . amor de pendejos! Nena won't think about it, not yet. Will not allow it to spoil the present.

Maíz

*N*ena rushed to the public phone booth to call Paco, still smarting from the incident that made her feel so alien in this land that is not hers. She wanted to hear his voice, to feel grounded.

It was her own fault, she concluded. How could I even dream that such a thing would happen? Someone at the tertulia heard her ask about where to find corn masa for making tortillas. Yes, Nelson piped up. I know a place where they sell corn. A friend of his had told him about it. He gave Nena the information.

Nena so yearned for corn tortillas! The flour ones she made often offered a comfort, a consolation, but the corn ones were nowhere to be found. She had found canned tamales in the gourmet section of the Corte Inglés. Awful! No semblance of what a tamal is. After a couple of bites she had thrown the whole can away. So that day, determined and on a mission, she went to the place Nelson knew about. She took a metro and walked for blocks on end. Finally she arrived at the place only to find it closed; it was still lunchtime. She waited for the store to reopen at four o'clock and rushed in eagerly.

Yes, the man said. They had corn. But it was only for pigs and Mexicans. She felt herself blush and received the insult with anger. Furious, she wanted to lash out, to shout at him, but she didn't; she just turned around and walked out and kept saying to herself, I should have said this and that. Told him off. ¡Viejo gordinflón! ¡Ignorante! El maíz es la vida.

She cooled off and calmly went back in and asked to see the corn. It was just the grain, not even cornmeal, and she realized she didn't know how to prepare el nixtamal for making the masa. How would she soak it in lye and then grind it and finally have it ready for tortillas? So she left the small business with its crowded shelves and dark interior, with the owner wearing a white, bloodstained apron, for he was also a butcher. The musty smell of too old, too dank, too poor. The odor of sadness. The feel of prejudice and bias.

Still smarting from the incident, she rushed to call Paco and tell him about the insult. He comforted her: They are such scum. Son unos cagapalos, no les hagas caso. Tarados. Estúpidos. Forget about them. Gilipollas.

She confides that the corn is part of her being, that she misses the smell of the corn tortillas on the comal, cooking. Even if she cooks a pot of beans, the tortillas are missing. Tells him that the corn is who she is. Corn is in my DNA, she jokes, I am a daughter of the corn goddess. Chicome-coatl. I miss it more than I miss anything else. Corn. Maíz. It is me.

Of course, flour tortillas are also you, he chides, reminding her of a recent conversation about wheat and how in South Texas the flour tortilla is more common than the corn.

Yes, she concedes, but I can easily make flour tortillas here, but not corn. I feel as if something is missing, as if I had no hair, or had lost my teeth. I feel a void. A deep void. Me duele. A hurt so deep I want to cry.

The very next day Paco shows up at her piso with corn tortillas from a Mexican restaurant he'd found in a suburb of Madrid. He had scoured the city looking for them. He was like that. Thoughtful. Loving. As she took out the package from the bag, unfolded the butcher paper to reveal the golden orbs, happy tears came, and she couldn't contain them.

Ya, ya. I want you to be happy, Paco crooned as Giovanna and

Ronnie, who knew nothing about the incident, sat perplexed at the dining room table where they had been preparing their monthly budget.

Nena went to work immediately; she rarely cooked, preferred to wash the dishes and let Ronnie or Giovanna cook. In no time she had fried the tortillas and made tacos with some chicken that they had in the fridge. The enchiladas were a little harder to prepare as she didn't have the right cheese, but they weren't too bad. The big hit was the big pan of Mexican rice cooked with chicken broth and canned peas. He had also brought Mexican beer he found at that same restaurant—a rare find indeed! Everyone agreed: this was by far the best Mexican dinner ever. They also made plans to go have a meal at the restaurant where corn tortillas could be found.

Heavenly! Divinas! Ronnie exclaims.

Nena agrees. The tortillas are exactly right to erase the bad taste of the incident. She chews the carefully cut bite-size pieces of the enchilada and takes a spoonful of rice with a banana sliced in it like Mamagrande had taught her. She is transported. This is home. This food. This moment. He made it happen. Then the realization hits her. She has fallen in love with Paco. No. She almost says it aloud. No. But it's in her heart, in her mind, in her soul. He is special, thoughtful. Yes, she has fallen in love. The butterflies flutter in her belly, and she is no longer hungry. No. She looks around the table and is both joyous and sad all at once. No one seems to notice. But.

Her cravings for her comfort food, those delicious tortillas, has satisfied her craving, eased a bit of the homesickness. But on the other hand she is even more homesick, yearns for the hand-patted ones Bueli would fix. Nena looks around the table and jokes with them to try to ease the pain of saudade: I could eat a hundred and not have enough!

After the meal and a long sobremesa, where Paco tells jokes and Giovanna recites a poem from memory, he leaves alone. Come with me, he pleads, but is not upset that she decides not to go but instead decides to stay and finish working on their budget and taking care of their plans for the next month's trips and tasks. That night in bed, as she writes in her journal, listening to the radio, Nena discovers that she chose to stay because she doesn't quite know what to do with the realization that she is in love.

The next morning, as they are getting ready to leave for the Biblioteca, talking to Giovonna and Ronnie, Nena says, I can't imagine the trouble he went through to please me, to find the tortillas. She confides, I think I'm in love. I don't want to leave.

Possibilities. She could become an immigrant. Overstay her visa. Teach English, at least stay until . . . But. No. She mustn't even consider staying. It is not an option.

So, stay longer, Ronnie urges. Or go home and come back, Giovanna suggests. They keep talking about her options as they walk to the metro. On the ride, Nena's in a daze. The Biblioteca and her work will help. She can't dwell on the matter. It will have to wait. But.

Part III   Jugar con fuego

Board Games

*N*ena stays in Madrid one weekend in April to celebrate Giovan-na's birthday. It's Friday, and she's come home early from the Biblioteca. Taking a break to get herself organized and ready for her next few trips.

Paco picks them up in his Seat; they pile in and go to a Lorca play at the Teatro María Teresa. *La Casa de Bernarda Alba*, one of her favorites! The production is fabulous. The cast stellar. Nena is not disappointed. It's part of an international theater festival, and the company is from Mexico. She loves to hear the melodious Spanish coming from the stage. Even though it is a Castilian play, the actors' Spanish is different, familiar to her ear.

After the play they go to a bar for copas. Paco is quiet and doesn't engage with them. Giovanna asks if anything is wrong.

No, just tired. A long week, he responds.

They take it as sign to call it a night although the Madrid nightlife is just taking off. He jokes about how he is becoming an old fart, not wanting to stay out with such pretty women, go dancing or perhaps bar hopping.

Both Giovanna and Ronnie insist that they too are tired; they want to go home. So they do.

On the way to his place he tells Nena, I have a surprise: tomorrow night we have tickets for a zarzuela. A young tenor has the lead, and I hear he's terrific.

Nena has never seen a zarzuela and wants to know all about the genre.

This one is a classic, *Jugar con fuego* . . . playing with fire. He tells her, I have not seen it in ages. In the south, when I lived in Andalucía, I saw many.

On Saturday night they arrive early and find their seats when the orchestra is warming up. She marvels at the theater. Almost as splendid as where they go for the opera. The audience is different, though. His friend Luis, who also loves opera and plays violin in the national symphony, arrives with his partner, Astrid, a tall German woman who is an artist. Nena feels comfortable with them although she's usually shy around Luis.

At the tercera llamada, about fifty people, all Norteamericanos, come in and sit as a group. It is obvious they are on a tour. Paco seems upset. Are you okay? she asks.

Sí, sí. ¿Pero qué no ves lo que están haciendo? Can't you see the travesty?

But before she can respond the music starts. Each is immersed in thought, Nena wondering what the travesty is. The tourists? As the story unfolds, she wonders if this is their story, hers and Paco's. The music by Barbieri and the lyrics by Vives. The message is not lost on Nena: it's the story of finding true love and the dangers of playing with fire.

Paco holds Nena's hand as they listen. There amid the tour groups and the local aficionados, Nena feels alone with him in the world the music is creating on stage. She can tell he is sad, not just upset. He is sad. Later he will confess that yes, he is sad. Triste. Feels like his heart is breaking and he can do nothing about it. He remains sad at the way the tourists treat shows, as if they were spectacles commodified for their convenience. Sad. The office of tourism is doing it, he is sure, to rake in the money. Sad. How she'll leave and he'll be sad. Triste. Yes. Sí, triste. Sad.

During the intermission Paco and Luis go off to have a drink, and Nena and Astrid decide to stay. They make small talk. Then Astrid asks,

Why don't you join us for lunch tomorrow? Come over to the house. We'll make it a day.

Paco gets home from playing his Sunday morning soccer game. He's picked up churros and they are having their coffee, reading the paper, when he suggests, Let's go for a stroll before we drive to Luis's. As they are walking through the nearby park, she asks, Why were you so upset last night? What was going on?

For various reasons, he explains. Mira, it's the tourism that is ruining the arts in this country. They sell tickets to the travel agencies who then sell packages, and you get busloads of Japanese or Germans or British attending events they have no interest in whatsoever. It's just because it is their way of experiencing Spain—one night of flamenco, one night of zarzuela, a visit to the Prado and another to Plaza Mayor for bacalao y ya.

Nena counters, So? I don't see anything wrong. I wouldn't do it myself—tours are so rushed and you don't really get to see what you really want. There's no time to explore a place on your own. No, I wouldn't do it. But why not support it for others? At least the tour guides have jobs. The ticket sales must keep the performances going, ¿no crees?

Maybe you're right. No sé. I just don't like some of the changes. It was never like that. The events were there for us, for the aficionados who know about it, who can appreciate it.

Soon they are in the car, driving out to the afueras de Madrid to a neighborhood full of small chalets on their way to lunch at Astrid and Luis's. Paco has been there before, so he quickly finds the house and parks. The lunch proceeds without incident. Everyone is very kind to Nena. Another friend, an Asturiana, is there, so Paco and she sing the himno Asturiano, as good nationalists do every time they come together. After lunch and after an extended sobremesa, that wonderful custom of lingering at the table talking, laughing, commenting on the food, or whatever comes up, Astrid asks, Who's interested in playing? And then come the games. Apparently Luis and Astrid like board games, and their re includes numerous games from Spanish Scrabble to Monopoly. They choose one Nena has never heard of or played. It involves partners throwing dice and traveling along a route that the board dictates, a trip that can take you around the world. Nena and Paco travel to and fro on the map that is the board game. But soon they are divided, and Nena ends up going to Africa, on safari, and then by way of Australia she ends up in Tuscany. He goes to Galicia and then to Andorra, and in a few more turns is in Beijing, and then he's visiting the Taj Mahal. A shiver runs down her spine. Goosebumps. She knows it is an omen. They will never be together again. This time in Spain is their time. This time of love will end, and they will not share another such; not in this lifetime. But. She knows they have been together before, perhaps in Italy. Perhaps. Quizás. They continue playing this game that has given her chills, that has reminded her of what is to come. He takes an after-dinner drink but is soon feeling sick.

See, that is why I don't drink, Paco tells Luis, who had insisted that he try the sherry they brought back from Jerez, the tiny hamlet famous for the drink.

Nena suspects he is sick because he also knows the game is prophetic, that they will never have the life they tease and joke about sometimes. His body is reacting.

Just a few nights ago they were engaged in such talk. What kind of children do you think we will have? Mestizos, she answers. Como los de la Malinche. A Spaniard and a Chicana, what else could they be?

True. True. But what color of hair, of eyes, of skin?

The most beautiful in the whole world: hazel eyes, black hair, and cinnamon skin.

And super smart, intelligent, and with a great sense of humor.

They have dream-talked about their ideal home. She prefers a house, he an apartment, so they compromise. They will have a house in the city and a condominium on the beach.

But, Paco says, the furniture must be modern. I can't stand all the antique-filled homes with other people's memories, other people's energies—people who have died—still there in the drawers where they kept their stuff, or in the wood, the scent of a person's cologne.

She agrees. Modern. Contemporary design it will be. All new. All Italian.

Everything brand new, and she would have it made for them, by her friend who designs and makes furniture. They dream like all couples do of what their life would be like if they were to be together forever, grow old together. I am older, he says, so you would take care of me in my old age.

No way, Nena smiles. I would care enough to find someone to care for you, but I too will be old.

They know these are only words, only dreams, only hopes and wishes. And so they construct lives for themselves, lives that will never be. The board game of life is but that, trial and error, luck of the draw, a roulette wheel where one finds love is a game. We only know the rules that we want to learn. The game has many layers, many rules. The game is rigged, and one can only win, never lose, although it means not always getting what you want, but choosing what is to be. No wrong choices. But.

Is there free will? she asks that night as they settle in under the chenille bedspread that she has come to love.

No, it is all predetermined as with animals; we're subject to nature and her rules. There is no free will.

Pero, what about choices? If I want an apple and not an orange, that is free will, no?

No. You chose according to what you were programmed to choose. Por algo you choose the apple. Could be you identify with Eve, he says with a wink. Or it could be in childhood your parents would peel the apple and cut it into tiny bite-size pieces, so you identify apples with your parents caring and doting on you and, of course, that can be very satisfying, so you choose based on your deep memory. Cellular memory. There's no free will, he says definitively.

Pero, Paco, what if you are right and all choices are predetermined y aún así I choose against what would lead me to choose one way.

No, that's just it, there is no choice. ¿No ves?

Pues, no. I can't see it.

Vale. Let me put it this way. Free will is the religious groups trying to guilt trip you. If you have free will, then there is sin. Adam and Eve chose to disobey and eat of the tree of knowledge. La manzana. But truly they did as they were programmed to do. If you tell someone, Don't do this, that is exactly what they will do. Don't fall in love with me, you said, and here I am. See? I have no choice. There is no free will.

Pero. What if that is the choice? Isn't not choosing a choice? Nena asks.

Of course not. It's all semantics. But believe me. There's no such thing as free will.

But. What if?

Quizás. Perhaps.

Alcoy's Moros y cristianos

*A*lcoy. Alicante. A magical space, full of surprises. Nena arrives by bus to find on the main square a reconstructed castle and a battleground where the Moros y cristianos will engage in mock battles. Certainly akin to the ones in México, she deduces, but, as she has read, with a different focus and significance, for here it takes place on the very ground where the battles were fought, and the participants are the descendants of the very families that fought one another, the Christian and the Moor, fighting with sword and word over five hundred years ago. In Mexico the mock battles are Spanish and Indian, and the masked participants assume the roles of conqueror and conquered. In Spain the subsequent inquisition erased any trace of dissent, banished any non-believer. How can the fiesta not resonate with old battles and old resentments? The contests are between the various cofradías to keep the fiesta "pure" and not change a word of the parlamento spoken by the kings and the queens of both the Moor and Christian forces. There are battles won by the Moors, as there were going back centuries ago when they first came and conquered with their superior culture and ruled for eight hundred years—changed the language and the land and the people. Continuous battles two hundred years later changed it once again. The mock battles are staged, frightfully loud so children run and dogs bark. The horses are groomed and made ready for battle. Always the fiesta ends the same way. The Christian king and queen defeat and triumph over the Rey y Reina de los Moros.

Too soon, it's over, the series of mock battles, the parlamentos, the festive lunches and dinners, and the music and the partying. The families who have gathered to remember past celebrations move on, the children outgrow their costumes, and the elders reminisce with nostalgia. It's time to go back to daily tasks, at the bank, at the market, at the drugstore, and at the office or the fields. The workers and the students and even the retirees look back at one more year and cherish the photographs and the videos that record it for posterity. An enterprising photographer has posted thousands of photographs each day of the fiesta, and people come by and select the ones they want to buy. The photos hang on clotheslines with clothespins and form corridors of images.

Nena mingles with the crowds, with the ghosts of past fiestas, and observes it all, records it with her Pentax.

La entrada Mora y la entrada Cristiana. All in honor of San Jorge, their patron saint. The desfile is not really a parade but a procession, as each bando walks along the route to the center of town where the mock battles take place. Each day the deafening sound of the guns and the smell of gunpowder take over the town.

Nena stays at an hostal; she had the foresight of reserving a room weeks in advance. While she trimmed Rose's hair one Saturday morning, they were talking about the upcoming trip, and Rose warned her and insisted that she call and reserve a room. She's glad she did because the town is packed.

Nena's letter to Paco explains:

> I love the fiesta in Alcoy. I felt so much a part of their world;
> I was invited to have lunch with one family then dinner with
> another. I felt I belonged. But only for a bit, then I went back to

being the researcher, the scholar trying to theorize the ancient battle between Moor and Christian, how it has played out in the Americas, where the Moors are the Indians. It's a kind of give and take, no? The substitution of one "infidel" for another, no?

I took a photo of a bull, just for fun. One of the comparsas had it outside their office. You'll love the image!

When she returns to Madrid, anxious to see Paco and to be with him, she notes a change. He is not as warm, not as loving. She is sure that he has seen someone else. She can feel it. ¡No puede ser! A few weeks is all? How can that be? Es que he knows I'll leave. So why not? She counters, Well then, I'll do the same. Find another friend. Make him jealous. We'll see. After all, I've been insisting that this will end. Must end. He's as free to see others as I am.

At the tertulia on Wednesday there's bound to be someone who will be an interesting companion on my next trip, she thinks. Someone who will offer a way to keep it in perspective. Prove to me that I am not really in love. And there is someone: Nelson. Nena sees him as a big happy puppy who needs attention. He's in exile from Uruguay, an expatriate fleeing the political persecution in his country, working as a journalist, writing poems, and working on a novel. And they begin lunch meetings in restaurants on Recoletos. En el Café Gijón. Or some other expensive café where she has manzanilla and he coffee, un cortado. He gives her books by Cernuda and Cela. ¿Qué se cree? That I haven't read them? she ponders. I'm not going around giving him books by Chicanos. En fin. She keeps quiet and lets him offer gifts. But she knows this Latin American expatriate is not for her. Resists his advances. Nelson is a good friend of Manolo's. Manolo who has already left Madrid and is living in A Coruña. But Nelson is a handy distraction, and Nena will not confront Paco. To do so would only indicate she is interested and maybe even jealous. No. Better leave it as it is. Unsaid. She has no proof. Has not seen anything. Ojos que no ven, corazón que no siente. What the eyes don't see the heart can't feel. But.

Washington Irving Cultural Center

At the library of the US Embassy's Washington Irving Cultural Center, Nena finds books and magazines. She reads *The New Yorker*, *Newsweek*, *Time*, *Saturday Review*, *The Atlantic*, and *Harper's*, trying to keep up with what's happening in the States and not lose touch with her English. Immersed in Spanish, she finds herself forgetting words now and then; it is disturbing. Her roommates tease her and note that there are even some hints that she will begin speaking como Española, ceceo and all.

Nena refuses, says, No, I will never pronounce the *z* or the *c* with that strange lisp. Nor will I drop the endings the way Andaluces do, the way some folks speak at home. But she notes it herself. How she seems to imitate the Spanish of a region when she is there. In Valencia and Barcelona it is the Catalán intonation that creeps in. In Andalucía it's the relaxed consonants and dropped syllables. When she thinks about the influences, the changes, she also thinks of her sentimientos. Feelings, not sheltered, but open and raw. She is allowing herself to feel. To love. She is changing. Becoming more herself, perhaps. Quizás. The library is a kind of home, a respite and a refuge all at once.

A well-stocked library for sure, but the books are old. Classics of American literature—Faulkner, Hemingway, Twain, Hawthorne. She wants to read the contemporary writers, Rita Mae Brown and John

Cheever, Canadian Alice Munro. And these come to her in the mail, gifts from a friend in Lincoln who knows her love of books. Who writes brief cryptic notes: "All is well, but here we have some rumblings about changes in the department," or, "Hope you are well, one of our colleagues collapsed when running laps and died of a heart attack."

Who? Nena wants to shout. Is it someone I know? But she only gets to fill the gaps weeks later when her own letter gets answered, for it is the time before email, even before phone cards that make calls affordable. The husband of one of her favorite professors was jogging during the lunch hour at the university track where Nena used to jog. He just literally collapsed. Dead of massive heart failure. Nena remembered seeing them holding hands at a concert and thinking how romantic it would be to grow old together like that. They seemed ancient to her although they were probably only in their mid-forties. And now he is gone. Just like that.

Years later, another colleague would also just suddenly collapse and die. In the middle of a tennis game with his brother. Healthy, seemingly full of life and with a full life ahead of them, people die, just like that. At least when someone is sick you expect it, await it, let yourself grieve for what is to happen, but when it happens so suddenly the only feeling is that of betrayal. How could he just up and die? How could she just collapse and check out? It's not fair. Is it fate? Is life also scheduled?

Does one reach the allotted time and then that's it? Can one choose death the way one supposedly chooses birth?

The Center's library is a quiet and welcoming space. Once a week, usually on Wednesday afternoons before heading to the tertulia, Nena will walk through the glass doors and go through security to sit for hours in the comfortable seats in the reading room. She meets others there who are also drawn there for similar purposes—to read current magazines, newspapers, and journals. She feels at home in that environment. But she resists, writes in her journal of the contradictions—how can I be so colonized that I feel patriotic to a country that has so mistreated my people? We are a colonized people in South Texas. And yet Nena is comforted to hear English. My linguistic self is multilingual, she muses—English, Spanish, Tejano, Spanglish, and others in between. Why can't Paco understand this basic fact about her? She is Norteamericana, but she is not a gringa. She is Mejicana, but she is more Tejana. She is a mestiza. She encompasses all who have made her who she is. Including her languages. Including her Spanish. Including her English. Including her Caló. Including her Tex-Mex. Yes. All of it.

Nena sees a notice that James Baldwin will be reading on a Tuesday afternoon at the library and makes plans to attend. She arrives early and finds a good seat. There's only about twenty people in the audience, mostly Spanish students and a few Norteamericanos. No one in her Fulbright cohort, she notes. Her roommates had other plans and couldn't make it. Paco was at the opera. But he understood her choice. She arrives alone.

Right on time, in walks the cultural attaché for the embassy and a short, slight black man with the most engaging smile. He wears a gray wool sweater over a plain blue shirt and dark-gray slacks. Nena is tickled pink, as her friend Sally would have said, to be there, to hear him. She has read all she could get her hands on, not for a class but for herself. She loves the way he uses words. She idolized him from the start. Now she wishes she had his books with her to get him to sign them, but alas, they are back in Texas, neatly placed on the makeshift bookshelves in the living room of her childhood home on San Carlos Street, worlds away.

After he concludes his talk, she stands in line to shake his hand. When it is her turn she expresses her admiration, tells him how much she loves his work. He humbly looks into her eyes and thanks her as he takes her hand in both of his, cradling the thin, bony hand as if tenderly holding a bird.

He asks, Where are you from?

Texas, she answers. He smiles. Tough place.

Yes, it is, she agrees.

Semana Santa in Cuenca

$\mathcal{H}$oly Week en Cuenca. María José tells her that it's fitting that she shies away from the showier and more studied Andalusian celebrations in Sevilla or Granada. She chooses to spend Holy Week in the quiet town with the hanging houses built into the mountain, apparently suspended in midair. Nena gets off the bus, quite a stretch from the center of town. She begins walking, her backpack weighing more and more with each step. Then a car stops. A couple, an older man and his wife, well dressed and perfumed, offer Nena a ride to town. They live in Madrid, have come home for the celebration. It's Thursday of Holy Week, the day when the church elders wash the feet of the poor, of the monaguillos, and of those selected to participate in the ritual. I think I'll skip it, she says, and asks that they drop her off at her friend Sarah's house.

In Cuenca Nena finds herself among friends, others who have come for the fiesta. Friends of friends who take her in and show her the ropes. There's a party to go to—indeed, the whole town is one big party. The pasos every day for the religious—the hooded men of the cofradías, the ancient guilds—remind her of the KKK, and she can't shake the image, although these men don such garb as prayer and atonement. A group of drummers wear wigs and berets.

Penitents wear deep berengena, eggplant-purple or deep-chocolate-brown cassocks and hoods, peer through holes with piercing eyes. Some

even go barefoot, carry the heavy pasos with holy images, so heavy up to forty men are needed on each side, and they walk in perfect synchronicity. The smell of incense in the church reminds Nena of the Holy Week celebrations in Laredo, her father's booming voice as he reads the siete palabras, the long biblical passage of Good Friday services. Here there are outdoor services as the processions wind their way through narrow streets.

At her friend Sarah's house, she meets Ángela, a fellow Laredoan married to an artist whose name is Ángel—who with his halo of curly light-brown hair truly looks like one. But. Ángela can't believe Nena is from her hometown, that they have mutual friends, acquaintances. They know the border town so well. Even Ángel has visited Laredo—he found it dry and hot and inhospitable. He who comes from this hidden town up in the hills where there is nothing, not even a theater, criticizes her hometown, and Nena feels ire. But she lets it go. No point fighting. Would Paco think the same? she wonders. Of course.

Nena buys a postcard with the hanging houses and writes a brief note: Paco, Missing you and wishing you were here, el cariño de siempre, Nena.

Ángel and other artists work in an old converted hospital that the government has made into studios for artists; his studio is there and so is Pepe's, who makes his own paper. Ángel's work is good but won't ever bring him the fame or the money he yearns for while saying all he wants to do is make art; he is naïve about the business of art and remains unknown. Ángel Cruz, a minor artist with a major heart and a major talent. Alas, he lived to paint. And he did. When Ángela leaves with their two sons, goes home, settles in Dallas, he stays behind, won't follow. Ángel dies a few years later. His studio passes on to another artist who also paints and remains unknown. But some are lucky; they know the business of art and make it big, go off to the Biennale and galleries in Madrid and New York, show their work. Cuenca is like that. Full of artists. Full of life. Full of potential.

Nena had read all about Holy Week, the Semana Santa celebrations all over Spain from Andalucía to Navarra, Catalunya to A Coruña. But she chose Cuenca. Paco had insisted that she go to Sevilla for the truer, more authentic fervor, but she felt it might be too studied, too touristy.

Now she knows it was her destiny to meet up with Ángela and Ángel. She can see herself in a few years: married to Paco with a couple of kids. Never going home, never feeling quite at home. But.

The Semana Santa crowds are immense on Friday for the turbas. The solemnity turns rowdy, and there are real drunks who spit and cuss and lift their fists in defiance of the Christ figure carrying the cross. The eyes seem real, the hair real on the Christ figure on the centuries-old paso. Some pay dearly to carry the weight, to go barefoot and to suffer the procession so that vows can be fulfilled, so that favors granted are repaid. It is tradition. It is the way it's always been. The authorities try to control the crowds. Children become disrespectful, and one small boy shouts at his grandmother, abuela pocha, and is hit by a parent's hand; discipline is harsh in this land. The child shouts even angrier and stomps away. And the adults laugh. The term "pocha" strikes home with Nena. The same insult that her Mexican cousins will hit her with when she visits because of her pocho Spanish, her pocho ways: won't eat chile, wants cereal for breakfast. And in Cuenca it means something entirely different, this insult. It means rotten, old, and useless. Still, it's an insult.

Nena takes photographs of the pasos, of the crowds. Talks to matronly women, grandmothers, matriarchs who rule over sons and daughters and grandchildren with a look. She talks to young men who have vowed to carry the heavy pasos, talks with the vendor selling plastic toys, balloons, and reguiletes, whirlwinds that flutter in the breeze. Little girls dressed as Verónicas precede the paso.

At times she thinks of Paco. Asks herself, What is he thinking? Why doesn't he want to come with me? Why not share these adventures? They had a minor argument about her leaving this week. He wanted to go off to the beach and have a holiday; after all, it's Semana Santa, and he is off from work.

If you must work, why not go to Sevilla? he asks. But she insisted on going to Cuenca. He's not happy and takes off with Luis and Astrid to Torremolinos. She finds the partying would've fit his plans, but the religious fervor wouldn't. Knows he would chide and insult with his caustic

criticism of the church, of the religion that preaches one thing and is another. Typical for many Spaniards raised during the Franco era, he has rebelled, is not a *creyente*, not a believer. She knows that. Accepts him as he is. She's not sure what she herself believes. She toyed with being a Buddhist, then an agnostic. That lasted the longest. Now, she's not sure.

It's Good Friday, but the parties are everywhere. Most visitors have booked hotel rooms, but many are out in the streets: everything is full, *hostales*, private homes. She is lucky to be staying with Sarah. Students and tourists camp out in front of the church with bottles of wine, and they sing and dance. Ángela can't go with her, so Nena joins Sarah and Erica, who serendipitously was on the same train from Madrid. They attend a party in one of the "hanging houses," and Nena is surprised at how cozy it is, like being in a cave. She observes it all even as she tries to carry on a conversation with Sarah above the loud music—Led Zeppelin! She feels that she has entered a scene in a hip movie, an indie made with very little money and with stoned actors and crew. A tiny old man, must be in his eighties, sits on the lap of a tall, blonde twenty-something. He is in his glory. His face is one big toothless smile above his long, white, Rip Van Winkle beard. The young blonde is stoned, plays with his long gray hair, cradles him like a baby on her lap. It is surreal. Why? Nena questions and looks away, a bit upset with the scene. Erica has disappeared, joined some of the partygoers in another room. Nena drinks her red wine in a corner, talks with a photographer from a newspaper in England who has come to photograph the most somber of all the holy week celebrations. He has photographed in Sevilla and in Valencia, but this is something else. Too serious and at the same time, this—she waves her hand to indicate the scene. Linda, that is the photographer's name, wants to photograph the old man and the young Norteamericana, but Nena stops her.

Why?

Don't, she says. It is so dissonant. It looks putrid, and it feels pornographic. Yes.

They will surely go off together. She, stoned and in love. He's in ecstasy.

But probably won't perform in his impotence. This gives him power to have the rubia Norteamericana in his bed.

It's a dead-end conversation. Suppositions. Conjectures. Is it real? Nena wonders. Probably not. But it could be. She believes. Linda, the photographer, smiles and asks instead to take her photo.

Nena declines the offer. I don't like to have my picture taken.

Why?

No sé. It's been years since anyone took my picture. I had to get a little drunk to allow a friend to take my passport photo and all those pictures one needs for the innumerable carnets—for the Biblioteca Nacional, for the museo, hasta para la catedral en Sevilla. Some were not so bad. I'm kind of glad he took them. But. Still, I get queasy standing in front of a camera. There's one I especially like where I stand in my apartment back in graduate school, photos and books behind me. I like that one.

The photographer smiles and says, I understand. I don't like to be photographed either. That's why I am behind the camera!

And as they talk, Nena takes a couple of photos of herself reflected in a mirror. She holds the camera in front of her, half hiding her face. She looks at the mirror. She stares back at herself. Long hair pulled back, Nena's wispy bangs frame her face. Long, tourqoise-ringed, thin finger. Long, skinny hands. The camera doesn't lie, captures the look in her eye.

El día de la coneja

It's Easter in Madrid, and Nena's group of Norteamericanos has planned an Easter meal; Paco has agreed to attend. Nena had promised Ronnie she would be back from Cuenca in time to do the shopping for the meal. Ronnie had been smart, and weeks before had contacted the butcher and ordered the turkey. Good thing she did, too, because it turned out that turkeys are hard to find in Madrid. Although the turkey the butcher hands them turns out to be the size of a large chicken!

Ronnie wanted a traditional home-cooked Easter meal for their group. Nena and Giovanna help her, but it's not the traditional Easter meal either one of them recognizes. Giovanna is used to a huge Italian meal her grandmother prepares for their forty-plus relatives. For Nena, Easter in her south Texas home consists of a carne asada out on a picnic at Lake Casa Blanca with the whole family gathered and Tejano music blaring. Cascarones—the carefully prepared, colorful, hollowed eggshells filled with confetti—in Easter baskets full of marshmallow peeps hidden in green cellophane grass. No, this is an adult Easter, no Easter egg hunt, no cascarones to break on your friends' heads, no confetti showers everywhere. It's an Easter meal served up north in Michigan and Minnesota or Nebraska, probably in the East, too, and the West, although Nena has no way of knowing, as she's never had that kind of meal, never experienced Easter outside of south Texas. Giovanna prepares the baked ham with apple sauce, and Ronnie cooks up a soufflé that she agonizes over—what if it collapses? She even bakes hot cross buns! It's the kind of Easter meal Nena has only read about in books.

Easter morning, Nena insists on going to mass and gets herself out the door and to the nearby church in time while the others are perplexed. Isn't she an agnostic? Why the sudden devotion? And she tries to explain that, yes, she isn't quite sure what she believes, but Easter mass is a must. That's all. It just is. Her family would expect her to attend. Estrenando a new dress and shoes. Of course, here she only wears a new pair of shoes that she's bought for the occasion.

Estrenar, what a concept. And what a word. What's the English equivalent? Ronnie asks.

Not sure, Nena answers. I only know it is essential for many feast days, for one's birthday, of course, and on New Year's Eve one wears brand-new red underwear, for good luck, and new outfits for Easter, New Year's Day, and Christmas. Always for the first day of school, too, new shoes and socks and new clothes.

No wonder Mami sewed all their clothes, so many new outfits for so many children. How could she afford it otherwise?

In Madrid there are no Easter eggs, no cascarones filled with confetti, although it appears to be a custom in Valencia and other places in Spain. She yearns for the familiar shrill of the children chasing each other and searching for hidden cascarones, the Easter egg hunt, Laredo style. The cascarones lovingly prepared, saved for weeks in advance, and dyed and filled the night before to surprise her brothers and sisters. And some mean kids fill them with flour or with rice, while some families insert a coin, un daime, a ten-cent piece, o hasta una peseta, a twenty-five-cent piece for the lucky one who gets it. The tostón, the fifty-cent piece, is too big to fit in the hole. Some even stuff wadded up bills, one dollar, five dollars, or even ten dollars, inside the egg shell—what an Easter egg find that becomes!

But in Madrid she must be satisfied to have Paco join them for lunch. He came back early to be with her. He brings the wine, and it is exquisite. Although he doesn't drink, he knows about wines and selects the best for her celebration from a friend's little-known reserva from an unknown vineyard in el Bierzo, better than the more common one from la Rioja. The meal is a success, but no one says grace or prays over the meal, although several of her friends do joke about how Christian this meal is with the cross marking on the beautifully browned buns. The soufflé is a hit, and the ham is rich and tasty. Ronnie beams, pleased with the compliments. Nena rarely ate ham at home—too expensive! Except when Papi went accident free for a year and the smelter gave him a ham as a reward at Christmas. What a feast that was! Most of the time, strips of bacon was as close as they got to pork—and of course the pork for tamales, although her mother prefers to mix in some beef, or if nothing else is available she'll prepare tamales with jabalí or venison from a neighbor's hunting trip.

Nena calls home to wish everyone happy Easter. Her sister Azalia, who is home with a cold, answers. She is glad to have Nena all to herself. They talk and talk. Azalia says that everyone is out on a picnic at Lake Casa Blanca for el día de la coneja. Nena feels drawn across the miles to that picnic scene; she can smell the requisite grilled chicken, carne asada, brisket, fajitas, sausage, and onions wrapped in foil. Her brother-in-law has camped out at Lake Casa Blanca so the family can have a choice spot. The lake, where the music blares loud and where spontaneous dancing erupts now and then—polkas, cumbias, rancheras, and some ballads, too, for good measure. Little Joe and Sunny and la Sonora Santanera along with local groups who manage to get KVOZ to play their songs. Impromptu games of softball or volleyball spring up. Some overdo it and invariably suffer heatstroke— Mami must be careful lest she get a migraine. Grandmothers take care of young babies while young people dance and play. In some cases there is too much to drink. Fights break out.

In their dining room in Madrid, the party is in full swing. David, a guest of one of the Fulbrighters, has had too much to drink. Starts quizzing Paco.

So, what do you do?

Paco answers in his heavily accented English, I'm a graphic designer. I design book covers, layout for magazines.

Y ¿eres de izquierda?

Paco gratefully switches to Spanish: Claro; who isn't after what we've been through?

So, what are your intentions? Marry and move to the US? David says, indicating Nena with a nod.

That does it. Paco gets upset and wants to leave. Won't even engage the drunken David, who is innocently smiling and can't even understand what he has said that is so wrong.

Nena walks Paco to the door. Don't get upset, she says. He's just drunk. They all think that everyone is trying to get to the United States.

I know, he says. Lo sé. They agree that she should wait until the guests depart, and then call him so he can come get her.

He kisses her on the forehead. And walks away. Hasta ahora, chicanita.

She goes back in and avoids everyone's questions about why he left and why he got upset. After all, it is true, the Spanish are full of contradictions—they hate the US and then they buy US stuff, music, jeans, any and everything American. But not everyone. Her leftist friends from the tertulia, Paco and his crowd, and others, they resist and deny the seduction of capitalism. Such hypocrites, one of her friends opines, and she defends the Spanish, defends Paco, just as she defends her friends when Paco criticizes them for being so American, such capitalists, such parasites of the world. Paco understands her leftist politics but can't understand how she tolerates the Norteamericanas. Racists, he condemns.

She's disappointed that he got upset, but also she can't believe how her friends were quizzing him, giving him the third degree. Before David it had been Ronnie. But she understands their position too. She senses some kind of protection. They are protecting one of their own, although she doesn't always feel as if she is one of them.

He doesn't wait to get her call and comes back in about an hour. It is still early; they can catch a movie or just go home and listen to an opera.

He's picked up a new recording. It's Montserrat Caballé. He smiles. I want to share it with you. You'll love it.

As they discuss the day's events, she excuses her friends. Her roommates are not like that, she explains. It's only the one guy, and he's not even a Fulbrighter, he just invited himself. I don't even know him.

It is 1980 and Carter is president and she is not proud of what her country is doing in Central America—but she is proud to be a Tejana, a Chicana, to be free to criticize and to change what needs changing. She must stand up to both. If Spain is hypocritical so is the US, and if the US is a capitalist state so is Spain quickly going down that same path. At least they are moving away from the oppressive dictatorship. But the politicians in both countries are the same, out for similar things and in power for similar reasons.

Clearly she can never reconcile these two disparate worlds and her own even more complex position in these worlds. A Chicana with one foot in México, the conquered nations all behind her; Paco, a Spaniard, an Asturiano no less, a member of that colonial power that conquered her antepasados and who now resents the imperialist power that is her country, the United States. Los Estados, they shorten it. USA, they say—use! And laugh at the appropriate acronym.

Immigrants

ut it's not so bad, Tomás, the Mexican poet who's in Europe on a Guggenheim, tells her. Spaniards like Mexicans porque Mexico received those expatriates who fled Spain as a result of the War when Franco's forces took over. Mexico granted asylum to many a Spaniard and allowed them to remake their lives. Por eso, the Spanish love Mexico.

Tomás's own family found refuge in a land that could've easily said no, go elsewhere. The last time we welcomed you, you destroyed our ways and took our land and our people became your slaves.

But now the Spanish who went to Mexico forty-plus years ago are free to return, as are the ones who found refuge in France. Nena meets returning expatriate writers at the tertulia on Wednesdays and at the feria del libro, the giant book fair where authors mingle with readers. Expats, writers, artists, and even many regular folks coming home. Even the Guérnica de Picasso will find a place in this new Spain. And now it is their turn to flee dirty wars, to find refuge, the Latino Americanos, Uruguayans, Chileans, and Argentinos and the Central Americans, Salvadoreños, Nicaragüenses, Guatemaltecos. All will come a la madre patria, the motherland. From Peru and from Ecuador in a subtle reconquest that will end who knows when or how. In the '80s that truth of refugees isn't quite the crises it will be in the next century, when thousands from the Americas and from Africa seeking residency and legal status will find the Spanish as adamant as the North Americans and as racist in their ways. While the shifts in Europe occupy a greater threat for globalizing cultures like the US, wars loom small and large. Wars that will devastate and displace people, refugees who will die and live in refugee camps, who will seek refuge outside and take to the sea or trek by land to reach a promised land. Grenada. Somalia. Ethiopia. Iran. Iraq. Afghanistan. The Balkans. Sarajevo. Samara. Kabul. Someone said wars teach us geography, and Nena agrees but wishes it were not so. War on a grand scale, nation against nation, and war on personal scale, men against women. Domestic violence in Spain is rising, *El País* reports.

Unheard of places fill the TV screens and the newspapers bylines. Nena feels as if she is in a bubble, wants to get back in the classroom to discuss these current events with her students. She imagines that the Refugee Assistance Center she and her friends established is brimming with cases; she has not heard from her friends who staff it. Laredo's Amnesty International chapter must be engaged in numerous campaigns in so many countries. The increase in international crises as the United States is about to go into a presidential election makes her nervous.

She questions herself: Am I deluding myself by working on the fiestas project? What good will it do? Who will benefit? I should be home working with the refugees, preparing for the election. She fears that with the hostage crisis debacle, Carter will not win reelection. Ronald Reagan is running. She can't imagine how that could be. Why would an actor want to be president? Of course, she never imagined him as governor either.

Caravaca de la Cruz

*N*ena travels by bus to Caravaca, the tiny town in Murcia. Arrives to find the now-familiar bustle of townspeople readying for the fiesta. Los Caballos del Vino. That's the opening of the fiesta that has different contests: the horse race, of course, and the decorations that include the fancy embroidery and beadwork. The fiesta exists in conjunction with the celebration of the Holy Cross. After all, the town houses a holy relic, a piece of the real cross where Jesus was crucified. The race and the contests are all under the domain of the bandos or peñas, the groups that will compete in the races for the decorative prize. The recognition of having the best makes it all worth it—the expense, the unending work, the stress and the effort. The celebration honors a historical event and the Holy Cross. As the story goes, when the castle was under siege and out of water and food, the horsemen from the town braved the Moors and secured food, water, and wine for the townspeople. All that happened in the 1200s, and few people can give Nena details. All they know is that there is such a legend, and that is why the Caballos del Vino exist as part of the fiesta honoring the Holy Cross.

The Moros y cristianos mock battle and the parlamentos were added later. From time immemorial the pregón and the parlamento, the horsemen and the horses, grace the fiesta. People prepare all year. In April a drawing determines the order. The awaited ceremony sets the process in motion. At the fiesta in May, dancing is everywhere—even the horses

wear festive garb and seem to dance in the procession. The celebration was muted during the Franco years, but it is back now in full force. Nena predicts it will surely grow, will develop beyond the three days as already the children are taking a prominent role and the women are in the procession. It is indeed the town's main fiesta, although Nena has read that they also celebrate Corpus Christi and Holy Week. But this one is all theirs, not the liturgical celebration that happens all over. It's unlike the celebrations of the neighboring towns and villages, their very own fiesta. Nena stayed in a private home as there were no hotels or hostales in the tiny hamlet. Theresa, a friend of María José's mother, welcomed Nena and eagerly talked about the fiesta and invited her neighbors to come and meet her guest. They all contribute something and talk about their youth and how the fiesta has changed. How their fiesta is the best. Unique.

A proud Theresa explains, No one else has the Caballos del Vino even if they have the Moros y cristianos. No, this is different. She pulls out a huge bottle of wine made just for the fiesta. Concludes, We honor our past, celebrate our present.

On the train back to Madrid, Nena falls asleep and dreams she and Paco are climbing a mountain. The higher they go, the easier it becomes. It reminds her of hiking to Pike's Peak in Colorado. Or that one time she hiked outside of Santa Fe. The air crisp and clean. El campo. They hike effortlessly, under a hot sun. They finally reach the top. At that point in her dream, Nena realizes she's dreaming. She spreads her arms and effortlessly lifts, flying high above the trees and the river below. The deafening river wakes her up with a jolt, and she realizes it is the roar of the train. The train zooms past villages and countrysides and finally arrives at the station. Paco is waiting for her. I've missed you, he says as they drive to his piso.

Cuentos

*N*ena doesn't like to watch TV much, and even less the dubbed episodes of US shows—*Charlie's Angels*, especially. But tonight, on canal 2, the educational channel, there's a documentary on the Spanish Civil War, and Paco wants to watch it. She drinks a glass of sherry; Paco drinks an infusion, hot mint tea. They settle in to watch the documentary.

The program is over, and they slip into nightclothes and snuggle in bed. Nena says, When I was studying for my master's degree, I had a friend who was German. Her uncle had been one of those Germans that had killed Jewish babies. She told me how he would tell her stories of killing children for fun. Hitting them against a tree or using babies for target practice. He also killed cats, and my friend remembered how he killed one of her kittens—drowned it in a water tank in front of her. When she told me, she watched me carefully to see my reaction. I was horrified and felt sorry for her. She expected rejection, and I offered sympathy. She told me that later.

Paco asks, Why are you telling me these horror stories?

No sé, se me ocurrió that you might have heard stories from your family about the war, about Franco's troops, o la Guardia Civil. Must be the program we watched.

Yes, he begins, the stories are there. Always, there are stories. History is one thing. Family stories another. My mother told me stories of my

144

father's heroism. How they killed him. They came into the village and rounded up everyone they suspected of being communists. Even after the war was over. Since my father never went to mass, and he was never close to the church, they assumed he was a communist. Who knows, maybe he was. He was a journalist, you know. He owned the town's small newspaper in Asturias. His grandparents still spoke Bable, the dialect from the region. He was very much a nationalist, ethnocentric, I would say. According to what my mother described. All of that condemned him to death. No trial. No judge. Nada. Just a firing squad.

Nena counters his pain, his anger, with another story.

Ever hear of Emma Tenayuca? she asks. She was a member of the communist party in Texas. A labor organizer and one of my heroes. In San Antonio, at age seventeen, she led a major strike. In the '60s, a los Chicanos también. Everyone assumed we were communists because we were leftists and we were working for civil rights. I'm sure some were, but I don't think I ever met a certified communist party member. And with the Cultural Revolution in China, I'm not sure I wanted to. Marxists, yes, I know many. And sure, we were leftists, I still am, but the revolution doesn't have to be communist led. That's what they don't understand. You don't have to sacrifice your life to achieve change. To achieve true revolution. Then the Chicano nationalism caused even more problems. Strange thing, nationalism. Mira Méjico. The Revolution ended when it became institutionalized. And then in the '60s a failed attempt. Have you read Elena Poniatowska's *La Noche de Tlatelolco*?

Nena continues, Without heroes there's no revolution. It is all about image! Look at Che. And Fidel. And Ortega.

Paco smiles and seems almost condescending. He says, But, flaca, I tell you there are no heroes. Revolution or not. Life goes on and life ends, como dice tu poeta, Eliot, with a whimper. That's the way it is. Revolutions come and go. Small and big. True and false.

The word tells you: RE Evolution. It's all for moving forward as a people, as humans. ¿No? O ¿sí?

The Cruelest Month

A mere three months in Madrid and Nena already feels at home, has fallen into a routine. The servers at the café know her, the clerks at the grocery store know her, the gypsy selling flowers knows her. She has ensconced herself into the routine of life in her small world within the larger world that is Madrid. Her Sunday phone calls home tug at her heart all week long; she hangs up and feels homesick. Saudade. The very trip to the Telefónica to place the collect call has become part of the ritual of life in Madrid. The saudade lessens each week; time heals all wounds. But.

It is April. If she is not to return to her position at the university, she should let them know so they can find someone to teach her classes. But she delays. Not sure. At least she will be in Madrid through the summer. Should she choose to stay, what will she do? How can she survive? She will certainly get in trouble if she overstays her visa. But.

Nena and Paco get back to his apartment one Tuesday in early April after *Tosca*. She notes two tiny glasses on the coffee table. The bottle of sherry. She knows he had company the night before. She asks. And he answers too quickly, too guiltily, No, really, it was a friend who stopped by to have a sherry after dinner last night. No one you know. And she notes the lipstick stain and says nothing. Could ask if he got sick from drinking or why he didn't mention he had had company. But she chooses not to be the jealous girlfriend, a Tosca. Decides not to make a scene. After all she's leaving soon, only a few more months left. I won't think about it, she tells herself. Let him have someone else. It's better all around. And she doesn't let on that she is hurting. But. He knows it. Is gentle. Kind. Loving. More than ever, he whispers. Flaca, te quiero.

Nena checks her calculations. The Cabañuelas are spot on! January 4 had been breezy and cold, and so it is in April mostly breezy and cold. The month has turned out to be as expected. Nena remembers that the day after her birthday was a good day. She wrote in her journal that April would be a good month. Full of joy and with a little bit of sadness. Here she was enjoying it all. The fiestas. Paco. Her friends. But. She was also wondering how her family was doing. How her friends were getting along. Whether her students missed her. But. A sweet and full month with a little bit of sadness sprinkled in for good measure. Can one expect fidelity under such circumstances? Yes. But.

Lhardy's

One Saturday Paco and Nena are out walking as they often do on weekend afternoons when she is not off on one of her trips. They slip into Lhardy's for a cup of soup. It's rainy and cool outside, and people crowd before lunch into the tiny space. It feels comforting; the scent of perfume from the patrons mingles with the warm cinnamon and cardamon. He has been wanting to have her experience this most madrileño of locations.

She watches him walk away to get their order, and she studies him from afar as if he were a total stranger, which he was only a few months ago. Never would have noticed him. He's not her type. What is her type? ¿Quién sabe? Y él, ¿quién es? ¿Por qué él? He seems full of himself. Struts like a rooster, she notes, as he walks back to their tiny table. Still. He can be so gentle. She sits on a stool, and he stands next to her. Close. Very close. Uncomfortably close. She can smell him as she sips the soup and is warmed. The mild scent of sofrito now familiar. He holds her cold hands in his. So close. So comfortably close. He says, Your hands are always cold. Warm heart?

So they say.

I will warm you up. Totalmente. Cuerpo y alma.

Don't think so. My feet, my nose, my hands—always cold. It's normal for me.

Por eso. Y con más ganas. And he looks into her eyes. She looks away at a matronly woman dressed to the tees in a mink coat. Gold and pearls adorn her robust neck, her earlobes, and her wrists. In April! Too many pearls. Too much gold. Her makeup garish and her hennaed hair too red. The woman is staring unapologetically, noting their jeans and long, unstyled hair: Nena's long, black, and curly; Paco's long, the color of wheat sprinkled with gold. Her black and his brown locks touch as they talk, whisper quietly. Her whole being smiles.

She's jealous, he says of the woman.

No, she's offended, Nena replies.

Same thing.

Really?

Yes.

But. Mira, "Lhardi" on one sign, "Lhardy" on the other. Which is right?

No sé. A hundred years ago, aquí venía la reina a tomar su té.

¿Qué reina? Which queen would come here for tea?

¿Cuál otra ha de ser?

She slips a paper napkin with the Lhardy logo into the pocket of her blue jeans, un recuerdo. They slip out into the Madrid afternoon and look for a restaurant around Puerta de Sol; he knows just the place where they can have a good meal and sit quietly and talk. It's too noisy in here, he says.

They go to Plaza Mayor and dawdle for a bit. They go into the feminist bookstore near the Plaza, and she looks for a book of poetry by Nuria Amat that someone mentioned at the tertulia. He looks uncomfortable. Nena could spend hours in this place; the space feels like a woman's bookstore in Austin, Lincoln, or San Antonio—has the same feel, the same energy. She buys the Amat book and a collection of Gloria Fuerte's poems. She picks up a new writer, at least new to her, Ana María Moix, a Catalan writer. Nena likes the bookstore, has come for a couple of readings, met some of the women who work there. But. She doesn't feel at home, not welcomed. Same thing as in Lincoln. She didn't feel she belonged with all the white women. Here it is more a matter of class or something that is undefinable—these feminists are just as elitists as the ones in Lincoln. They stare at her brownness, at her Spanish when she asks a question during one discussion.

When they get to the restaurant, he is full of questions. So, are you a feminist?

Claro, she answers. Of course, why do you ask?

And he doesn't know why he is asking, or if it matters.

Biblioteca Nacional

*A*fter months working at the Biblioteca Nacional, in the Sección de Raros, which is as quiet as a meditation center, reading centuries-old manuscripts in difficult-to-decipher script, Nena feels at home. Her work as a researcher is rewarded: she has uncovered ancient secrets, reading texts of plays from the nineteenth, the eighteenth, and the sixteenth centuries. Some even older. She finds references to fiestas, finds the old medieval play where Santa Elena finds the Holy Cross— the same story the matachines told her back in Laredo. The old folks' Catholic tradition is rooted in the centuries-old story of how Constantine is converted, how the entire Roman Empire is converted to Christianity.

Nena marvels, smiles at the simplicity of the text. Another major find is the pastorela from the late nineteenth century, where the devils are capitalists and the shepherds are the proletariat. A Marxist pastorela, how appropriate. She smiles. This part of the work is a joy. It nourishes her soul.

During the quiet of siesta, when most businesses close, she stays working at the library, trying to use the time well, but leaves by seven to enjoy the evening strollers. Most days, though, she finishes her daily work in the early evening, walks to meet Paco for dinner and perhaps a movie or just a walk. Alone, she cherishes the time to roam the streets in the hustle and bustle of people meeting in bars before going home to dinner. Sometimes, though, she works late into the night until they finally close the library. The stern, serious-faced usher comes to walk her out.

Nena arrives every morning by nine and eats at around two in the afternoon, un bocadillo and a glass of wine. Some days it's a treat to go with her fellow researchers, Ronnie, Sean, Giovanna, and Steven, to the nearby restaurant that caters to working folks, good food for a low price. A full three-course meal—el menú del día—for a few pesetas. At that time, no more than a dollar. De primero, usually two choices— judías verdes or guisantes—strange words for the familiar ejote and chícharo—green beans or peas. For el plato fuerte, usually two choices—chicken or beef. For dessert, melocotón en almíbar, the sweet canned peach halves in even sweeter nectar, or a fresh fruit, usually an orange. She always chooses the orange over the canned peach. Always chooses the chicken over the red meat. No choice on Friday; it is always merluza, the white fish Nena learns to love. Sometimes she chooses only the vegetables with the bread and wine, confusing the waiter. Ronnie fears her friend is too thin, perhaps anemic. You need to eat! And Nena complies but still doesn't gain the weight.

It's hereditary, she explains. There's a reason they call my father palillo. He's thin as a toothpick!

Rarely does Paco come by for lunch. He too works through lunch so he can go home early and not work in the evenings. Lunch rituals are changing. Things are different. In Franco's Spain the work place always closed for lunch, but now, especially in an office like his, workers have a semblance of flexibility. Some work straight through lunch and then don't have to return in the evening. It is a time of transition. Shops still close at two for lunch and reopen at four. But in some sectors they don't close at all. The big department stores remain open, and so does el Prado. So Nena has options if she wants to take a break and go see the latest exhibit or shop at el Corte Inglés.

La Biblioteca. How she loves the smell of books! She dreams of having a library of her own. Her books are stored at home, carefully placed on makeshift bookshelves her father built, long boards that he secured for her—discarded planks from a construction site—held up with cement blocks. But to her they are perfect, at least for now. Some day she will have proper bookshelves, custom made of fine wood, worthy of her books. Books, her treasured friends. Books that hold precious memories only she can find. Each one like a jigsaw piece that completes her heart.

Reminders of Home

$\mathcal{E}$ vening meals at the piso with Ronnie and Giovanna often turn into debates about proper foodstuff and culinary predispositions. Dinner or supper? La cena! Her roommates prefer yogurt and perhaps a slice of tortilla Española for dinner. Nena prefers a soup: garlic soup, so Spanish! Or lentejas, the rich Italian lentil soup Giovanna makes. Or a simple consomé de pollo, the chicken stock that is rich in nutrients, with her slice of tortilla española. Some evenings, when she's especially homesick, she makes her kind of tortillas; she rolls out round, flat flour tortillas and prepares a cinnamon tea flavored with brown sugar. Her saudade is abated by these reminders of home. Comfort food.

Back home things are progressing predictably. Her father writes long letters, filling her in on what is going on, letters written in his flourished script detailing what each sibling is doing, signed "Vale." She has the sense that her world is changing and she is not there to witness it. Her siblings are growing up, each is finding her or his own path. One is working and attending college. Another has found a job at JCPenney. Her brother who's in high school is working at la Posada Hotel as a bellhop. The youngest is doing well in school; he's brilliant, so accomplished already. Papi shares his worries about illnesses, about the daughter who is graduating and has no plans for college. How the youngest daughter is a cheerleader. He even fills her in on the stats for the baseball team from Nuevo Laredo, los Tecolotes!

Food is home, Nena tells Ronnie, who agrees enthusiastically. The smells. The tastes. I miss aguacates, watermelon, Mexican candy. I miss the feel of ripe avocados. The sound of ripe watermelon when tapped. I miss Mami's mole with the chocolate and peanut sauce over chicken breasts. Food feeds the body and the soul, like music feeds the soul.

Tortilla making has always been a going-home space and time for her. But. Not tortilla Española but the thin, breadlike discs made with wheat flour. Her thin hands measuring the flour, the salt, the lard, and even the warm water. She feels the smooth lard as she crumbles it into the flour; she finds the sensuality comforting. Kneading the dough and setting it aside for a few minutes she feels a sense of accomplishment. Then the testales, round little doorknob-size patties, rolled out into wafer-thin discs that puff up on the hot griddle, a makeshift comal, made from the burner of an antique wood-burning stove she picked up at the Rastro, the flea market she loves to visit on Sunday mornings. Three turns, no more. Violante, a friend of her mother's, taught her the trick, claimed her husband knew if the tortilla had been turned more and rejected it as imperfect. What a brute, Nena had thought then, but now she remembers and attempts to do it perfectly each time. Each orb a golden disc puffed up to signal that she is a jealous person. Not true. She talks to herself. I am *not* jealous.

Nena daydreams as she rolls out the tortillas and multitasks cooking them on the comal. She makes enough for herself. What a trick that had been in Kingsville, to relearn the process making only a cup of flour instead of the whole five-pound sack. The memory seeps in like a watermark, and Nena goes back to her childhood. How special she felt performing this most necessary of tasks: kneading the daily dough and making the stack of tortillas for dinner. She also recalls the dank, putrid smell of dough gone bad if left out in the heat too long. A day was all it took. How proud she was to help Mami, making the dozens and dozens of tortillas the family consumed daily.

And you never count them, Mami instructed, otherwise no te rinden, and we will not have enough.

Miércoles de tertulia

*W*ednesday es día de tertulia. She goes with friends to the weekly gatherings, has her vinito at the bookstore where they gather: aspiring poet Manolo Montesinos, who is also a lawyer; visiting Mexican poet Tomás Segovia; various visiting scholars and writers; and of course the host, Don Luis Cano, who takes her seriously and likes to talk with her about US writers. As if she knew them personally, she discusses Welty and Updike with Don Luis. He regales her with stories of writers he has met and their antics in Spain. He is working on the poets de la generacion del 98. He bemoans the fact that Spaniards have no access to her literature. How no one in Spain reads anything by Chicanos, not even the works of those who write in Spanish. It's the '80s and no one is reading Chicano literature anywhere except in the rare Chicano Studies classrooms here and there. In Germany there's a scholar who is translating works into German, but it will be decades before the Spanish take Chicano literature seriously. Don Luis urges her to translate poetry, but Nena remains fearful of not measuring up, remains unsure of her Spanish. When she was in graduate school she translated Alfonsina Storni's poetry and published it in *Prairie Schooner*, the university literary publication—but that was from Spanish to English and not the other way around.

After the tertulia they go to a place where the Republicans, the "good guys," those who opposed Franco, used to gather—some still do—for bacalao and more tinto. Casa Labra serves the best fried codfish and tortilla española. The house wine, served in carafes, flows as the writers meet each Wednesday night. The night stretches long past midnight when the metro will stop running, so Nena and her roommates head home just before, walk the quiet streets and feel safe as the street cleaners hose away the day's grit and trash with powerful jets of water. Montesinos or the Uruguayan writer, or the young journalist, or the university professor, or one of Cano's students accompanies them. A las damas hay que acompañarlas, someone says, and Nena cringes but doesn't complain that someone always accompanies them at least to the metro stop and sometimes all the way home.

Nena notes how Don Luis is surprised to be greeted with kisses on both cheeks, but soon he gets used to it. Not all the Norteamericanos like the tertulias, but Nena loves them. After all, it's about politics and literature, about reading and writing. About jokes and the most recent plays and movies. The literary chisme of Madrid and Barcelona! The talk is about what she loves—politics and literature. How can she not love it? How can she stay away?

She gets to share her "theories" about literature, about life, about politics. About how Reagan is throwing his hat in the ring for the presidency—she can't imagine him at the helm. An actor! Bound to be a puppet for sure, someone at the beck and call of others who control the real machinations of the world. He's just an actor, and a good one, too. Someone predicts that he will no doubt act the role well.

Paco doesn't like such gatherings. But. He doesn't say anything. Knows she will go with or without him. He holds back. He knows she'd go anyway. He feigns interest, asks her who was there. What did they say? Maybe he's curious, she thinks. But. He never attends, yet he never says, Don't go.

Everyone agrees Spain is just awakening to this world and Felipe González, the head of the PSDOE, is going to be the one to usher them into the new Europe. The new world order. Everyone hopes that their democracy will be different, more socialist. Hopes that they have learned their lessons. But. Soon everyone is disappointed.

Nicaragua, too. There was such hope when Ortega won fair and square. But. Now rumors abound, multiply and spread. Like leaves in the wind, stories scatter everywhere. Excesses of power. Corruption running rampant. Is it true he paid $150 for a pair of sunglasses?! Is he really only hiring his supporters, members of his family? The new government, riddled with corruption, plain and simple, is no better than the old. But Nena refuses to believe that and argues that it is the capitalist system that is flawed. No matter who occupies the seat of power, the dispossessed remain so. What's needed is a true radical revolution—a change in the system. Her friends share her views but can't agree with the ETA terrorists, whose bombs go off and continue killing innocent people. The Guardia Civil is still in charge, and Nena witnesses beatings of peaceful demonstrators, sees the familiarly dressed guardias hassle a group of gypsies. She sees that they are abusers and generally act with impunity against whomever they wish. But she cannot say or do a thing. She is a guest in this country.

No te metas, Tomás advises. Let things be. But.

She's a scholar come to research, to work. Frustrated that she cannot participate, she also feels inadequate. What good is researching fiestas, innocuous cultural events? How can she reconcile this work with her passion for political activism? At least in Laredo she felt she was doing something. Working to combat illiteracy, working to support the Central American immigrants. Working for change. She's come to reconnect with her past. Come to learn. And she does. Along with learning and analyzing the structures of the celebrations, both religious and secular, her hypothesis is proven true—the roots are in the traditions of Spain. She learns so much more. About Spain and politics, about her own psyche—what makes her tick. Nena discovers the essence of her being one morning while walking to the Biblioteca from the metro stop. She looks up and is catapulted into the past. Once again she feels a shift in herself—a realization so strong that she shudders and hears a loud ringing in her ears. Her home is not here. She knows it in her heart, feels it in all of her being. As much as she loves Madrid, loves Spain, its people, its customs, the way she can come and go and feel safe; as much as she loves the hustle and bustle, el trajín; as much as she loves Paco, this is not her home. It can never be her home. But.

Talking with the Norteamericanas who criticize Spain and express their ethnocentric views, she reminds them of how in the States there are abuses too. How politically corrupt Chicago still is . . . and Laredo! How bad it still is for Blacks everywhere. How the Native people were slaves to the masters. In Laredo for sure, she says. The abuse of power, the political machine that was only recently exposed, has given way to new leaders who also hire their buddies, their cronies. Corruption plain and simple. She knows. Her own students who graduate with teaching degrees are not hired by the local school district because they—or their family—don't support certain candidates. One student came crying to her. I'm moving to Houston, where I can get a job, she informed Nena. My father is a foe of the superintendent, and I've tried and tried, applied repeatedly to job after job, y nada. Denied.

Yes, the corruption persists. Gas prices in Laredo are higher than anywhere because the monopoly is so strong; the powers that be will not allow independent owners to open gas stations. Yes, it is not just the fiestas that are similar. Reminders of home are everywhere.

April in Paris

*V*ámonos a París, Paco says one morning as he is driving Nena to the Biblioteca. What? What? Estás loco, tengo que trabajar, she exclaims. I'm transcribing and translating an important document for my work. I can't just up and leave.

Why not? It's been there a couple of centuries, it will be there when you get back. Besides, te mereces un "break."

How romantic! Her roommates gush when Nena gets home that evening and is packing. Ronnie asks, Can I come along?

Sure, Ronnie, but do you really want to come with us? We are taking the train to Barcelona and spending a few days there before taking a night train to Paris.

No, I guess not. I've already been to Barcelona. Maybe I'll go later and meet you in Paris, or maybe not. I don't want to be a third wheel.

Don't be silly. Paco likes having you around. I do, too. It would be fun. Think about it.

Luis drives them to Chamartín Station and with a wink wishes them feliz luna de miel . . . and thinks it is the funniest joke to wish them a happy honeymoon!

Nena worries that Paco might think this trip will make their relationship more serious than it is. After all, traveling with someone is getting to know them even more intimately. They have already discussed the reality of her leaving in a few months. It is clear and simple. She's leaving at the end of summer. Y ya. But.

Paris doesn't disappoint. It's everything it promised to be—magical, romantic, historic, perfect! They stay at a quaint hotel on rue Daguerre, where Paco has stayed previously. They arrive around noon, and after resting a bit Nena wants to go out, to see the sunset from the newly built Georges Pompidou Art Center. They take off and make it just in time to sit on the stairs outdoors, at the highest possible level, and see the enormous saffron balloon sink on the horizon with the city lights blinking over the rooftops like a scene in a postcard.

He holds her hand. What do you think? Do you like it? I had it scheduled just for you.

Thank you, sir, yes, I love it. Now can we go have some dinner? I'm famished!

But before dinner they stop at the enoteca, the wine shop that her friends recommended near Montparnasse, and she has a glass of a most expensive red wine. Paco chooses for her. Nena wishes she knew more about wine, knew how to tell what makes it so good. She loves the taste, the way it stays in the mouth, in the taste buds. She loves the buzz, the giddy way she feels. He abstains and drinks tonic water. The wine works its magic; she's euphoric.

They walk along the placid and calm Seine, and she knows that this moment has been destined for them to enjoy. She utters gracias to the spirits of the place and her guardian angels that have led her here to this perfect night, this perfect city, this perfect moment.

Paco holds her hand, and they join other couples strolling along the river banks in the city of love. She hears the traffic go by and the birds settling for the night in the trees and thinks, It is all so ordinary, and yet so extraordinary. They go to a small restaurant he knows in Montmarte, where pale-pink linen tablecloths are covered with crisp white ones. He carefully repositions the bud vase that holds a white rose and a bit of green and the tiny candle that the waiter lit when he brought them their menus. I want to see all of you, he says. She feels glamorous wearing black jeans and a plain, black, long-sleeved top she had bought at the Salvation Army Thrift Store back in Lincoln. Still one of her favorite "de salir" outfits. The fabric has the tiniest metallic threads woven through about every half inch. She remembers packing it back in Laredo and thinking that it would be for a special occasion. And it is. Perfect.

She orders medulla soup, a delicacy that she remembers reading about in some novel. Fresh asparagus drenched in a wine sauce. A three-course meal. Just as Paco had predicted, the food and the ambience are all delicious.

Nena notices that there are no prices for the dishes, and she asks Paco about it. Don't worry about it, he says, just enjoy it. But she can't and does worry, remembers how her father always tries to figure out how much a meal will cost at restaurants and is ever so conscious of the cost of things. How he keeps a running tally of what is in the grocery cart so that he has even caught the checker's mistakes.

But she tries to do as Paco asks. She has paid for her train ticket and insists on paying for half of the hotel bill, but he insists on paying for everything else. Claims to be hurt that she is not letting him pay for everything. So she reluctantly agrees that he can pay for meals and bar tabs. She doesn't like to owe anything, she explains.

But you won't owe anything. Believe me. It is my gift to you. Just say, "Gracias." Nothing more. ¿Vale?

Thank you, she whispers.

Every day that week in Paris is glorious, even when an unexpected rain shower finds them strolling along a boulevard and the sidewalk artists pick up their easels and rush inside. She takes photos of buildings: Notre Dame, the Eiffel tower, Musee de Orsay, Church of Saint Denis, the Louvre. They spend two whole days at the Louvre; he's been there several times and shows her his favorites. The great masters, including some Spanish artists—Velásquez, Ribera, Zurbarán.

Nena loves strolling through the Prado and has her favorites—Bosch, Brueghel, of course Velásquez and Goya and Titian and others, but here it is different. She can't explain it. It just is. In front of la Gioconda, the Mona Lisa, a tear slips down her cheek. Paco gently wipes it away.

I'm such a chillona, she says, a crybaby. Paco, this is a dream come true. And I never imagined it would be so tiny! I guess I knew it from art history class, but look at that.

Then she asks to see the Venus de Milo, and they amble to the sculptures, Greek and Roman. She marvels at the hands that shaped such beauty.

After the Louvre they go to St. Etienne du Mont, and she goes directly to the tomb of Ste. Genevieve, her patron saint. She had insisted that they visit the small church. But. She finds a sheet that explains how the saint's bones had been either thrown into the sewer or burnt during the French Revolution. All that is left are shards of bone, and these are encased in glass to be venerated. Paco can't understand why she wanted to come to this small chapel.

I was born on her day, Nena explains. She's my protector. She saved Paris, not once but several times, from famine, from attacks by Hannibal and others. She is like Guadalupe for Mexico City or la Virgen de Zapopan for Guadalajara in Mexico.

Nena kneels reverently in front of the relics, the remains of the saint. Paco seems distracted, uncomfortable. As they walk away he asks her for details.

What do you mean she is your protector?

Well, she's my patron saint. I was born on her day, January 3. I have always had an affinity for her, felt that she was looking over me. You know, at the spiritual level. I can feel her sometimes.

He remains perplexed. Looks at her quizzically and shrugs.

It's April in Paris, and the tourists are everywhere. Paco and Nena are two more lost in the crowds. One afternoon they climb the Eiffel tower, but it is cloudy and there is barely a semblance of a sunset. No matter, she got her wish. Plus she took pictures from up there, the wind blowing her hair everywhere. But no pictures of her or of Paco.

They walk up the stairs at Notre Dame, and she takes more photos.

The Seine looks like a small canal from up above the treetops. Nena says, Look, people look like ants down there. And the rooftops! Just like I imagined it would be.

Paco takes a long nap that afternoon while Nena writes in her journal. I need to rest, he said, the show at the Moulin Rouge starts at midnight. Indeed, the show is spectacular and overwhelms her. Right on stage are live animals, hundreds of beautiful people, women who are like mannequins, so perfect. The emcee translates the gist into English for the benefit of the tourists, and Nena is grateful, although she would prefer he didn't. Her French is good enough to catch most things, but he doesn't translate the jokes. Paco explains them to her. Then it's over, the dazzling dancers, the beautiful bodies—which she doesn't even notice are bare-breasted until he points it out—the lights and dry-ice smoke. Each number a spectacle unlike any other. It will be years before she sees anything like it, on a trip to Vegas with her sisters.

Too soon it is over and they are streaming out into the Parisian night. A hot-dog cart is parked, ready for the crowd exiting the theater. Paco asks, Do you want one? All of a sudden, she is starving. Yes. It is the best hot dog she will ever eat—of course, French sausage in a wonderful baguette with French mustard! They share one because it is at least a foot long. They sit down on a bench to eat it.

I'll never forget this, she tells him.

Good, he says. That's what it's all about.

Suddenly it hits her, and she panics—he is setting her up. Wants her to be so much in love she will not leave. That must be the plan. She says nothing. Waits for more signs. And sure enough, the clues are everywhere. He talks about the future as if she will be there. He buys a beautiful piece of glass by a new artist in one of the galleries along the Champs Élysée, near the Arc de Triomphe, asking her opinion so he can choose the one that she likes best.

Glass. It is so fragile, she says.

Yes, he answers, like love.

And when they are back in Madrid she asks him, Do you really think I will not leave?

No, he says. I know you will leave, you must. But I believe you will come back. We will be together again. I just know it. Ya verás, you'll see.

Mira, Paco, this isn't that kind of story. Not even in the movies does that happen. There's *Annie Hall*. Or *Casablanca*.

Bueno, sabes, I have always identified con ese tío, el Woody Allen. I feel like him. Just as insecure. Just as, as, as, coño, I don't have a word for it. Maybe the word is *lost*. Just as lost. Just as needy of love. Plus I am just as neurotic, ¿no crees?

Well, now that you mention it! They laugh. She let's go of the topic, stashing it away for future action.

She returns to the previous comment. Sabes, it really is like a movie. No matter what happens we'll always have Paris, like Rick and Ilsa. ¿Qué cursi, no?

They fly back to Madrid, and Nena returns to her routine of working at the Biblioteca during the week and traveling to see the fiestas on the weekends. Paris haunts her dreams, and she's often atop Notre Dame with the gargoyles. They had climbed all four hundred steps because she wanted to see them up close. What artistry! Paco humors her and tells her a joke about a gargoyle that comes alive, a monstrous dragon with claws and wings like an eagle but the face and body of a tiger. He teases that perhaps she is looking for the hunchback.

It's not that. I just think of the workers. Those who labored centuries ago and whose work survives. True artists. Plus I just want to be high above the city. Like at the Georges Pompidou. Makes me feel as if I can fly like the birds, and she signals with her hands the many birds circling and flying—doves, swifts, others she doesn't recognize.

When they were up there he took her hand and slowly, gently traced the cold, hard sculpture of the gargoyle. Nena thought of the long-gone stone carver and how he must've felt.

Paco says, It is now yours. Forever in your memory.

Recuerdos y lágrimas

*J*n late April she goes to Belmonte for their fiesta. There, Nena
meets local historians, young professionals who invite her to their
home for dinner. Their young toddlers Aranxa and Mercedes, named
after their grandmothers are already in pajamas when Nena arrives,
want to play with her. Nena misses her young siblings, her nieces and
nephews, yearns to hold a baby and cuddle it, smell its baby scent. The
children love her and hang on to her. They misbehave because there is
company and won't go to bed.

They ask Nena to tuck them in, tell them a story. Nena obliges and
changes a familiar story, tells them of a little girl who lives by the river
and is scared when she hears a woman wailing in the night. Leaves out
the part of the dead children and ends it happily. It was nothing but
the wind that howled at night, sounding just like a woman crying.
Pilar says, But it probably was a woman who cried because she was
afraid of the wind.

And the children want more, so she makes up a story about two little
girls who want to see what the moon is made of. Not cheese, they don't
believe that, and certainly not a cloud, for it doesn't disappear like clouds
do, and when have you seen clouds at night? No, the moon must be
made of marzipan, or some other sweet, Nena tells them, for doesn't it
get eaten a bit at a time until it disappears? Silly stories that keep the
children entertained.

Finally they settle down, and Aranxa drowsily asks, Where you come from is the moon the same as here?

Yes, Nena answers, then hugs her and continues, and children, too, just the same; they ask questions and like stories just like you. She teaches them a short poem that Mercedes learns first: "Yo tengo un gatito, muy blanco y muy fino, se llama Minino, se acuesta en el costurero y le dice mamá, ¡quítese grosero!" The children's rhyme about a white cat quickly becomes a favorite. It was Nena's favorite, too. She gets weepy remembering her youngest sister, Xóchitl. Nena rues that she was gone when her youngest siblings were learning such rhymes, listening to such stories. Saudade. She can't imagine not being there for Azalia's graduation coming up, and the new niece will be baptized soon. She misses them all, wants to be back in Laredo, immersed in the life of her family. According to Papi's latest letter, Tía Licha has two new dogs, her cousin a new job. One of her mother's cousins, Mase, died of a heart attack. Nena remembers his throaty laugh, his nonstop jokes when they were making tamales on Christmas Eve. If she had stayed home she would be attending the parties, the velorios, the wakes and funerals. She knows her absence is noted. Anda en España, her father must explain when people ask about her. And she imagines him being both apologetic and proud.

At the dinner table in Belmonte, Nena tells her hosts of the other fiestas she's been to, and they tell her that theirs in Belmonte is older, better, and more authentic, not mired in religious myth, not commercialized like the fiestas in Andalusia. She listens and doesn't argue, has learned to accept the local version of things, and asks for the story again. Like a good ethnographer she absorbs it all, allows them to speak as she listens, soaking it all up and asking questions to elicit the more complete story: What's the history behind it? What king was it? Was it during the Muslim reign? Why don't they celebrate with Moros y cristianos here as they do in Alcoy?

She walks a few blocks to sleep in the back room of Rosario's house, which is full of antiques, crocheted doilies, and a tiny TV. Nena had found her through a friend in Madrid whose cousin was one of Luis Cano's students. She rented the room for the three nights of the fiesta. Rosario's wrinkled, parchment-thin skin reminds Nena of Mamagrande; she even has the same sky-blue eyes behind thick spectacles, but not Mamagrande's verruga, the mole, next to her mouth on her left cheek. Rosario's hair, so white it looks blue, is pulled into a bun at the nape of her head with peinetas holding back the stray hair around the temples. Dressed in navy blue, even down to her cotton stockings and blue wool slippers, Rosario, or Chayito as everyone calls her, in a sudden burst of conversation, confides that she doesn't go to the fiesta events anymore.

It's for the young; it's all a waste of time, she claims. She admits that she does go to the church services in the morning on Sunday, and sometimes she might go to the caballada. In her youth? It was quite different; she went all the time to everything. But. Not now. Not anymore. Ya no.

Rosario is quiet, barely talks, but when she does she asks Nena all sorts of questions, awestruck by Nena's freedom, her ability to come and go, alone in the world. She's lived in the same house all her life, she lets slip, with her mother and sister until they died. And the afternoon before Nena leaves, after the noon meal and the sobremesa, the woman Rosario, Chayito, sits at the old piano in the tiny sala de estar and plays "Bésame Mucho." She sings, Bésame, bésame mucho . . . her high alto, almost a falsetto, a voice that surprises Nena. Suddenly she stops midway through the song, weeping uncontrollably. The tears have forced her to stop singing, to stop playing.

I'm so sorry, she apologizes, Lo siento. Not sure what's happened. Surely it's the memories. When you believe it is in the past and it doesn't hurt, see how it all comes back so clearly? The pain lives in one's memory. In one's heart. Still hurts.

She resumes playing, María Grever's music. Nena imagines this lonely woman's life. She's like the nuns in the convent, tucked away from everything. Obviously she has lived a hard life. She remains alone, with her memories that have settled along with the dust on the ceramic figurines on the TV set and alongside the lit candle on the altar by her bed, memories crocheted into the intricate pattern of the bedspread.

Nena waits for more, for Rosario to tell her story. But there is no more. The woman Rosario, Chayito, keeps her story in her heart, like a treasure safely hidden, so well guarded it is almost forgotten until a song digs it out. Nena invents a story—a love story, of course—about how a father had died leaving a house full of women. Rosario was the youngest daughter, born when her mother was forty-five or so and her father fifty-five. Twenty years later the mother prohibits el noviazgo, perhaps her marriage, to a poor but handsome man. Chayito saw him once riding on his horse in town, and she fell in love with him on the spot. They looked into each other's eyes and knew. They recognized each other from another lifetime, reunited once again. Her soul mate. She was sure.

But when her mother opposed the match, no one supported her, not even her sisters. He went off and married one of her girlfriends, and she was godmother to their firstborn against the mother's wishes, her one act of rebellion. A different ending for the *House of Bernarda Alba*, Rosario is left alone in the old house. Alone with her memories. And the story Nena invents for Rosario could be truer and more believable than the real one.

Why won't she tell Nena her story?

Nena writes Paco a long note about her encounter with this town so full of characters. She writes about the town's pride in its past. How the young people are so energetic, so full of hope. She writes of how the children make her yearn for her siblings. Her family. Maybe she should reconsider her decision not to be a mother. Not to be a breeder, as the feminists say. In her journal she writes about her fears of ending up like Chayito. Alone. As she writes she knows she will never mail the letter. Instead she'll send him a postcard. One with a picture of the castle. She'll write a cryptic note: En este castillo se encuentra una dama encantada. Yes, an enchanted lady waiting to be rescued!

As she is falling asleep, Nena thinks of Paco, imagines him next to her, his warmth, his scent, his being by her side. She dreams they are on a trip and he gets lost and she can't find him. Then she sees him on a ship sailing away. He waves and wants to get off to be with her, but the ship's too far out to sea. Nena wakes up with a start.

On the train back to Madrid, Nena relives her visit and ponders Rosario's life. What lessons she's learned. What is her karma? Her role in life? She vows that she won't allow that to happen to her. When I am eighty, she thinks, I will not cry over what was or might have been. No. I won't be singing "Bésame Mucho." I Won't. Of course not, she smiles to herself. I don't even know how to play the piano!

Part IV La Cruz de mayo

La Cruz de mayo

*A*ll over la Mancha small villages like Almagro and even Toledo celebrate the Holy Cross; towns and individuals build and decorate crosses on el día de la Santa Cruz. La Cruz de mayo. May 3 it is. In the town center, usually in the plaza across from the main church, folks set up a wooden cross, dressed in spring flowers. Purple, yellow, red wild flowers. Dancers dressed in traditional dress, white lace and black sateen velour, and wearing shiny gold jewelry honor the day. The devotees bring their prayers, their candles, and honor the Holy Cross. They decorate community crosses; barrios have their own, too. In some places the priest blesses them; in others it is not a church-sponsored feast day, and the people bless them with their celebration. The tradition may harken back to when the Celts inhabited this land, some say. Perhaps. Nena finds the same story as the one told by the matachines in Laredo. How Santa Elena went looking for the true cross where Jesus was crucified. All over the Holy Land she travels. When she finds it, Constantine her son converts and becomes a believer, shifts the history of the Roman Empire. In some versions the conversion comes first, after Constantine dreams that the cross will grant him victory over his enemies. In others it is Santa Elena who convinces her son Constantine to leave the old pagan ways behind and follow the Christian God, who sent his only son to die for sinful humanity. Constantine prevails because of the Holy Cross and its power to defeat his enemies. Miracle of miracles, the same Romans who had been killing and torturing Christians became Christian. In one telling, Santa Elena appears to help the hermit from La Pastorela. She gives the matachines their Holy Cross. Ever since, they dance on May 3 to honor the Holy Cross.

But. Even during the Roman times, not all agreed, and some remained faithful to their gods and goddesses and worshipped the new religion in name only. They built Christian churches on the same sites where Greek and Roman temples once stood.

The same as in Mexico, Nena muses. The Spanish built their Christian churches where ancient temples stood honoring the gods and goddesses. Tonantzin. Huitchilopotli. Quetzalcóatl. Like at Notre Dame in Paris, where the Celts worshipped, then the Romans built the temple to Jupiter, and then the Christians to Mary. Overlapping devotions on sacred ground.

She must go and witness the celebration away from la Mancha, see how else it is celebrated. Roman Catholic Church. The Roman persists in the language of some prayers as Nena learned in catechism as a child. Vestiges of previous rituals remain. Por la señal de la santa cruz, de nuestros enemigos líbranos señor, Dios nuestro . . . she learns to say as she makes the sign of the cross with her index and thumb, touching her forehead, her mouth, her heart. A powerful symbol, the sign of the cross protects. Shields. La Cruz de mayo celebrations in Spain and in the Americas attest to the persistence of belief.

Sonny in Pamplona

Nena chooses none of the more accessible and more studied Holy Cross celebrations all over la Mancha with the decorated crosses in the plaza mayor. Instead, she reads of another fiesta where the penitentes carry crosses. It is not strictly a Holy Cross celebration, as it honors the Holy Trinity and the pilgrimage is a Romería de la Trinidad. So she foregoes the fiestas closer to home, and she heads north to Navarra, to a celebration in the tiny village of Lumbier. It takes her an entire day of travel to get there. By train from Madrid and then by bus from Pamplona until she gets to her destination, a tiny village in Navarra.

In Pamplona she has a few hours before the bus leaves. Walking along the street by the main plaza she meets a Chicano who is a Vietnam War deserter. A mass of unruly curls frames a face that shows sorrow and a kind of peace reflected in his dark, deep-set eyes. He asks where she is from. At first she takes him for a homeless man begging. However, he speaks perfect English and a different Spanish and doesn't ask for money, just asks where she's from.

She answers, Texas.

Where in Texas?

When she answers, Laredo, he lets out a whooping yell that scares her. Is he a madman?

I knew it! Me too! That's where part of my family lives, he says with joy. Come, I'll treat you to some wine and some lunch. By the way, I'm Sonny.

After stopping by a small grocery store where he picks up their lunch, they walk uphill to a nearby plaza where they have a view of the town below them and the hills in the distance. Come sit, he says, we'll have a picnic and you can tell me all about Laredo. But she doesn't say much because he won't let her get a word in with his continuous flow of stories, of how he came to be here after years traveling all over Europe and Asia. Amsterdam most recently. He shows some clippings from newspapers that he has picked up at the small grocery store—That's where I keep my things, he says, confirming in her mind that he is homeless.

I have been all over since 1970. For ten years I've been rambling, like that song says, a rolling stone gathers no moss . . . así soy yo. And I don't know if I'll ever go home. Home is where the heart is, no? I had my picture in the paper in Amsterdam. See, here it is. También in Portugal, and in London, and now I am here making my way to Madrid, but maybe I'll just stay here. In France they were super nice, and I had a good place in Paris, but I had to go on, had to ramble on.

He wanted to know what had happened to the Chicano movement, because he'd been in it at the beginning back in California, because his family had moved from Laredo to Fresno back in the '50s when he was a child.

You are from Laredo? Nena asks, incredulous.

Sonny tells Nena his story. Yes, but I haven't been back for a long time. Left the day after graduation. It was the '60s. El movimiento, la raza. It was calling me. I left and never looked back. Barely out of high school. No money for college. I volunteered. The draft would've taken me anyway. Didn't have much choice. Uncle Sam was happy to take me, and off I went to fight a war that was not mine. I just couldn't stand it. Thought I'd go mad. Commit suicide. Or kill my commanding officer or my own buddies. So I just left. Found a way out and left. All the training and going to Nam, and all that was supposed to make me into a killing machine. But I knew I couldn't. So, instead, I just left. I went AWOL when I was on R and R in Japan. While my friends were buying stereo equipment, I was plotting my escape.

Listen, thank you so much for lunch, Nena interrupts, worried her bus might leave.

Isn't it great! We can both eat for less than three bucks, bocadillos de jamón serrano and cheese along with good wine.

Yes, but I must go. The bus leaves for Lumbier, and I have to go.

Sadly, he agrees. Bueno, give my love to my cousins in Laredo, one of them is a policewoman in Laredo, there aren't too many of them, so I'm sure you'll find her. And he gives her a name that Nena recognizes.

Ciao.

Adiós, Sonny.

At the bus station, a kiss and a hug, and Nena is off. As she settles into her seat, she can't contain the tears as she thinks of Tino, her brother who was killed in Vietnam, and how he would be about Sonny's age. The pain of his absence is still there. That war! She is angry, and sad, and cries into her journal as she writes about Sonny and jots down his cousin's name so she won't forget.

Sonny was put in my path for a reason, she writes. But what is it? To make me realize that life is what you make it? That one must have courage to do what one must do?

Lumbier and the Holy Cross

*S*he arrives in Lumbier. It's a small village with a priest and a congregation's devotion to the Holy Cross that stretches back generations, to a time no one remembers. Nena walks to a home that someone tells her will surely have a room she can rent. The woman at the station had said, You just go down the alley and yell, doña Mela, and a woman will poke her head out the window and ask what you want. Just tell her you are looking for a room. She'll let you in.

Amazingly similar to Chayito's home in Belmonte, Mela's house is clean and smells of old people. Nena remembers her grandaunts' home in Monterrey, the same smell of camphor, a certain mugginess, the same crucifix over the bed, similar brass bed and lumpy mattress. Even the old women, two unmarried sisters in their '80s, remind her of her Tía Chita and Tía Toña, Mamagrande's elderly sisters. We must arrive early to church, Mela tells her. Muy temprano.

Is there a mass? Nena asks. No, not until we get back from the romería around noon, Mela's sister Alba answers.

Buenas noches.

Before sunrise the bells of la Iglesia de la Asunción call the penitentes who will carry the heavy wooden cross up the path and those parishioners like Nena's hosts who want to make the pilgrimage. The hermitage is up on the hill, la ermita de la Trinidad, on the outskirts of town, and

it beckons in the early morning light. For about an hour Nena follows the townspeople who hike up the hill after them, praying and singing. The elderly make their way slowly while the young sprint up and the children skip and jump, romping like young puppies happy to be outdoors, to be on an adventure. Nena notes that there is an order—the old folks go last while the young penitents, barefoot and carrying the heavy wooden crosses, lead the way.

The elderly recall the many years of making this very same hike, remember old favors granted, prayers answered. They remember all their relatives and pray for an easy death when it comes. They don't think of themselves much anymore; they have seen so many die they know their own mortality. The young are making vows and keeping their promises. Please grant that I may pass all my classes, that he notices me, that she will answer my calls, that my wedding will be beautiful, that my new job is wonderful. They are thinking of themselves and planning lives full of yearly treks up the hill to worship, to thank, to pray. And those in between? Those who have not yet lost too many friends, too many elderly relatives?

They pray for success still, they ask for peace and quiet and for time to enjoy the grandchildren newly born, they ask for patience to be able to care for elderly parents. Pray for wisdom to know what to do with the daughter who is off in Madrid, working and so independent, or the son who is married and drinks too much. The youngest, still a teenager and acting rebellious all of a sudden. The son who will not marry and is living with another man in Barcelona. The daughter who refuses to go to church.

Nena does not give herself the luxury of prayer; this is work, she reminds herself. I must be a participant observer, take notes, take photos, interview people. Talk to them, get them to tell me their stories.

She respects the men who carry the crosses. Barefoot and wearing dark-brown tunics with their alpargatas or tennis shoes hanging from a rope strung around their waists, they don't seem approachable. She will wait until they arrive.

As the procession reaches the first of fourteen crosses that the cofradía has erected, they are stunned to find that some vandals have turned the crosses over, destroyed the work they had so lovingly and laboriously done for the past year.

The vandals didn't succeed in all cases, but most of the crosses have been felled; the newly erected new-color cement taunts the pilgrims, who pray and cross themselves and cannot fathom who would do such a thing. Must be someone from outside, perhaps even ETA, trying to disturb our celebration, our rituals. They are always talking against the old ways, against the church, against the state. Must be. And the excitement rises—what will they find when they get to the top? Did they vandalize the hermitage? La ermita that has withstood Goths and Visigoths and Moors and the onslaught of centuries?

When they get there the hermitage doors are open, and three tiny candles are burning in the dark and dank interior. The sun is so bright outside it blinds Nena as she steps out of the hermitage. No one takes care of it anymore, although in centuries past a hermit always lived there, spent his whole life in prayer.

Finally Nena prays too, why not? Can't hurt. Prays that her family is well and safe. That Paco will understand and not hate her when she leaves—she couldn't bear to have him hate her. She thinks of their leave-taking a few days before. How he held on to her and whispered, Don't leave, you don't have to go.

Her heart stirred, and she had to force the tears away as she hugged him back and said, Yes, I do. I must go. It's my work. It's our destiny. The weight of her family and the love of her land is ever present, but never as much as when she has these conversations. Why can't he see it? Her duty. Her commitment. Her love.

They both knew they were playacting what would happen a few months later. The leave-taking that must come. As she sits quietly meditating, a glimmer of an idea comes to her: maybe I *can* stay. I could teach English and delay my return. I could ask the university for a leave of absence. What if I stay at least through December? That way I get to observe the fall fiestas too. It's worth a try. She can't imagine what her family will say, how her father will react if she stays longer. How she herself will feel to be gone an entire year

In Lumbier the town's fiesta is celebrated as it is in other places. But. It is a romería like a hundred others in Spain. But it is different. Lumbier's is somber not festive. So unlike Caravaca's or the Laredo Holy Cross celebrations, with dancing and eating and the procession by the danzantes or matachín dancers. The faithful reverence and the ritual procession to holy sites—to the hermitage and to the church—seemed to be the only similarities. Both the same. But everything else so very different. Lumbier has not attracted the tourists yet. Few outsiders have come to take photos, awed by the spectacle, by the devotion, by the faith of the devotees. In Laredo she was accepted, as she was one of them. Here she was a stranger, a foreigner, her presence suspect.

It's late in the afternoon after they come back from the romería, and everyone retires to their homes. Nena goes with the elderly Mela and Alba. Another year, another visit to the ermita, a memorable year with all those crosses turned over. What a sin! May God forgive those responsible.

That evening she walks into a café, and everyone turns to look at her. She sits at the bar and orders a café con leche. She can feel their questioning eyes on her. Who is she? Why is she here? Was she involved in the desecration? But soon their fears are allayed as she interviews the priest who is there with the men. He offers his support for her research project.

She talks to some teenagers who didn't go up the hill that day. It's for the old folks, they say and giggle. The young men and women who want to speak English, who want to know all about los Estados, ask her more questions than she asks them. What a contradiction. Despite all the Yanqui Go Home graffiti everywhere, so many are learning English, want to dress in jeans, watch US movies, listen to US music. They share with her their dreams for Euskara. They want to separate from Spain. Have their own country. Have their language honored once again. But. Still they want to know about the United States. They listen to music from England and the United States.

But the young men who carry the heavy crosses and walk barefoot up the hill to the hermitage, what do they think? Nena finds they too embody these contradictions, are conflicted but have faith and sacrifice for a purpose. In thanksgiving or in prayer, their sacrifice a quid pro quo. Faith. We have that, one bearded young man tells her. And we believe, says another, somos creyentes.

Still. They are certain that the best thing for their part of the world would be independence. Free to be who they have always been. Proud Basques. But. They like wearing jeans. Yes, they like to drink Coke and to listen and dance to American music—Michael Jackson, Fleetwood Mac, the Eagles.

Such contradictions! Cultural imperialism triumphs where the politics can't. And as in the past, it all works out in the end. The next morning Nena takes the bus back to Pamplona and then the train back to Madrid. Back to Paco. Back to her room in the piso she shares with Ronnie and Giovanna, back to the safety and comfort of the library's sala de raros with its warm wood walls and quiet old carpeted floors.

She is beginning to see how her project has changed and will become either a book or a treatment for a documentary. She's not sure yet. Maybe she can get her friend the filmmaker to take on the project. In any case she'll write the book and theorize about deterritorialized traditions, how they move across space and time and yet remain the same. Her focus can easily be the secular and religious celebrations, the fiestas that function as social glue in these communities, whether in Texas or in Spain. The fiestas, the faith-belief of the folk.

The Power of Faith

*N*ena ponders the power of the Holy Cross to change lives. For two thousand years such a symbol has survived—a symbol that, even earlier, was for the Native people of the Americas a symbol of rebirth, of new life. And the agony of such a death. Crucifixion—strange word, strange spelling. An *x* for a *sh* sound. From the Latin. Of course. In Spanish it made sense.

Crucifijo becomes crucifixión. The *x* is the *j* . . . so much like Galician. Is that why Mexico is spelled with an *x* or a *j*? At one time it was a *sh* sound: Mechica, Mexicas. The languages change and the people change. Yet they remain the same. This too shall pass, and the cross will remain. Or not. In five hundred years will the symbol mean the same thing? Almost five hundred years ago, the conquistadores, the Spanish, brandished it aloft as they killed the indígenas. In the name of Jesus. They called out to Saint James, Santiago, Saint Iago, to help them in battle against infidels in Spain, in Mexico, and in New Mexico. But.

These celebrations spill over to the Americas and bring faith there, too. It is not a whim that someone will dance the matachines sones for hours barefoot in front of a Santa Cruz decked out in flowery finery once a year for the fiesta. The power of faith works in mysterious ways. Here and there, in Spain as in Texas, people's indisputable evidence of healing, of favors granted, remains the motor driving the celebrations.

Nena has a quick dream as she dozes in the train, lulled by the conversations in Euskera, code-switching with the Castellano of the Basque families all around her and the grating, turning wheels, steel against steel. Earlier they had shared their bread and cheese with her; she even took a swig of wine as they passed a bottle around. In the dream she is wearing flowers in her hair, and Paco is holding her hand and speaking Italian. She can't quite make out what he is saying, but she knows it is a poem. If I can decipher the poem, translate it, she thinks in her dream, we will be together forever. Magical thinking.

The train's rhythm is hypnotic and constant as her heartbeat, so loud it seems to be inside her, in her head, in her blood, in her very soul. The wheels turning, turning, turning. On and on and on and on. Until she is in Madrid. Until she is in Paco's arms at the Chamartín train station. Until.

María Izquierdo

*I*t's a rare weekend when Nena's not traveling and is instead working at Paco's all weekend. From Friday morning until now, Sunday morning, she has been writing. Her back hurts, and she goes to bed at almost five in the morning. Sound asleep, Paco doesn't feel her sneak into bed.

She doesn't hear him as he leaves at seven for his Sunday-morning soccer game, but she awakens when he's back and ready to go out and get the fixings for the dinner he wants to cook for her. But before they shop for dinner, they go out for café con churros; his a cortado and hers a café con leche.

They shop at the nearby outdoor market where they know him. Puerros, acelgas, patatas, aceitunas from the vats full of ten different kinds of olives, various sizes in green and dark hues. Leeks and spinach, greens. Her mouth waters at the sight. At the butcher's, they pick out a chicken. Or would you rather have the rabbit? Paco teases her, pointing to the poor dead animals strung along the top of the butcher's market stand.

I don't know how to cook much, he says, but this chicken I will cook with a red wine and with prunes.

Sounds disgusting, she says. And do you really know how to cook?

No, trust me, it's good. You'll love it.

They shop some more, and then they separate. He goes home, and she takes the metro to a gallery where she sees the artwork of Mexican artist

María Izquierdo, a rare exhibit of the work of the Frida Kahlo contemporary who is mostly known for painting alacenas, pantries, saints, and what interests Nena most, traditional celebrations like the day of the dead. Nena knows her to be a feminist contemporary of Leonora Carrington and the Spanish exile in Mexico, Remedios Varo. But she finds nothing of this history in the catalog or in the signage at the exhibit. The artwork stirs her ruminations about Mexico, about Kahlo and her tragic life. Izquierdo too. Such powerful, talented women. Such tortured lives. Nena is taken with the images, the still-life paintings of lush fruit. María's painting of her nieces makes Nena take pause, and she is homesick for her nieces. Her sisters Esperanza, Dahlia, and Margarita already mothers! The two oldest nieces are only five. Nena wishes she could start painting again. She would paint her nieces, too, their bright smiles, laughing eyes, and pulled-back, long, pony-tailed hair. Dolled up according to their mother's wishes with matching pastel pink, blue, and lavender, the outfits all color coordinated down to the lace-trimmed socks.

And she thinks of another idea for a series of portraits of the border folks. Los transfronterizos, she would call it: a cartonero with his bicycle stacked with cardboard; la tortillera, sitting outside the Mercado Maclovio Herrera selling tortillas; el Guardia, the border patrol officer with his dog. So many characters on both sides of the border. It would make a great series. Perhaps she could accompany the portraits with narratives; their stories would also paint a portrait. Or maybe create a border lotería! Or she could match each with a poem. Or all three—portrait, oral history, and poem!

Of Stars and Santa Teresa

*N*ena returns and finds Paco still busily working on the meal. All afternoon he prepares the sauce and the salad, even dessert, a flan, while she works on her manuscript out on the terrace. The same spot where most mornings the breeze gently caresses her hair, her body, as she does her yoga asanas. She imagines the gentle breezes at the beach on the Gulf coast, where her family goes every summer. They swim and frolic in the warm waters of the Gulf. They camp out on the white beach sand, find seashells, and eat shrimp and fresh-caught fish.

Paco calls, Dinner is served. The chicken, delicious in the delicate wine sauce, is the centerpiece of the meal adventure he has toiled to prepare, complete with candlelight and jazz. He plays a new album, Alberta Hunter's warm, syrupy voice singing "Old Fashioned Love," and the candles burn and glow. Nena feels pampered.

After dinner they sit outside en la terraza, where she had worked most of the afternoon. He lives on the top floor, the seventh floor, so his terraza is filled with pots of geraniums, hibiscus, palms, ferns, and large pots with various flowering plants; it feels like home to Nena. She tells him how her mom has the same plants in her yard and on their porch. Paco confesses the housekeeper keeps the plants watered and trimmed, for although he loves plants he has little time for such things.

They watch the stars and the sliver of a moon and talk. Nena shares her fascination with Orion. Her father taught her about the constellations, told her stories and quizzed her to make sure she learned them well. Mighty Orion, his belt clear and bright, looms overhead. She shares her father's prayer for a new moon—but it must be but a sliver, the first visible sign of a moon after the darkness. She tells him of the full moon rising over the Gulf of Mexico and of how the beach glistens with the moonlight. She mentions that the sky in Spain looks lopsided to her. The constellations are not in the same place as they are at home, she explains.

He tells her how the sky up north in Asturias or even Galicia or A Coruña is so much more familiar to him. He speaks of his father, the father he barely remembers, who taught him to look to the stars for direction. No matter where you are you can get home if you know where the stars lead, he had told him one wintry night when they had gone to visit a sick uncle and were walking home in the dark. Look for the North Star to guide you.

Nena shares her father's lesson, too: in the dark, when there is no light whatsoever, don't look straight ahead; look to the side and you can see what's in front of you, her father had instructed. As a child she had been amazed at how it worked. Now Nena thought it was good advice for looking at everything. Look around it, from different angles, to see the full impact, the full image. Don't just look at things straight in front of you; you may not be able to see them for what they really are.

Paco talks of childhood pranks and of his mother's love of music, how she still sings some of the old ballads—and in the original language, too. Nena excitedly says, I would love to meet her, to tape her singing the songs in Asturiano, in Bable.

No, he says, that can't be. She would never agree to that. She's too shy. Too afraid of machines; she barely uses the telephone. And Nena doesn't ask why, accepts his explanation.

Nena thinks of her mother, who is not shy, not afraid of machines. Loves technology and got herself a Brownie camera to photograph her kids. Suddenly she remembers that tomorrow is Mothers' Day. Tomorrow she'll call home, wish her mother a happy Mother's Day, hear the tears in her voice, the beloved voice that tries so hard to sound happy, joyful, to hide the sadness of not having her daughter with her. Mother's Day.

Ávila

*P*aco gets up early to go play fútbol with his friends. Nena is lazily reading the *El País* Paco bought at the kiosk on his way home last night. Nena's still drowsy and falls back asleep, dreams of traveling to a foreign land where she doesn't understand the language but where a translator whispers the messages into her ear. The messages all say the same thing in different ways. Warnings. But. Also contradictory messages encrypted in dichos, sayings from her youth: Más pronto cae un hablador que un cojo. Más vale pájaro en mano que ver un ciento volar. Al que madruga, dios le ayuda. No por tanto madrugar amanece más temprano

She awakens when Paco is out of the shower and showering her with kisses. It's still early. Must be around eight, Nena guesses.

You were dreaming and talking in your sleep, Paco says accusingly.

No es cierto. I never talk in my sleep.

Sí, hoy sí.

And what did I say?

Nada. It was impossible to understand what language you were speaking.

Of course.

Come on. Let's go out for a drive.

Where?

A donde quieras.

Well. How about Ávila?

Ávila it is.

But before we go, I want to call my mother. Es el Día de las Madres.

Pero it's too early, you'll wake her.

Right! I'll wait until we come home tonight.

Ávila is only a bit more than an hour away; they talk and sing on the way. The drive is longer than she anticipated. But the highway is almost empty this beautiful Sunday morning. Ávila is all she imagined. Walled and majestic. They arrive early and park in a spot that is convenient for walking. The walled city welcomes them. A stork's nest teeters on the steeple of the church. The impressive bird's size makes Nena wonder what size the eggs must be. Over a doorway into the walled city is a saying that Bueli used to recite: Cuando una puerta se cierrra, otra se abre; When one door closes, another opens, she translates for herself. She gets goose bumps, tells him of her Bueli and her sayings.

Celia Becerra. My mother's mother. Wise and beautiful. She died when I was twelve. La velamos en casa, right there in the house, Papi set up the coffin. I keep her with me always. She shaped who I am with her dichos.

Like my mother, he says. She too speaks in parables and sayings. As if words didn't tell the things enough. They need to use the sayings of the old ones.

The old ones, Nena repeats. Los viejos.

And he shares stories of growing up in Asturias. How is life up there? Nena asks. Cold. People are different. I must be Celtic, he claims, not like the ones from around here. This is la Mancha. Or Castilla, da igual, they are in the center, we are in the north, we are purer. And she detects an ethnocentrism she detests.

How can that be? Didn't others go by there? There have been so many occupations of Spain.

Yes, but not Asturias, he maintains. And she remains quiet, won't argue, but is disturbed by his rationale. The Iberian land is an ancient one, there must be mixing, must be mestizos, she tells him later. He argues and finally concedes that she has a point, but for the south, not the north.

In Ávila Nena wants to see the saint's finger. Santa Teresa de Ávila. It's here, she tells him, I read about it.

And they search for her home-turned-museum where the child Teresa and her brother played. With the ear of memory Nena can hear her Tía Licha, who had a special devotion to Santa Teresa, praying the novena to Santa Teresa. She buys postcards to send home. Tía Licha will be thrilled to get the card. And her sister Esperanza, too.

Es una bobada, silly and stupid, he claims when Nena is telling him the story of Santa Teresa that he claims he's never heard.

True, the church didn't do well by her, Nena agrees. But my tía loves her, and I have read her work. I really like what she said. I wrote a poem for her once.

Spiritual ecstasy? Nothing but sexual orgasm, he mocks.

Yes, but it was also spiritual. She was praying and God spoke to her.

You can't be serious!

Well, yes, I do believe some of it. She was ahead of her time. Was better at what she did than the others, that's why the church didn't want her preaching. She was truly in touch with God.

Y ¿quién es ese dios, eh? he asks, wanting her to give him proof that there is a God.

Well, I don't know who God is. But. It is both he and she as Ometéotl, el dios de los Aztecas. One God, the creator.

Now I know you're not well. ¡Estás ida!

Maybe, but how do you explain it all?

Why should I explain anything? We live, we die, and that's it. In between we have some fun, we suffer, we live as best we can. Y ya.

Is that really what you believe?

Yes. Pure and simple. ¡Joder! Have you gone religious on me?

No, not religious, but spiritual. I have to believe. I must. At one time I didn't, I was an agnostic, even an atheist, I think. Also tried Buddhism. But.

Doesn't religion answer all the questions? he asks sarcastically. For sure Teresa didn't have all the answers.

No. Of course not. But she had answers for her time and place.

For sure she was getting it on with San Juan or with any of the men she hung around with.

No, I don't think so. She was celibate. Why can't you believe that?

I can't. It's impossible. Believe me.

Nena retorts, But of course it's possible. If one really wants to be celibate one can be.

But sex is normal, it's part of life. Like eating and shitting. See?

Pues no. I can't see it. One can abstain from food, of course for a period of time, ayunar, and I am sure that it's tied in with the penance and with the desire for purification, to be able to talk with God. So, yes, one can abstain from sex, too.

¡Joder! Paco insists. There you go again. I tell you, those who talk to God are only delusional, they are talking with themselves.

Yes, with their higher selves, the godhead in each one of us.

You're impossible! No te entiendo. You're an intelligent woman, a feminist. How can you believe in God?

Sí.

Pero.

But.

Es cuento de nunca acabar, this debate must end, or else.

Or else what?

You are leaving at the end of the summer anyway. You will bury yourself in that town of yours. What are you going to do with your life? Nothing. There's nothing for you there. You have so much to offer. Stay with me.

So, that's where your anger is coming from. You know I can't.

Okay, go, but don't go back to your town, that place you love so much. Go elsewhere. New York or California.

No. I promised I would go back.

Promised who?

My family. Myself. The university.

And so what. They will understand, seguro.

No. I must go back.

And do what?

Not sure. It's my destiny. I must return. The Fulbright was meant to give me a break from teaching to do my research, not to be a way for a permanent move out of Laredo. I must go back to do the work I've been doing with the refugees, with the literacy program, with the students at the university; I must go back for my family most of all.

¡Joder! Don't you see? You make your destiny. Nothing is predetermined. Or doesn't your God give you free will?

Sí, I know I have free will. I know you don't believe that, pero por eso, I choose to go back. To go home. To do the work I have to do. It's important. En esa frontera, that borderlands where I am from, that is where I belong. That is where my home is. Ahí. Con los míos, with my own people. That's where I must do my work.

Bah! You're impossible.

Nena feels her heart close against him. They have been walking in the small museum. They are now standing in front of the case that holds Santa Teresa's reliquia, a tiny finger encased in a gem-studded reliquary. Nena feels protected by it. Centuries of devout followers have come to adore and to pray in front of this artifact, at Teresa's birthplace. Where is the rest of her? Nena wonders. Like Coyolxauhqui, she is dismembered. Who will put her together again?

A cigüeña sits passively atop the enormous nest perched on a church steeple just like the ones in Alcalá de Henares. She looks up at the blue sky, speckled with white puffs of cloud, above the red rooftops and the whitewashed walls. She yearns to be home.

Nena remembers it's Mother's Day. Does the mental math and figures out that they will be about to sit down to lunch at home. Everyone has come home to wish Mami feliz día de las madres. Her sisters will be preparing the meal—maybe a carne asada that her brothers are grilling. One sister has prepared her famous potato salad and the other her famous rice. Her father will no doubt be beaming to have all his children home, all but Nena.

Home. In May with the mesquite newly blooming bright yellow and new leaves sprouting chartreuse green. Where the odor of carne asada fills the air of the barrio. She imagines how it was that morning back home, with early morning serenatas honoring mothers. The musicians throughout the day at the cemetery, the cemetery that's certainly abloom with flower offerings. Dogs barking and roosters crowing in the early dawn. Nena can almost hear the serenatas: Estas son las mañanitas que cantaba el rey David, hoy por ser día de las madres, te las cantamos así. Despierta mi bien despierta, mira que ya amaneció, ya los pajarillos can-tan, la luna ya se metió.

Atienza y la Caballada

The fiesta in Atienza happens the week of Pentecost, although it's a secular fiesta based on an event that happened over eight hundred years ago. One day in 1162, the story goes, the horsemen of the town helped the king out of some trouble. Apparently King Alfonso VIII was fleeing from his uncle, Ferdinand II of León, who wanted to seize the throne from him. But the brave men of Atienza saved the day. Ever since, the town in the province of Guadalajara commemorates the fateful ride with a caballada, horse races reenacting the historical ride. The horses are beautiful. Roan and bay, Arabian. Horses that prance and dance around, richly adorned with bright ribbons. They wear their finery while their riders dress in plain black with white shirts, ride bareback and perform tricks. The elders wear capes. Others wear embroidered jackets. The young men are so beautiful in their masculinity, in their roles of loyal subjects to a king that exists as a footnote in the history of this place. Atienza.

It is all so primitive, someone says.

Nena refutes: Not any more so than what we do. All fiestas have elements from the past. A newfound friend agrees—You want primitive? Boxing matches! An Olympic event, even! But Sweden forbids the sport, and when they hosted the games there were no boxing events. See, even the Swedes know that it's primitive. I certainly think so, if you ask me.

The horses are beautiful, and the Caballada de Atienza shows them off beautifully. Nena notes it all down in her field notebook, takes photos with her trusty Pentax. Photos she will never see, lost by the developing center back in Madrid. Only the memory remains. Atienza in springtime fills with flowers, the smell of new blooms, the fields awaken with green of grass and bush, and the streets overflow with visitors who come for the fiesta. Her friends from the tertulias—Roberto and María Jesús—have invited Nena and Paco. They ride in their tiny car, a dos caballos, called that because it has only two horse-power. Paco holds her, wishes they were in his car. It would be more comfortable. They would not be squeezed in so tight. They sing and laugh all the way. Arrive right before the mass starts so they get to see the entire event. Paco doesn't go in but stays at a bar with Roberto, who is from Atienza.

Lunch in a small café consists of a new delicacy for Nena, tortilla de espárragos. The two-hour drive back to Madrid takes almost four hours. They stop in Sigüenza on the way back, arrive in Madrid exhausted. Nena enjoyed their company but had not felt free to do her work. Felt compelled to be with them and worried about how they were doing. She thought how much better it was when she traveled alone and could come and go as she pleased. But then, she had loved their lively conversation, and the way they helped her see things she missed. Roberto had broken down the parts of the event, and María Jesús offered to take photos while Nena interviewed one of the church elders. Yes, a team worked well. But.

True to las Cabañuelas, May has turned out to be springlike, rainy but not too much. The liturgical fiestas on the calendar, Easter, Pentecost, have come and gone. Nena spent Semana Santa in Cuenca. Reading in the library about cascarones and about the church plays that are still per-formed, about the feasts around Pentecost and the coming of the Holy Spirit. She found some old stories in the hemeroteca about the fiesta, but nothing prepared her for being out in the country and in the middle of the Caballada. The sounds and smells all encompassing. The passion and pride the same as she observed in other fiestas. Pride and joy of the people in charge of those making it happen, of keeping it alive—even of those who have nothing to do with the fiesta but who are proud of their town, of their pedacito de tierra that is home.

Tomás and Maru

$\mathcal{N}$ena travels to France to visit friends she met at the Wednesday-night tertulia. Paco was supposed to come with her but got a last-minute job he couldn't decline. He is designing a new magazine that a friend is launching. It was all set. Someone else, one of Paco's friends, was supposed to do it, but then he had to pull out. So Paco is stuck. Can't travel. Must stay and work. Nena almost cancels her trip, but he insists: No, you go ahead. I will be working day and night; we won't be able to do anything anyway. Go. Visit your friends. Enjoy the south of France.

Tomás, the poet from Mexico, and his young wife, Maru, have invited her to their casita in a village near Arles. From Barcelona she takes the train. Settled in her seat, she writes in her journal and talks with a woman who helps her translate when the conductor asks where she is going and Nena misunderstands, can't understand his non-Parisian French. Nena finally arrives to a warm welcome from her friends. The casita seems to smile, nestled in the quiet street of the village where Tomás and Maru have settled in. That first night, cuddled up under crisp white linen sheets, Nena writes a letter:

Paco, querido, my darling, I arrived last night to this enchanting place. You can't imagine how much I miss you. How much I yearn for you. Chingos, as we say in Laredo.

As soon as I got here, I knew it was the right thing to do! I'm so glad I came! So glad you insisted.

I had no problem on the train from Madrid to Barcelona. But from Barcelona to France—that was another story. At the border, in Perpignan, we had to change trains, and with my rusty French, well, you can imagine! I had several confusing exchanges. Apparently France and Spain have different train tracks, and the trains can't travel in each other's tracks. I can't imagine!

But a nice French woman who spoke a bit of English came to my aid. I can't believe that, knowing both English and Spanish, I still had problems. But it was as you warned. The French are not tolerant and expect everyone to speak French. They also don't like Norteamericanos and will not even try to speak English. But my French isn't that bad, or at least that's what I thought. I never let on I spoke English, but maybe they don't like Latinoamericanos either! Or Mexicanos! I finally arrived with the help of a couple of viejitos, an elderly couple, two men that I think are gay! They saw that I was ready to walk the three kilometers from the train station to the town where Tomás and Maru live. They drove me in no time. All I had was the address, and no one uses street names in the village, so it was a real challenge. But we finally found them thanks to good luck and their asking everyone we ran into. We finally arrived at a stone house, the kind that are so common in these rural towns in southern France. Wonderful fireplace and exquisite lace curtains. Maru looked out one of those windows when she heard a car and she ran out to welcome me. She explained they were not sure I would come. But she was very happy to see me. Tomás was out, but he arrived shortly after I did, and he too gave me a hug and welcomed me. They asked about you. We ate dinner in the small kitchen. Something light. Cheese, bread, wine, and then we had biscotti with some excellent coffee. Maru promised to take me shopping in the market tomorrow morning so we can get food for the week. They fixed a bed in the room that serves Tomás as a study, where he writes. He's finishing up a collection of poetry. I feel bad, displacing him, disturbing his writing rhythm. But he assures me it's okay. That he can still work at the café downtown. That's where he was when I arrived.

Good night, yoltzin, little heart. Todo mi amor . . .

Another letter the next day:

Dear love, today we ate out en la enramada, the arbor, under the grapevines. It is a special space, with beautiful flowers all around. A white tablecloth and embroidered napkins. I know you don't care about such things, but I write this so I won't forget, not necessarily because you may be interested.

I know, I know. You love me very much and you are interested and want to hear all about where I am. If I go on and on about tablecloths and such, it's because I want you to picture my surroundings in detail. I am sure you would've loved the dinner. It was spectacular. I helped Maru cook! Can you believe it? Fresh fish from a nearby lake, beef, and locally grown asparagus with butter and mayonnaise she made right then and there.

She's an excellent cook! We also had a light soup, a consomé. Dessert was the sweetest watermelon I've had in a long time. Imagine! I had the first watermelon of the season in France! Wonder what my father would say, he who loves and grows the best watermelon. The table is under an enramada, una parra, a beautiful old grapevine with bunches of succulent green grapes not quite ripe. None of us will get to enjoy these grapes, Tomás declared. They too will be leaving at the end of the week. To Paris. That made me sad. Those who will enjoy the ripe fruit will not have seen them as they are now, full of potential. Full of life. Tomorrow we will go visit the surrounding towns. Hadrian passed through here, and so did the Etruscans, the Goths, and the Visigoths on their way to Spain. So much ancient history!

I am so happy to be with Maru and Tomás. Their Spanish is

so like mine! Although Tomás keeps correcting me, and I have to patiently explain that I speak a different Spanish from his. Just as I did with you! I have to educate. Explain that in South Texas and Northern Mexico our Spanish is our own. Like yesterday, he was complaining that the town has no sidewalks—aceras—and I said that it's the same in my barrio in Laredo; we have no sidewalks—banquetas. He knew what I meant, but still he asked me: What are banquetas? Same as you! Why can't you understand that my Spanish is the same but different? With its own vocabulary and unique grammar that mark it as border Spanish? That's all. I told him how you don't want me to say "mande," and he laughed, saying, Pues, sí, he's right. We Mexicans ask that others order us and we introduce ourselves by putting ourselves at the service of others. But watch out if someone tries to order you or ask for your service. I once again explained that it is a positive not a negative custom.

. Well, for now, my love, I must say good-night. I send my love and many, many kisses . . . yours, Nena

ps—I'll send these two letters in the same envelope.

Driving through the countryside with Maru, Tomás at the wheel, Nena snaps a photo from inside the old Volkswagen van. It shows their backs: Tomás smoking a pipe, Maru's hair held back in a bun, a postcard of Velasquez's *Las Meninas* pinned to the front the way Mexican bus drivers pin pictures of holy images, saints, and virgins for protection. The moment remains frozen in time in the black-and-white photograph that has vanished from Nena's files but not from her memory. A photo. Silent witness. A memory.

On the train back to Madrid, Nena ponders her situation. Should she stay? Come back next summer? She is learning so much. She has merely begun to scratch the surface of the traditional celebrations. There's so much more. But.

She wishes she could bring her siblings with her to enjoy the sights, the history, the food. She wishes she could show her mother the beautiful handiwork, el deshilado, and the embroidery, wishes she could interview the lace makers. Maybe she can stay after all. Get a job teaching at the Complutense in Madrid. Then her family could come visit her. One by one they could spend time with her . . . and Paco. She has not told anyone about him, not even her close friend, her sister with whom she shares everything. No. Why worry them? Why let her father know she might not come back? He who is always fearful of letting her go. Since her brother came back from Vietnam in a casket, her father has become overprotective, wants to keep them all in Laredo, all within arm's reach, or at least within a fifty-mile radius. No. She will not mention anything. Besides, it may not be so. She will go back and resume her position at the university, go back as if nothing has happened.

Only she will know, will harbor the experiences. Her book on the fiestas will be published; she will add to the scholarship that she is beginning to call transcontinental, transfrontera, the intersection of time and space and the development of cultural artifacts that help communities live and hope. Survive. But.

Erasure

$\mathcal{A}$ few weeks after her return from France and a few weeks before her departure, it happens. Nena has stayed at Paco's to work on her manuscript. She goes into the bedroom and looks in the nightstand for a pen. She sees one of her postcards from Segovia. She reads it and begins to cry. She cries for herself and for Paco. Before she knows it, she is on a search-and-destroy mission, rummaging through drawers and shelves, looking for letters and postcards she has sent Paco over the course of the last few months. In a crazed frenzy she pulls out everything—postcards from all the places she's been: Pamplona, Alicante, Santiago, Belmonte, and Segovia. From Andalucía and Galicia. Letters, too—long, wonderful, loving letters telling of all the adventures she was having and how she missed him. She piles them on the bed and sits down to read them. As she reads each one, she tears it up and drops it into a trash can. Once she is done she takes the trash can out to the terraza, lights a match, and drops it into the trash can; the papers burn with life. She feels possessed. Not quite in control. The fire runs its course, and only ashes remain.

She rationalizes her behavior: I don't want another woman coming into the house and finding my intimate expressions of affection and reading them. No, it's better to destroy it all. She would be a memory but leave no evidence. Of course, I'll have to tell him.

When Paco arrives that evening, she's writing out on the terrace.

Didn't you go out? he asks.

No. Decided to stay and work here. I still have so much to do. The book is all laid out. I think I'm not going to pursue the film, the book should be enough.

And . . . did you get much done?

Oh yes, lots. And I feel really good about the direction it's going. But I have something to confess, she hesitates.

Let it out. I can take it, he jokes. You are leaving me for another man. He laughs as he hugs her and kisses her neck.

No. I destroyed my letters.

He disengages and, looking into her eyes, says, You what? What letters?

The ones I sent you.

What? Why did you do that? They were mine, not yours.

No, I wrote them, so they were mine. Now they are gone. I burned them.

But why?

It's that . . . I didn't want anyone else reading them.

Pero, Nena. I loved those letters, your words, you. How could you?

It was hard, I must admit. I reread every single word, in a way I relived all my trips and my love for you that was in them. I am leaving, and I can't bear the thought of someone else . . .

But. Who's going to read them? That's a strange kind of jealousy!

Maybe. I just don't want another woman going through them and reading my words, words meant only for you.

Ay, Nena. Do you think I was going to be so careless, leave them around so anyone could read them? They were my treasures, mis tesoros. You just don't trust me, do you?

I guess I trust you up to a point. But I know how women are. Someone is bound to go snooping and find them and read them. No. It's better this way.

Well, what's done is done. As you say, Ni modo. But I am not happy. You'll just have to write me new letters from the States, he teases.

Ya veremos, Nena answers, relieved that the exchange wasn't as volatile as she'd feared. Glad she told him about it.

So, what will we have for dinner? What plans do you have for this evening? Let's go out. Okay? We can go see a movie.

Si no te importa, I'd rather just stay and work some more. There's so much to do before I leave. Maybe I should go home. Ronnie's expecting me.

Why? Call her and let her know you are staying with me. Seeing her serious look, Paco continues, But, okay. If that's what you want. Still, we have so few nights left, I really want to spend as much time together as possible, ¿no? I'm not sure how I can live without you.

Nena smiles, Como la canción que canta Chelo Silva, "Perla Negra," I think it is.

She sings, Como una perla negra eres tú, no puedo vivir sin tu cariño . . . sin tu mirar.

No la conozco, pero sí, así es . . . although I don't get it, what does a black pearl have to do with it? But. If you prefer to go, I'll be okay. Or, si prefieres, we'll just stay in.

Bueno. Let's just stay in. But I do have to work. You can drop me off in the morning so I can get to the library early.

Sure. Good idea to stay in. I too have work to do for Nico. His company is really doing well. Hes's starting a new magazine, de la farándula, he says.

But it's not part of your job.

No, this is separate. I like freelancing. Maybe I'll start my own business. Resign from the company and go at it on my own.

Wow, that's serious stuff. Are you serious? Will you be able to make it?

Yes, that magazine contract went really well, and there's others wanting me to design for them. To do layout and create logos and such.

Pues. If you feel drawn to it, do it.

No sé. The book company offers security. If I go on my own, who knows how long it will take to really become established and make the same kind of money. Perhaps years.

And so they spend another evening at Paco's apartment. She had learned to think of it as home as well, this space up on the seventh floor of the building on Marqués de Zafra. She had come to love the writing space out on the terraza. She was beginning to feel more at home there than in the shared piso downtown with her roommates and the landlady who with a mere look made her feel guilty for not being home every night. Nena felt warm and tingly and wept that night after Paco had gone to sleep. The tears surprised her. Are they tears of joy? Of sadness? What is going on?

He must really love me, she ponders. And he was upset, and hurt, but by his actions he forgave me. What possessed me? she wonders. Can't be just jealousy. Or can it? He is right; I destroyed his property. And she imagines a book with her letters to him. And his letters to her. Must be in the future when she writes about this part of her life, this part of the story. No. What's done is done. But. Perhaps she won't write at all. Who knows who will read them? No. I'll see him or call him occasionally, she vows. But no letters. That's all. But.

Corpus Christi in Toledo

ena will leave soon—late July or early August—so a sense of dread overwhelms her. She fears she won't have done all she planned! So many fiestas still to document, to experience: the Romería a la Virgen de la Cabeza, San Fermín, San Juan, Santiago, a trip to Granada. There's too many! In her journal Nena lists several: the beautiful carpets made with flowers—Las alfombras de Elche in Albacete; the community altars for Corpus in that place everyone knows for its beautiful embroidery, Lagartera; the dancers, las danzas de Porzuna in Ciudad Real; and in Guadalajara, the danzantes de la Octava de Valverde de los Arroyos. And that's just near Madrid! Too much! But. Nena must decide, so she chooses to visit the Corpus fiestas in Toledo and Camuñas; they're not far apart and she's confident she can manage it. Jueves Santo, the feast of Corpus Christi, on a Thursday in Toledo, and then she can go on to Camuñas for the Pecados y danzantes. The latter offers the most similarity with the matachines in Laredo that she has seen so far.

Paco offers to take her to Toledo—he'll take the day off from work, and they can invite Luis and Astrid to come with them. So, it's all set. The day begins gray and rainy in Madrid, and they drive in Paco's apple-green Seat, listening to cassettes of his favorite music. He is happy, singing along and laughing. Luis joins him. Astrid and Nena exchange looks that say, What can we do? Along the way the weather turns sunny, and by the time they arrive it is a bright, sunny day. Nena notes how quickly the weather changes and makes a mental note to check the cabañuelas.

Toledo is but a short drive from Madrid, but there's traffic. During the drive, in her usual morning quiet, Nena just listens and retreats into herself. Last night's dreams are still with her, although they slowly fade as she looks out the window at the countryside. Red poppies and yellow wild flowers. So appropriate for this country, whose flag has those very same colors, the same shades of red and of yellow. If she half closes her eyes they appear as streaks on a canvas. She has an idea for a painting. It's been so long since she's done any artwork. She misses it so much that for a moment it feels like physical pain.

They arrive and park away from the Plaza Zocodover. Traffic is already quite heavy, and Paco wants to make sure they can get out when they choose to leave. Paco has made this trip before. But it's been years, he confesses. I'm not a believer, and this fiesta is too much. ¡Se pasan!

The residents have readied the Casco Viejo for the celebration. An herbal scent rises as people tread on the sprigs of rosemary and thyme that carpet the streets and the plazas of the historic town center. A kind of canopy, a toldo, has been strung overhead so the custodia, the monstrance, will be shaded during its journey through the streets during the procession. Nena considers that given the heat of the day the toldo also offers shade for those in the procession as it is strung high above, along the route where various guilds will travel. The narrow callejones, alleyways and streets, are full of excitement even though it's only about eight in the morning.

They walk away from Zocodover and stop for chocolate and churros at the churrería on calle Santo Tomé—the best churros in all of Spain! Paco proclaims. The narrow sitting area accommodates only a few of the many who are in line waiting for the delicacy.

They walk back to Zocodover, and Nena wants something more substantial, asks if they can stop at the Café Toledo. She wants a bocadillo or at least a ración of a tortilla española. The others laugh.

That's not for breakfast, Luis chides.

I know, she says, but I like it, and she goes in and asks for a ración de tortilla. She enjoys the freshly made tortilla with eggs and potato and a dash of garlic, fried in olive oil. They continue walking along the streets of the Casco Viejo, enjoying the bustle of the crowd. Paco says, We must find a good spot before the procession. Seemingly out of nowhere comes a group of gigantes y cabezones followed by a small drum-and-fife band and, at the end, a dragon or gigantic turtle—Nena can't decide what it is.

Centuries old, the figure of the blonde puppet atop the green monster—dragon or turtle—confuses Nena; she had not read anything about such a figure. She asks people milling around. The kids stare in amazement and awe. No one seems to know much about it except that it is la Tarasca. Finally, an old man tells her that the doll atop the dragon is Anne Boleyn.

The Tarasca and the gigantes, the giant puppets some call mascarones, parade down the path as they did the night before. Nena catches them as they are entering the courtyard by the Cathedral where they are placed to observe the festivities.

The figures of the gigantes everyone seems to know: the Moor and the Christian queen and king, the Chinese and the others. Giants as tall as the toldo that covers the area where the procession will parade. Nena is surprised by a cabezón that appears suddenly. It's Groucho Marx! The young boy takes off the head and poses. His friends take off their cabezón heads and pose, too.

The outside walls of the cathedral are draped with rich tapestries depicting biblical and mythological scenes. The annunciation with Mary amid the angels. The child Jesus before the rabbis in the temple. Over fifty tapestries grace the cathedral walls; they are old, and Nena has the impression that they are not as well cared for as they should be. The next day, the workers will pull them down and put them away for next year. For eight hundred years Toledo has been celebrating Corpus Christi. Of course, she had to come!

Nena wants to attend mass, and she goes off alone after they find a spot where she will join them afterward. As she enters the twelfth-century cathedral, she feels dwarfed and insignificant. The main "Organ of the Emperor" in the transept of the cathedral stuns her. The choir is singing in Latin. Nena has read about Cardinal Cisneros and the great influence he wielded. Fernando and Isabella protected him and urged Rome to make him a cardinal. Isabella called his children "his three beautiful sins." The small Corpus Christi Chapel for the celebration of the Mozarabic Rite intrigues Nena, and she makes a mental note to tell Paco she wants to come back. There's so much she doesn't know. So much that piques her interest. The faded-red bishops' hats hanging overhead. The burial plaques everywhere. The beautiful cloister where she found the first-communion children lined up. So much more to see, to learn.

She must come back to study the cathedral with its priceless artwork and so much gold—must be from the Americas. The magnificent organ sounds. The various cofradías are lining up for the procession that begins at the end of mass. Some women are wearing fancy mantillas, the elegant, exquisite lace head coverings that in some cases reach to the hem of their skirts; an elegant comb, a peineta, holds it in place.

Nena remembers the custom before Vatican II, and how many times she would have to use a hairpin to hold a piece of Kleenex tissue on her head to hear mass because she forgot her head covering. She smiles to herself, remembering the time in Monterrey when she was escorted out of the church for being bareheaded. How things have changed! But she loved to wear the fancy lace mantillas, too—the small, circular lace ones and the fancy longer ones. She owned a number of them in various colors. She remembers the Easter crocheted hat her Tía Luz made for her when she was nine, the many hats and head coverings her mother had bought or made for her. What acts of love, she thinks as she daydreams, waiting for mass to begin. She wonders if her family will attend mass at San Luis Rey Church, for Corpus, together once again.

She finds a seat upfront, right behind the authorities—military and civic—where she can observe the archbishop, the bishops, and the visiting priests. There must be over twenty officiating mass. It's a ritual she knows well, so she mouths the prayers and stands and sits and kneels in unison with everyone. The solemnity of the event touches her despite her apparent distancing so she can study the event. Such deep devotion, such faith! She's in a building built in the twelfth century, participating in a living legacy, a celebration that has drawn the faithful for centuries.

At the Biblioteca Nena had read about the origins of the liturgical celebration: how the cult to the Body of Christ originated with a nun, Julianna was her name, who had a vision and was told to begin the worship of the Holy Eucharist. That's how so many things begin—with a woman having a vision!

As soon as the mass is over she dashes outside with her Pentax, ready to shoot as many pictures as she can. The first-communion girls, all lined up, stop their giggling as Nena takes their photo. They've dropped off flowers and now are waiting for mass to be over so they can take part in the procession like their parents and grandparents and ancestors for many generations.

Along with the first-communion boys and girls, adults line up, the cofradías, the old guilds that have been around forever; they are lined up in order of the year when they were founded. A brand-new one intrigues Nena. It was added this year, los Investigadores! Scholars, researchers like herself. She feels a kind of déjà vu and sees herself decked out in the

fancy pastel-blue cloak with the funny headdress. Many years later, as a guest of the Universidad de Castilla la Mancha, she joins the faculty and marches down the same route that has been followed for centuries. She feels as one with the community, walking and pausing along the route, but also a sense of dread knowing the Inquisition used the same route for those accused of heresy.

The descendants of those early worshippers, these stern gentlemen and women, the nurses, the religious orders, the military, the young and old—everyone's in place. The horsemen in medieval dress escort the first guilds. At the very end waits the military band that will follow the custodia and end the procession.

Nena leaves the cathedral as if on a cloud; she walks the streets full of people already lined up, waiting for the procession. She finds her group. They have indeed secured a good spot and eagerly await the coming procession. She tells them of the mass, the choir, the monstrance that is over ten feet high, and how they are all lined up, who is coming in what order. Paco bought a program, and she consults it as the parade unfolds before her. He is helpful, telling her stories of what happened when he last saw the procession and how it seems changed and yet not.

The unending procession of group after group with banners announcing each cofradía bores the children and Paco. He and Luis discuss business and drift off, talking about sports. Astrid is quiet. Finally, the monstrance appears. The rich, gold and jewel-encrusted structure holds the Blessed Sacrament. Nena read that the monstrance was built in the sixteenth century by a German silversmith, Arfe, and that it took nine long years of work to create.

The appearance of the monstrance in the procession elicits yells of ¡Viva Cristo Rey! The military band follows and marks the end. Nena has shot two full rolls of film—seventy-two photos. Paco has been helpful, offering advice on how to hold the camera for certain shots, pointing to particularly interesting photo ops. For the first time Paco seems really interested in her work. When she wants to go interview some folks he tells her who the leaders are, but she decides instead to stay with the group.

I have a feeling I will be coming back to this fiesta, she says to Astrid, who's bored. There's so much to study.

She doesn't have much to compare it with, though. The Corpus Christi processions in Laredo have stopped, probably due to lack of devotion. The grand processions of Christ the King Church remain in her mother's memories and her own, though. Nena remembers walking along with the group, candle in hand, in the procession. The priest intoning in Latin, and the people responding. The old joke her mother is fond of telling: when the priest would intone, Ora pro nobis, Alicia, her mother's childhood friend, would interpret it as ¿'Ora por dónde? and laugh and say, Well, if they don't know where we're going, we sure don't! Her mother remembers the old women, Catalina, Simona, Sapopa, and Altagracia, singing off-key, the men shouting, ¡Viva Cristo Rey!

Since Nena decides not to interview anyone, they head to the Restaurant del Cardenal, where Paco made reservations. It is one of the fanciest restaurants, and it is full. The server is someone Paco knows—imagine the coincidence! He fills their wine glasses, and Paco raises his glass to toast: ¡A Nena, por su trabajo! She feels flattered and raises her glass. To friends! she toasts. Chin Chin. Amid the clink clink clink of glass against glass, Nena feels warm and tingly, knows that in the future she will feel nostalgic for this moment. She sips the red elixir and is glowing.

Some day she will come back. She will know this place that feels so familiar. Maybe she'll bring some students to study the fiesta. Or maybe not.

Camuñas–Pecados y danzantes

On Sunday Nena goes on to the small town in la Mancha to find another Corpus Christi celebration, markedly different from the solemn procession in Toledo. She has read that this one started later in the sixteenth century but can't find much more than that it is an ancient ritual that the townspeople perform on the Feast of Corpus Christi. While Toledo is serious and religious, Camuñas has an air of jubilation. The Pecados y danzantes are masked sins and dancers, characters who perform a narrative through dance, much like the matachines in Laredo. The Pecados signify evil and embody the main demons: it begins with pecadillas, little sins, and moves on to Pecado Mayor, or the head sin, then proceeds to the three temptations or trials of any Christian's soul—sins of the world, sins of the flesh, and sins of the devil. Above it all is the crucified Christ.

The sins wear cotton-print, clownish outfits and bright-red masks with a flounce of white cotton lace that covers the head, held in place with a flowered headpiece. In their right hand they hold a staff decorated with the same flowers and adorned with colorful ribbons.

Color is everywhere, except on Pecado Mayor, the head devil figure, who wears all black and reminds Nena of a black crow, or a raven, with his spindly legs. Suddenly all the dancers are birds in her mind, all colorful feathers and red faces and black beaks. But the image fades just as suddenly as the music begins.

The little girls in their floor-length, white communion dresses lead the procession. The musicians also walk along the procession—dressed in traditional garb—using panderetes, gourds made into rattles, and drums to beat the tone for the dancers, who line up and then one by one run up to worship at the monstrance, la custodia, or before personal altars set up along the way. The idea is that the Pecados attack the custodia and then are defeated and end up genuflecting in front of it. In the procession they stop at various home altars along the way just as the matachin dancers do in Laredo. The Danzantes similarly hold staffs and are attired in similarly colorful pants and shirts, but they also wear a kind of scarf that hangs from the head all the way to the floor. They perform various sones. One dance especially reminds Nena of one she has observed in the matachines. Tejer el cordón. The dancers face each other in two rows and dance, zigzagging in and out, following the lead dancers, here called Porra y Madama. Madama is dressed as a woman and plays the castanets. Correa is the last Pecado—dressed in red and with three crosses of Malta emblazoned on his chest—and he closes the cycle of dancing. Throughout the fiesta the conflict between Danzantes, good, and Pecados, evil, plays out,

although it is not confrontational as both groups honor and kneel before the cross or the custodia.

Nena asks about the masks—who makes them?

One dancer points out the master mask maker, who stands to the side. He doesn't dance. Shyly, he offers that dancing is not his prayer, making masks is. She buys a mask from him. He constructs them for the diablos and the dancers, he explains. He poses with the mask she will take with her. How far will it go? he asks.

To Texas, she answers.

Muy lejos.

Yes, very far.

Books and Writing

*P*aco and Nena are walking hand in hand down la Gran Vía one evening in June. It's a bit warm, but pleasant. They are headed to the Plaza España because Nena hasn't seen the Quixote statue that's there. Both have left work early to be together this evening, for their time together will soon be over. She has decided to leave in early August after she returns from Santiago de Compostela. She's let the Fulbright office know, and they have booked her ticket. It's all set. But she still must travel to the verbenas de San Juan and la Romería de la Virgen de la Cabeza. She and Paco have talked about going to Pamplona for the running of the bulls. Or maybe even to Italy for the Palio in Siena. All before Nena takes off across an ocean and they go their separate ways. Nena feels the tug of time rushing, pushing, and catapulting her into the future. Things seem to be moving swiftly, too quickly.

She and Paco stand before a bookstore window and, with a wink, Paco asks, Do you like to read?

Nena answers, Of course not! I don't like . . . I *love* to read. I have chosen to be a professor because I love it above all things. I could've been an attorney. Or a mathematician. Or a dancer. Or even a politician. They laugh.

No doubt the pay would be better, Paco says.

Of course, but would I be happy? I probably would be, being an attorney, but in a different way.

You read *El Quijote*, ¿sí?

Yes. And others by Cervantes. His treatment of certain things . . .

Paco interrupts, Remember when we talked about *Pedro Páramo*? Well, I never finished it, Paco confesses. Overall, I prefer nonfiction. History. Biographies. Memoirs, too. Travel and cookbooks, too. I feel I am traveling when I read travel books. And cooking when I read cookbooks.

You like cookbooks? I do, too, Nena pipes in. I dream up fantastic meals. I read the *New York Times* food section and clip the recipes and then file them away, but I rarely make them. Reading is a way of living other lives, a way of escaping one's life, no? Maybe that's why I love novels. A way of being someone else and knowing that it is not your life; it gives you a moral imperative. You can be judge, judged, and jury, y ni quien te lo reclame. Right?

Paco responds, But novels are fiction. They are not real. That's why I like history, biography, or memoir. They're real. Not invented. But I get it, why people want to escape into fiction.

Nena agrees. Right. That's how I see it too, but of course in the novel there's always truth, too. Another point. One lives the life of a character vicariously and enjoys her pain and her joy although it is not one's own. Sometimes a novel is more real than real life.

Or his! Paco almost shouts: I can't pretend to be an expert as you are, but if you ask me, it's shameless how some writers write their own personal lives into the narratives. A kind of cheating, not inventing characters, a plot line, just digging in their own stories. At least that's true of a friend of mine who writes novels—but he really is just writing about his own life. He even put me in one of his tales, called me Kiko pa disimular. Of course, it's just another nickname for Francisco—who does he think he's fooling?

Nena is circumspect. I'm not sure, she says. Some writers do that. Others don't. I think all writers draw from what they know, and what they know is what is closest to them. O por lo menos, that's how I see it. Even science fiction.

She continues, Sometimes truth is stranger than fiction. And after all, anyone's story is fiction, it's one's own fiction. My favorite dicho: Cada cabeza es un mundo.

Paco agrees, Cierto, it's true. Pero.

Mira, ¿qué te parece? he asks as they arrive at Plaza España. They have been walking along the major boulevard, la Gran Vía, as it will soon be renamed. It's been Avenida de José Antonio during the Franco years.

They look around in the late evening. There's still sunlight, but it is the sunlight of dusk, of sunsets, russet against a darkening sky to the west. The shadows look blue and purple.

Nena considers the people out for a stroll in the plaza. Some elderly, some young. Couples. Some teenagers smoking and laughing, immersed in their own intrigues, their eyes bright and luminous. The boys trying to be men, the girls preening and flipping their hair away from their pimply faces. But. Some have smooth, clear, ruddy faces. The boys too. All are just happy to be alive. The elderly walk slowly, wearing sturdy shoes; the men wear their berets, and some walk with a cane. Some walk with their arms crossed behind them. Sad looking, wise folks, wearing drab gray, brown, and mostly black. They are at that stage, she muses, remembering the riddle. What creature walks on all fours, on two, and three legs? They are all here for her to observe.

She and Paco linger a while before the statue, and she reads the inscription. Cervantes gets the big monument, his characters the smaller bronze statues. I don't recall too many statues to imaginary characters, she thinks aloud. Or for women. There's Rosalía de Castro in Santiago, Emilia Pardo Bazán in A Coruña, so few women. But they should be honored.

Paco adds, Of course, Agustín Lara has a statue, too, in that tiny plaza in Lavapies.

What a name for a neighborhood, eh, Lavapiés! Washfeet. Wonder where it came from. Our barrio names are just as enigmatic—el tropezón, el rancho, el tonto, and then los amores, el sal si puedes—some are more literal perhaps. Nena realizes she is thinking out loud, and Paco is looking at her quizzically.

Interesting, ¿a que sí? Paco asks. He tells her Lavapiés is the old

Jewish area of Madrid, and it probably derives its name from the practice of outsiders to the area washing their feet upon entering or exiting the area.

Are you sure? she asks.

Paco answers, Es lo que cuentan. Who knows if the stories people tell are true? ¿Qué se yo?

They stand before the monument to Miguel Cervantes de Saavedra.

Nena loves *El Quijote*; she read it on her own, not for a class, and she remembers how taken she was, how she wanted everyone to read it, to know the genius of the writer. She looked for his statue in Toledo and found it right off plaza Zocodover. She says, I want to go see his house in Alcalá de Henares.

Vale, Paco says.

Músicas

*W*alking along la Gran Vía, Paco and Nena arrive at the biggest bookstore Nena has ever been in, la Casa del Libro. Floors and floors of books and a whole floor of music, too. Paco gets off the elevator on the music floor. She mumbles, I'll meet you on the other floor with the literary criticism, okay? and feels sick.

No, wait.

But the door shuts between them. She gets off at the next floor and has what she later identifies as an anxiety attack. This has never happened. Why now? What is it? She finds a restroom and splashes water on her forehead and on her neck. It helps, and she comes out more refreshed.

As she is walking along an aisle, Paco is suddenly at her side.

You scared me. You went pale. What happened?

I felt sick.

Don't ever do that to me. I was really scared. I came looking for you and couldn't find you.

I was in the bathroom.

Come, I just want to find the new recording of Pavarotti. *El elixir del amor* de Donizetti. Then we'll leave, go out. Get some fresh air. Or if you're not well, we can leave right now.

No, no. I'm fine. Go ahead and look for the record, I'm fine.

They walk up the stairs, and he asks someone for the recording. He pays with a credit card. And as they wait for the transaction he holds her hand and looks into her eyes and says, What a scare you gave me. I thought, no, I can't even say it.

What? What did you think?

And he whispers, I thought you were nauseous because you are pregnant.

And she smiles. No, that's not it. I assure you.

But don't you see? I was glad. And that's scary. What if you are, and off you go and have my child, and I don't ever see you again? That can't be.

It won't. Don't worry. I promise you that would not happen. But I won't promise that I won't write about it.

Later, they are home listening to the new recording, in the living room with its modern furniture: built-in bookshelves on two walls, the other open to the kitchen area and the one opposite open to the terrace. They can see the lights of Madrid in the distance. The sound system pipes the music everywhere, and it's glorious to hear the music as if you are in the middle of the opera house. Una furtiva lagrima . . .

Una furtiva lagrima / negli occhi suoi spuntò / Quelle festose giovani / invidiar sembrò . . . Pavarotti sings, and Nena sheds a tear. Paco, teary eyed himself, moved by the music, the voice, the words, wipes it away tenderly.

I love this music. As much as I love jazz. It's not contradictory, is it? Paco says as the song ends.

No, it's not. I have learned to love it, too. That's probably why that floor of the bookstore gave me the creeps. I am such an illiterate when it comes to this music. All I know is what I like. I don't necessarily like Tchaikovsky, and I love Vivaldi. That I have learned from going to concerts. You must understand that it is not my music, and although I know it is not necessarily a class marker—at least here in Spain—for me it is. It is just not my music. In the States not everyone has access to classical music. I never heard it until I was an adult.

Come on, it's music for the world, for the ages. Don't tell me I can't enjoy jazz because it is a black music that originates in the US? Of course I can! And you can enjoy opera. And Sevillanas, too! What is your music?

Tejano. Mariachi. Rancheras. Boleros. Cumbias. Algo de conjunto, también. I have some cassettes. Pero, I don't play them much, because my roommate doesn't really understand why I like to listen to this music. It's not their music either.

Venga, bring them over and we'll play your music, ¿vale? I want to know all about you, what you like, what you love, the music, the food, todo. Before you go off across an ocean. Promise me. You'll bring me your music. ¿Vale?

Bueno, but it's not a quality recording. Just music I like. Tejano music. Little Joe y la familia, Sunny and the Sunliners, a duet that was popular a while back, René y René. Some women singers from the '40s, Chelo Silva, Lydia Mendoza. My cousin taped them for me when I left to Lincoln. She made me a cassette of what she knows I love.

Sure. I want to hear them all.

And she sings softly a few lines from various songs . . . Fui gorrión por querer ser gavilán . . . Don't even know the lyrics, she aplogizes.

Angelito déjame decir que antes que te vi no conocí el amor que
    por ti aprendí . . .
Las nubes que van pasando se paran a lloviznar, parece que se
    sostienen cuando a mí me oyen cantar.
Cuando a mí me oyen cantar, se paran a lloviznar . . .

I also like conjunto, the classics, como Narciso Martínez, Valerio Longoria, Santiago Jiménez, senior and junior. También Flaco Jiménez.

Flaco?

Yes, that's his name! At least his stage name, Flaco. He plays the accordion. Lydia Mendoza plays a twelve-string guitar. I have a cassette recording of her music that a group in California just did. I saw a documentary not too long ago about the music from the border, *Chulas Fronteras*. I loved it; they featured one of my favorites, Lydia Mendoza. Reminded me of home so I bought the albums, and my cousin taped them. Los Tigres del Norte, los Alegres de Terán. That's my music.

Paco asks, What about mariachi? It's Mexican. That's what I know. Yes, that too. I mentioned it. But. I don't have any of that music. The most famous group is el Mariachi Vargas de Tecatitlán, claro. My parents listen to Pedro Infante, Jorge Negrete, Antonio Aguilar, and José Alfredo Jiménez. They love Armando Manzanero, too. I like him, too; I prefer boleros to rancheras. Agustín Lara. I saw Lucha Villa and Amalia Mendoza, la Tariácuri, at the fair in Nuevo Laredo once. And, of course, el Piporro. That's my music. Boleros. Rancheras and Tejano.

Here we got to see Mexican movies.

Really?

Yes, from the '40s and '50s. Lots of music.

I also like music in English, after all I grew up in the '60s with the Beatles and the Stones. Also those slightly older ones, Dean Martin, Andy Williams, Frank Sinatra, Connie Francis. I guess I'm eclectic. De todo un poco. Igual Billie Holliday que Edith Piaf or Cher.

Can you pick one? Paco asks innocently.

Pues, no. I also like the '60s and '70s—mostly trova—Mercedes Sosa, Lucerito, Cher, Joan Baez. I even like certain country, a very special music. I like the way certain singers sing it, like Linda Ronstadt y Bonnie Raitt. Some country singers I really like. Also, Willie Nelson, Mel Haggard, and Patsy Cline. Claro, I love rock too, Janis Joplin, Led Zeppelin, even Queen and schmaltzy stuff like the Carpenters!

What's that, schmaltzy?

Cursi, tonto, stupidly sentimental.

Really? Well, it's a long list and pretty eclectic! Seems to me you are more Mexican, though. No?

It's what I've been trying to tell you, that I am both. I am Mexican and also from the US; I have both cultures. And the Mexican part is from the north, norteña. That means our food and our music, everything, is different. Get it?

And Paco holds her tight and whispers, Yes, I get it. But you don't have to apologize for anything, nor do you need to feel faint with my music. Unless it's because of its power. Music is powerful. So is love.

Well, of course, she whispers, slipping out of his embrace. The music does affect me in many ways. But today I can assure you it was being overwhelmed by your world that is not mine.

Listen, I want to get another LP, with José Carreras, he's a young tenor that everyone tells me will be a big name someday. If I had another life, I would've wanted to be a tenor, and he sings, una furtiva lagrima . . .

What about you?

Hmmmm, if I could be something else? A dancer. A ballerina. They are so graceful, and they embody the music. Or maybe a filmmaker. I love movies. Or . . .

Wait a minute, I said *one* thing, he teases.

Later he returns to the idea of the music of his world and wants her to know that it is for her, too. She responds, I don't want your world. I resist it with my whole being. Your world sought to destroy mine. Still does. How can I want the European, the Western way of being when my indigenous blood cries for my own? No!

Wait. It's the US that seeks to destroy my way of life. What do you say about a McDonald's in the middle of Puerta del Sol?

Yes, you are right, but understand that that is not mine either. I am a Chicana. We are a colonized people. They stole our land, our language, and I agree they are trying to dominate world culture, and I am part of them, too. Even as I resist. I can't deny that I am an accomplice. I buy products, wear clothes made in the Philippines by poor, underpaid workers.

It's complicated.

Yes, it is. Let's not think about it right now. Let's just enjoy this moment, okay?

Vale.

And they settle down to listen to the music. And Nena can't keep the thoughts at bay, they are at the door like the wolf that haunts her dreams and won't leave.

Of Gypsies and Orange Blossoms

*I*n Andalucía the doorways have curtains that sway with the breeze. Like at home on hot summer days when the mosquitoes seem to come through even though there's a screen door. Mami sews a long curtain, strings it up with a heavy cord across the doorway. Keeps the mosquitos and the flies away, she claims. The cloth is a print cotton, heavier than what she uses for Nena's summer frocks but lighter than the one used for winter colchas that she quilts all summer long, strung on the quilting frame and set out across the small living room, leaving little room for kids coming and going.

Papi makes the quilting frame from two-by-fours. The wool, bought from la Docha, the woman who has sheep and goats, is prepared the old-fashioned way, washed with ashes and rough soaps, until someone discovers that Stanley Home Products Degreaser works to get the lanolin out. The dry, clean wool is finally carded into three-by-six-inch bricks to be used as batting, lain across the base cloth, which will be the print one because the solid one has been marcada with a thin sliver of soap and will be the top to be stitched. One by one the tiny stitches shape the flowers and the leaves. Like magic they emerge from the cloth. These colchas are not the embroidered ones from New Mexico, nor the pieced quilts. They are more like comforters that will keep the children warm come winter. It is the same cotton fabric of the twenty-five-pound flour sacks that Mami transforms into curtains for summer, providing privacy on hot summer nights when the doors and windows are open, simple strips sewn together and gathered along the rope strung on the frame; they serve their purpose well.

Strange how a simple item, a curtain on a door, sends Nena back. It's 1965 and Nena has a date for the prom; Nena begs her mother to remove the curtain. Doesn't want to appear backward. Her home must look like the others. And Mami complies. After all, she was young too and remembers the way her mother understood. Bueli. So long gone, yet her life is still with them, the womenfolk, in the lessons and dichos and ways of cooking tamales or enchiladas, she lives on. She still cares. For Nena the memory of the prom is always tied to the memory of her mother's understanding. The old rose dress, thick satin and lace, that Nena sewed herself. Embroidered the lace bodice with beads. She remembers Tony, her date. How they danced that night. She led the bunny hop, and her friends laughed and held on as they went around and around the gym floor at Martin High School.

Nena and Ronnie take the long bus ride and doze on and off as the B-movie, and then the radio, plays on and on as they drive in to Granada. A British group Nena has never heard of is singing "The Devil Sent You to Laredo" in English! I must be dreaming, Nena thinks, but Ronnie confirms it. And she can't believe it. Is that what it says? Yes, that's right. How can that be? No sé. But so it is. Nice beat!

It's early July in Granada. Granada with its particular sweet scent that reminds Nena of her mother's garden. Gardenia? Jasmine? Orange blossom? She can't pinpoint the comforting odor of the city. Maybe it is the scent of the pomegranate. It's late morning when Ronnie and Nena arrive at their hostal. They check in and settle in at the hostal and go explore, do a bit of shopping. Nena buys a ring with garnets shaping a pomegranate. Un recuerdo, a souvenir of Granada. They make plans to visit the Alhambra the next morning.

That afternoon, as she sits at the café in front of the hostal, sipping her café con leche and writing her notes, someone asks to borrow her newspaper.

Sure, of course, Nena answers, barely looking up.

The paper in the café is gone, he explains.

No, no. Take this one. You can return it later.

Not from here, are you?

No, just got here from Madrid.

But not from there either.

No.

Mario, he says as he extends his hand. And you?

Azucena. And they make small talk. Nena has noted that folks here don't talk about the weather as they do at home; instead their small talk centers on what is immediate.

Look at that loose dog, someone should tie him up. He'll scare the tourists, Mario says. The caramel colored pup comes up begging for scraps. Lies at Nena's feet, content.

And before too long Mario is asking, Want to go see some flamenco? Tomorrow night?

Not sure. I'm with a friend.

Have him come, too.

I'll ask her, let you know later.

Let's meet here around ten, ¿vale? That way we can all go together.

Sure. If we're here, it's a yes. But if not, then it's a no, okay?

Vale. Aquí en la cafetería frente a la plaza de Santa Ana, a las diez mañana.

He reads quietly. Nena writes her notes for a while. Then they start chatting again.

They discover each other's paths.

He is a bullfighter, hopes to make it big. Just barely starting out. He's a novillero and will someday fight a bull en las Ventas, the big bullring in Madrid. For now it is mostly local rings, and not for ferias or anything, just plain novilladas for the season. And she shares how she is collecting fiestas and traditions to compare to her own from Texas. How she is a writer and wants to publish a book, or perhaps team up with a film-maker and film a documentary on the fiestas in Spain and Texas.

Ah, Tecksaas, he says with a heavy accent, very famous here en espain. He wants to practice his English, and they laugh at his exaggerated accent.

He says good-bye. Gotta go! A kiss on the cheek, awkward as she kisses once and he twice.

Ciao, see you. Mañana. Don't forget, at ten!

Adiós.

Hasta mañana.

Maybe, Nena answers as she waves good-bye.

The next morning, after their café con churros, Ronnie and Nena are ready to go visit the Alhambra. What's the best way to go to the Alhambra? Ronnie asks the waiter, who with a glint in his eye answers, ¡En taxi! and laughs heartily at his own joke. And Ronnie, without a pause, ignores him and clarifies, Walking. What is the best direction to go if we walk? And he points, Pa'rriba. Sigue pa'rriba. They head up the hill as instructed.

Nena and Ronnie arrive early to the grounds of the Alhambra. The pollen from the chopos falls gently, reminds Nena of snowflakes in the morning sun, falling in slow motion, falling in the sunlight. It is magical, Nena thinks. Alucinante, the word Paco would use. She has learned to call all awe-filled things with that magical word. ¡Alucinante! He is not with her. Has remained to work on an urgent project. She was there the night when the boss called and insisted that he not take the day off but come in and work on the design for the new magazine. Spain is boom-ing, and new magazines are springing up all over, and his designs and layouts are in high demand. He works with the emergent computer pro-grams to keep ahead, on the cutting edge. He must stay and work. Maybe I can go with you to la Romería de la Virgen del Rocío, ¿vale?

I'm not going, remember, I can only do one romería, and I went to la Romería de la Virgen de la Cabeza, she replies. She chose the Romería

of "la Morenita," as locals referred to the dark-skinned visage, because it intrigued her that there would be a version of Mother Mary that was dark, like Guadalupe in Mexico.

Nena had read the history. According to local legend the image was brought to the area by San Eufrasio; it was hidden away in the seventh century to protect it from the invading Moors, and then it was again hidden away during the Civil War to protect it once more. In the first instance she had surfaced when a shepherd saw bright lights and heard bells tolling nonstop near a hill. When he went to investigate, he found the image nestled in the rocky terrain as if waiting to be rescued. That was in August of 1227. Andújar treasures the holy image and pays homage once a year with a romería, a procession that leads up to the hill. Nena finds the spring festival refreshing and uplifting. Two men ride up near the image and bring up children to kiss it or touch items handed to them by people in the crowd. Nena was almost glad Paco was not with her as it gave her a freedom she wouldn't have had otherwise.

So it was for their trip to Granada. Except she was not alone. Ronnie had joined her at the last minute. That morning, Paco had dropped Nena off at the bus station where Ronnie was waiting. Hasta pronto, chata, he called out after her as she slung her backpack on her shoulder and looked back at him, pressed her fingers to her mouth, and blew him a kiss.

Nena had read Kipling's book on the Alhambra years ago, and she thought she was prepared for the magnificence of the place, but once inside the Alhambra, Nena and Ronnie can't reconcile the description with what is real. They spend hours in the magnificent gardens, the buildings, some in need of repair. Nena keeps thinking it is like a dream. As they exit the gardens, a gypsy, one of three who have been following them, offering to read their palms, reassures Nena as she reads her palm that the future is never certain. Remember, she admonishes, you have free will, but there is always light and love in your path. Luz y amor, maja, the gypsy says, looking into Nena's eyes, accepting the pesetas that Nena puts in her hand. She kisses the coins and turns away to join the other women, who are now accosting other tourists, offering rosemary sprigs, offering to read their palms.

But one stays behind, begging Nena to stop. They are now outside the Alhambra. A gypsy approaches Nena. The woman's cinammony skin glistens, her green eyes sparkle; she's wearing a long red skirt and a purple and blue blouse. She tells Nena, Your spirits are always with you. Looking over her shoulder, her eyes fluttering, the gypsy continues as if in a trance: Yes, there are angels and spirits that go with you always. Llámales y vienen a tu ayuda. She singsongs under the trees with the birds chirping in the background, Call on them, they will come to your aid.

Later, Nena will write in her journal about looking for García Lorca and finding Mario the bullfighter. She also finds Mariana Pineda, the martyr from the time of the insurrections, executed on May 26, 1831. She is all but unknown in the '80s but will have her own monument and a plaza named after her now that Franco is gone. Mariana will be known again.

And García Lorca resurrected through his work. He, who was also executed, will have a park and a museum in the new Spain that battles against the forgetting of that brutal war that is so immediate, even now, so many years later. In time Lorca's summer home will become a museum, la Huerta de San Vicente, where he wrote his plays. A museum that will house a drawing of García Lorca talking with Mariana—total anachronism, made real in dreams as Lorca writes the play about her life a century earlier, not knowing he too would be sacrificed, he too would be killed . . . different circumstances, but the same end. Martyrs, that is what they are. Nena senses the pain.

Wars. Why do they never end?

Nena vacillates—maybe she shouldn't meet Mario. But Ronnie encourages her. Yes, go and experience it. It will help you forget Paco, at least for a little bit.

But Nena is still not sure. She needs an omen. It comes in the form of a bird. A black bird cawing and signaling that it's okay. She is anticipating her departure. And she rationalizes, When else will I have an entry into this world? The world of flamenco? And in Granada, no less!

Peña de la Platería

*M*ario and Nena arrive at la Peña de la Platería, where they hear cantaores and watch flamenco until almost five in the morning. The food is good, but she somehow feels deflated. Wishes she could share the moment with Paco. She had wondered whether she would feel anything for Mario. He's good-looking and smart, funny. But as the evening progresses, she is disappointed, doesn't even feel like flirting, and he seems disinterested as well. There's no connection. Perhaps due to the wine, she's falling asleep, wants to head back to the hostal, where Ronnie waits worried and scared, imagining all kinds of catastrophes and bad endings. Although she encouraged Nena to go, she herself didn't want to go out so late, refuses to try new things, remains safe in her Midwestern ways.

Claro, Mario agrees readily when Nena says, I'm tired. Let's go back to the hostal.

He walks her home along narrow callejones, down steep stairways that are streets, and finally to her hostal along the Río Darro. He kisses her good-night, gently, as one would handle the nísperos so as not to damage them. Nena thinks of Paco. Will she tell him about Mario? No, she decides. Better not. It was only a sweet good-bye kiss, after all. Nothing to tell.

In bed, she thinks back on the entire episode. Why did I even agree to go out with him? I could've gone to the Platería on my own. I didn't really need an escort. Maybe I wanted to see what it's like to go out with another man, to compare my feelings, to see if I could be attracted to someone else. And she smiles. Guess what? she says to herself. You failed. Paco was in your thoughts all along. Right there in your head sharing the flamenco with you. ¡Tonta!

Nena falls asleep under crisp white sheets listening to the river rushing, rushing, rushing, a gentle lullaby that brings her dreams of flamenco dancers whose duende visits her as well. She dances in her dream, guitars strumming along with the river, passion and pain and jubilant stomping on hardwood floors clicking with the castanets in her heart. The sweet-smelling orange blossoms—the same azhares from her childhood en Laredo where the sweet scent perfumes the night air here as there, now as then. The morning comes too soon—it's 10:00 a.m.—time to get up!

Ronnie insists that it was stupid to stay out so late. Regrets encouraging her. Nena ponders; perhaps she should've been scared, been more careful. How could she just go off with someone she just met? But she remembers the gypsy's words and feels protected. After their café con leche and churros, they pick up their backpacks and take a cab to the bus station. She's anxious to leave Granada—didn't even visit the Cathedral where Isabel and Ferdinand, los Reyes Católicos, are buried. She just wants to go back to Madrid, back to Paco. Mario is soon nothing but a memory. And for years after in Mexico and in Spain, she looks in the paper to see if his name appears in the list of bullfighters, but it doesn't.

Granada remains a memory of flamenco and orange blossoms, of the Alhambra courtyards filled with light and almudejar ceilings, of the austere Carlos V habitat, the king who never really lived there after spending his honeymoon in the magnificent palace. His quarters, so sober and cold after the Nazarene king's lavish rooms, and one room where you can whisper in one corner and it can be heard clearly across the room. Nena and Ronnie try it, and it sends shivers down Nena's back. What genius. She smiles—all this for sport, and for the sheer brilliance of the décor, and she basks in the architectural wonder of the place.

Nena wants to fly with the swifts, birds that fly higher and higher, that go round and round and flock to the top and then seem to kamikaze down. The view of the town from up there is spectacular, white-walled buildings topped by various shades of red tile.

On a day like today, Nena writes in her journal, Federico was killed at dawn. Shot in the ass, some claim, for being gay. For writing poems. For being who he was. He didn't deserve to die like that, no one deserves to be shot by his own people—or by anyone—for being. No doubt they shouted insults and raised their own anger toward him. Otherwise how can one explain that one of his own would shoot him, just like that, as if he were an enemy, a stranger, a threat? No doubt they were following orders. But. One must not see the target as kin, as friend. Don't think it matters in some situations, though. Was this one of those? They killed others with him, a schoolteacher, too. They must've known them. Granada was a small town in the '30s. But they did it nonetheless. In the name of God, against the communists, the nonbelievers. Los Rojos. The Republicans. That is how it was when the poetic voice was silenced forever. That spring dawn, against a rock near an olive tree between two tiny hamlets of quiet streets and somber priests. Of old women dressed in black. The shots rang out, and a light was put out, a voice defiant yet afraid, silenced, but not forever because the writings live on, Lorca's voice is still there among the olive trees and the orange blossoms, hidden, woven in the intricate lace of the doilies in his childhood home, in the ink stain on his desk. And it shouts from stages all over the world and whispers on the page . . . verde que te quiero verde . . .

Regalitos

*N*ena loves to give gifts. Always has. As a child she would bring her small offerings to her mother, her Bueli, her siblings. Sometimes it was flowers cut from the garden, precious claveles y clavelinas that she learned to enjoy and not cut after she brought them to Bueli and got a regañada for it. And sometimes she'd steal a rose and take it to her third-grade teacher, Miss Villarreal, a perfect yellow rose cut from her mother's treasured rose bush.

On her way to see Paco, she often buys red carnations from the gypsy whose eyes shine with the light of truth and of pain. Red offerings for Paco, who always welcomes the gift with a kiss. The first time, he was flustered, didn't know how to react; no one had ever given him flowers before. And then there were the trinkets bought from itinerant hippie types who attend the festivals Nena is studying. Earrings and necklaces made from bits of wire and beads, seeds, whatever strikes their fancy. Nena calls it collage jewelry, and she buys them as gifts for her roommates and other friends, las Norteamericanas as Paco calls them, and her Spanish friends, María José, Marisol, María Jesús, others. In one of these towns, someone had a monkey that she almost bought even if only to liberate it from the apparently cruel life of going from town to town, fiesta to fiesta, begging for money. The monkey's wise eyes held hers, and then he scampered off to sit on his owner's shoulder, removed a tiny red hat that he held out to her.

Paco also loves to give little tokens of affection, as he calls them. A rose on her pillow. A miniature ceramic monkey the week after she told him of the itinerant monkey she had wanted to liberate. Gifts. Regalitos.

As her departure date nears, he surprises her with a clumsily wrapped cassette and a delicately wrapped box of chocolate truffles from the chocolate shop on Puerta del Sol. He is whistling one of Agustín Lara's songs that she loves as he hands her the packages. So you remember me always, he says. A sprig of rosemary on the crudely tied ribbon, and she knows he wrapped the gift himself. It's a Silvio Rodríguez tape.

They laugh as she reads the note. In a clear, crisp script: Música de tus tierras. She appreciates the sentiment, the penmanship as well as the message—the music of your lands. The thoughtfulness. No one writes in cursive anymore, he told her one day when she wrote him a note in her nearly inscrutable longhand.

¿Mis tierras? He's Cuban!

After all, isn't Texas over there near Cuba? he teases, reminding her of the old man who had told her as much. They laugh, and their laughter sounds to her like two rain sticks in unison, trickling along. He plays the cassette and Silvio's music, and his distinctive voice singing "Mujeres" touches her. She trembles as Paco sings along . . . me estremeció . . . lo que a mí más me ha estremecido son tus ojitos . . .

She asks, And the chocolates?

Pues, son para que cada que comas chocolates te acuerdes de mí. And he hums and softly sings the Agustín Lara song, Piensa en mí cuando beses . . .

But.

In time, she develops migraine headaches triggered by chocolates. So she stops eating them. Stops remembering him every time she unwraps a Hershey's bar. But. Every time she hears the songs, the scene appears to her inner eye as if she were still there in his arms and he was softly whispering . . . piensa en mí . . .

San Fermines–Running of the Bulls

*P*amplona in July. Nena joins people from all over the world, people who have come to witness an ancient ritual, the running of the bulls. Nena is considering a separate project focusing just on bull rituals. She might include the tauromaquia fiestas in her current book. But the tradition is so fraught with controversy and is so ancient and so complex, she feels it merits a book all its own. She could include the jaripeo and the corridas from Mexico and Texas as well as the corridas down narrow streets, like the one for la Fiesta·de la Candelaria in Tlacotalpan. She would have to expand the area to include Mexico then; the tranfrontera and transcontinental aspects would be fitting for such a study. Spain. Mexico. Texas. Theorize the fiesta as a transfrontera space. Why not?

Nena can't help but judge the apparent cruelty of bullfights. But she attends nonetheless, a guest of a couple who go back to Pamplona from Madrid to the fiesta every year. Javier and Montserrat, journalist friends she met through Manolo back in the spring. La fiesta de San Fermín . . . los fermines, everyone calls the fiesta. They arrive by car and go directly to Javier's paternal home, where warm hugs and kisses greet them.

On the road she tells them of a town in Mexico that also has a corrida, a tiny town near Veracruz. Tlacotalpan, the town on the river Papaloapan. On February 2, el Día de la Candelaria. Quite a sight: the image of the Virgen and canoes full of flowers in pilgrimage down the river. When she went there as an undergraduate, Nena was surprised to see that they had a running of the bulls. But. Obviously Tlacotalpan and Pamplona are different.

Six poor, tired bulls, persuaded to run down the streets that have been cordoned off to simulate a chute, chase men and boys who run ahead of the poor animals in that small town in Veracruz. The tourists are mostly regional and townspeople come back to Tlacotalpan for the religious celebration. The colorful houses that line the streets—bright orange, hot pink, lime green—seem to be celebrating, too. Nena finds the people as colorful as their houses.

Nena is transported back to the fiesta in Tlacotalpan. She stands next to a group from nearby Alvarado, the community notorious for having a populace of malhablados, people whose language is rich with cuss words.

¿Cuándo chingados viene la Virgen? someone exclaims that morning as they wait for the procession to come by where she stands, camera in hand. And her mind wanders to her mother's story of a comadre who went to baptize her child and was terribly embarrassed because the five-year-old let out, ¡Chingado! ¡Qué fría está la agua! when the priest poured water on his head. The whole church laughed, and her mother's comadre was mortified, quickly explained to the priest that they were from Alvarado, and so the child was only speaking the way all his familiares spoke. Amada. That was the comadre's name. Beloved. Like her mother's cousin, Amadita. Amada repeated the story many times, and Nena always smiled hearing it.

Now, in Pamplona, Nena remembers, tries to share the story with her friends, but Javier and Montse don't understand the cuss words, even after she explains it all to them. However, they do understand the fact that folks from a region are known for their colorful speech. Then they start telling Jaimito jokes, jokes so like the Pepito jokes that Nena has heard all her life. She makes a mental note to share the jokes with Paco. Surely he has heard them.

Paco is to join them later. He had a deadline and couldn't leave with them, but he will fly in and meet up with them.

Pamplona is resplendent with visitors and with festival energy. She looks for the Vietnam vet from Laredo, cousin to the woman police officer from Laredo—what was his name? Celso, was it Sixto, Simón? No, that was the other guy she met in Atienza. Sonny! That's it! She looks and looks, but Sonny is nowhere in sight. He may have moved on, she surmises. Suddenly she thinks she eyes him in the midst of the crowd. But she's not sure. And it's too far to go chasing after him.

The bulls come down a narrow alley, down narrow streets. The young men run in front or alongside. Yes, it's dangerous, someone says. The journalists are everywhere.

Nena can't really get any good shots and doesn't even try to get an interview. She has decided not to work on the bull rituals after all. Still. Here she is in the middle of the crowd, cheering and waving the red kerchief, like a local.

Paco has come in and now joins them and is poking fun at the locals, at the tourists. At the foolish young men. Paco smiles. Look at the sky, he says.

She does. A flock of birds flies against the blue sky, a message in a script she can't decipher.

Pilgrimage to Santiago

*A*fter several weeks at the Salón de Raros reading up on Santiago de Compostela, Nena finally takes the night train to Santiago for the fiesta honoring the apostle. She shares her cabin with three other women: a student who studies business administration in Madrid, coming home for the fiesta; an older British woman who now lives in the States and is traveling alone, off to see the world, she tells Nena; and a mystery woman, a redhead who never says a word, whose expensive luggage and clothing set her apart from Nena and the others. Nena had considered walking the Camino de Santiago, making the thirty-day pilgrimage—almost five hundred miles from France, across the Pyrenees, and across northern Spain—to arrive at Santiago de Compostela for the saint's feast day on the twenty-fifth of July. She weighed whether doing it was a necessary part of her research but decided there was no time to do it, postponed it for another year, perhaps a jubilee year, when the pilgrimage is more intense since it offers a greater reward. She knows a couple of professors in Nebraska who lead student groups along the Camino. Maybe she'll join their group.

Nena arrives with the morning dew and the lifting of the morning fog. She finds an hostal and drops off her heavy backpack. Walks out to bright sun and finds a tourist shop with postcards. She selects a few—of the cathedral for her tía and her parents, of a figure of a

witch for Paco. She sits at a café to write the messages to her loved ones. She observes the pilgrims who arrive with sore feet and uplifted souls to hear mass in the cathedral . . . la misa del peregrino. The whole town is decked out in its finery for the fiesta. The parade includes gigantes, which some call cabezones, similar but different characters than those that appear in Corpus Christi in Toledo. And the government dignitaries parade along with the bishop and the archbishop and the leaders of the cofradías as they have for centuries to the music of the gaita, bagpipes, and drums.

Along the same streets that afternoon the socialists and the communists will also parade. What a coincidence—a socialist gathering happening at the same time as the fiesta. Nena notes that Angela Davis is one of the featured speakers at the rally. She watches both and is amused to see the same somber-looking dignitaries participate in both the religious and the political parade.

The pilgrims honor Saint James, the apostle who came to Spain when Jesus, after being crucified and resurrected, sent his followers to spread his word. When the others dispersed to the various points of the known world, James came to Finisterre, the end of the world, to tell of the man who drew him away from fishing and to preaching, performing miracles. He returns to Rome, only to be martyred, to be beheaded by the Roman Herod Antipas. His trusted apostles then brought back his remains to his beloved Galicia, land of the Gales, of bagpipes and clog shoes, so close to the other Europe and yet so far. He lies buried, forgotten for centuries, in an obscure tomb while the marauding tribes come, and so the Moors destroy a world to build their own much finer world. The Jews settle every-where; after all, Santiago was Jewish too. And in the tenth century his tomb is found again, then again in the twelfth when the town is built around the tomb. Santiago of the twentieth century is a Mecca to hikers who trek over mountain and valley to arrive tired and with aching, blistered feet but with swollen hearts to the site rendered holy by their own personal voyage, their own personal path. Later, near the end of the century, Paulo Coelho, the same as Shirley MacClaine, will arrive and grow through the path's lessons. The Milky Way led the way in ancient times; a yellow arrow, sometimes hidden, leads in modern times. A path for those who seek.

But in 1980 the path is hardly noticeable. Nena arrives with her heart in her hand and stands in awe with everyone else as the giant botafumeiro swings back and forth, a giant pendulum suspended above the throngs of worshippers. It takes eight men, brown-robed as the apostle, to hold it and swing it. The pilgrims don't all believe, don't all worship, yet they all arrive to marvel at the spectacle. It is the never-ending path to the ends of the world that never ends, that Santiago believed ended with and began when his teacher, Jesus, who died and rose again and sent him forth speaking in tongues he didn't know, to lands he didn't know existed. While Peter went to the very heart of Roman space and others stayed in Jerusalem where they worshipped under Roman law and survived—or didn't—the dark and terrible times, James came to Spain. The rupture of the old ways was more painful than the disbelief of many.

Santiago lay buried in this place under the canopy of the Milky Way, in the land of miracles. Centuries later a shepherd sees the lights and is led to the remains of the apostle James and his apostles, the three buried beneath still another tomb safeguarded for centuries. Until the pilgrims were ready to come. Past plagues and past politics the city survives. Daily life remains rooted in the many services in and out of church to celebrate the essence of the place, the life-over-death battle of good over evil, of eternal life over oblivion. Such is the stuff of human essence, and the very rocks cry out and proclaim the message for those who want to hear it. The cultures mix, and people wear azabache black as protection from evil eye, and a vieira clamshell proclaims, I am a pilgrim on the path, and everyone wishes everyone, ¡Ultreya! Buen camino, may your path be a good one. Good luck and best wishes. Like the Spanish poet Machado wrote and Joan Manuel Serrat sang, Caminante no hay camino se hace camino al andar. Nena believes that in walking one forges one's own path. The pilgrims walk with their handy cane or walking stick, or is it a shepherd's staff? Hungry and thirsty, they arrive in Santiago.

In the olden days pilgrims burned all that they had worn over the long trek. Over time, industries were born to serve the pilgrims, shoemakers and inns and food vendors and those who would rob and steal, too. Thus the Knights Templar became caretakers, and the Knights of San Antón too; they protected the pilgrims and the road, the path, the camino. So once again it is the capitalist machine, the powerful money motor that drives the belief and the commerce that makes the soul-searching possible. Even this part of the church, so far from Rome, and with its very own martyr, a sainted apostle, is bound to money wrangling.

Archbishop Monroy brings the gold from Mexico for the extravagant gilded altar. He also brings a devotion to la Virgen de Guadalupe, so her presence reaches even here. A crowned image in a minor chapel, but a Mexican presence nonetheless. And Nena notes that there is even Guadalupe devotion in Ranxo, a small township in the area of Galicia, or is it Orense? But she is dressed differently and isn't quite the same; only the name remains. But Monroy was influential and brought Mexican gold and the Mexican worship of Santiago, and no doubt this

Saint Iago, this Saint James, this Jacob, is one and the same, so why not this Guadalupe, this mother of God whose name is both Mexican and Spanish. Coatlaxupe. Guadalupe.

Nena finds another devotion in a nearby hospital chapel; San Roque is also venerated in this land. He whose wound will never heal and whose dog brings him his daily bread, faithful to the end, dies in jail and is both a pilgrim to Rome and to Santiago. But he is persecuted. A case of mistaken identity, he dies by mistake in a jail cell where the angels visit and comfort him. But the structure they built to San Roque, who is also a martyr and a pilgrim, can never rival the one to Santiago. Nena finds it comforting to sit quietly and feel the centuries of pleas and devotion and the holy response. She meditates on the meaning of it all. How the fiestas honor the saints who help the town overcome adversity of some kind or another.

It is the same Santiago that helped the Spanish kill Indians. That helped them defeat the Moors—Matamoros is his epithet, or Santiago Apostol, or Santiago Peregrino. And he is depicted as all of these. Wearing the garb and signs of the pilgrim, or on his white horse slaying Moors or leading the Christians into battle.

For the fiesta the women don their traditional dress. They walk in procession, and dancing breaks out at certain times along the route. They are in the main plaza in front of the cathedral when Nena snaps their photograph. The wide-brimmed hats on three young women and the traditional headdress on the older women intrigue Nena. She attempts to interview them, but they are called to get in line for the procession, and she is left with the images and not the words.

She wants to write Paco a letter but decides against it, tells herself, I'll just tell him what it felt like, what I saw. What I observed. Besides, one can never fully transmit the feeling of awe, of surrender, of magic that Santiago elicits.

Paco asks, The saint or the city? when she excitedly tells him of her trip.

Both, she answers. Both awed and inspired me. Believe me. I'll return some day to walk the Camino. Some day. And I'll arrive in Santiago like a true pilgrim. I'll eat with the other pilgrims and cry tears of joy. In the end, it really has very little to do with the saint. It's more spiritual than that. But. El Camino de Santiago is not for everyone.

Adiós in Madrid

When Ronnie and Giovanna leave for the States, Nena moves into Paco's piso. She has taken care of everything—the good-byes have been said, the despedidas both formal and informal done with. Still. She can't reconcile herself to the imminent leave-taking. So the day before she is to leave Madrid, Nena goes for a long walk, as she tells Paco, para despedirme, to say good-bye to Madrid. When he leaves for work, she leaves too, intent on visiting the various sites she has come to love in this city that seems to be waking up to its potential after decades of stifled growth. Nena remembers the Victor Hugo story of the young boy stolen from his family and forced to live in a box until he grows misshapen; thus he can inspire more pity and be a better beggar. That was Madrid, stifled and held back. But now Madrid is resplendent in her newfound glory, reclaiming her place in the sun. Her former splendor returns, a phoenix arisen from the oppression of the dictator, Nena thinks. La movida has hit hard, and it is a young, vibrant city that Nena is intent on remembering and holding in her heart.

As she walks out into that warm August morning, Nena realizes it may take more than a day to walk to all the places she has come to love, or at least to recognize as important sites, lugares, where she has left a bit of herself. If she were to map it all out on a time pie chart, the Biblioteca Nacional would take up more than half the pie, followed by certain places like the filmoteca, el Retiro, Plaza España, and Café Labra. She walks from Paco's place back to her old piso, on Rodríguez San

Pedro—it takes her almost an hour as she walks along Calle de Alcalá part of the way. She veers off and arrives in Plaza España half an hour later. She goes by the filmoteca and notes what films she will miss this coming week. Goes by her favorite pizza place, just around the corner. Many evenings, after seeing a film, she and Paco would drop by for pizza. The summer heat relentless. She sits at a café and orders an iced coffee. Then she walks to Sol, peeks into Café Labra. She leisurely ambles over to Plaza Mayor, walks down a side street to Librería de Mujeres. It's been a joy to have this newly opened bookstore. Then she heads north, past Cortes, past the Retiro, she walks to the Biblioteca and meditates outside for a few minutes. She walks along Recoletos, goes past the post office building, says good-bye to Cibeles, resplendent on her chariot. She slips into Café Gijón. Doesn't order anything. Just looks around and walks out. Finally, she is tired. She takes a cab to the Complutense. She had not spent a lot of time there but feels that the university is an important site, too. She walks a good twenty minutes to the metro stop and heads to the Fulbright office to say good-bye. Everyone is gracious, kind. Nena knows they are getting ready to welcome the new batch of scholars who will arrive in September. Patricia hugs her and bids her good-bye.

Finally, at sundown, Nena finds herself at Casa de Campo, walking leisurely and remembering the open-air concerts and long walks she shared with Paco. Suddenly she notices that streetlights have come on; she should head back. She has covered a lot of ground and is as tired as if she had been walking along the Camino de Santiago. She feels accomplished and takes the metro to Paco's piso. Surprised that the metro car is almost empty, she settles into a daydream. Looks down at her jeans. Dirty—she'll have to do some laundry. She will be wearing the same jeans in just two days when she boards an American Airlines plane going home. She can't believe it's happening. So fast. Time spinning faster and faster like the rollercoaster en la feria in Nuevo Laredo. That is time, she ponders. Relative. She flashes back to an article she had read in the Biblioteca, one of the last ones. Serendipitously, it was on the Aztec concept of time. She had taken notes and memorized the Náhuatl words for past and future. She feels drowsy, and in that dreamlike state she can almost hear an ancient calling in Náhuatl repeating, In ompa tihuallahqueh—the time/place we've come from. In oc ompa titztihui—the time/place we're headed to. Time. The same concept, but not.

Nena slips into Paco's apartment, exhausted. He is waiting for her. She falls into his arms, tired, excited, happy, sad, regretful—so many emotions all at once.

I have a surprise for you.

What? she asks while he is setting up a record on the turntable.

The music starts, and Nena gets teary eyed to hear Flaco Jiménez's unmistakable accordion. She vaguely recognizes the song. But.

I tried to find something that was just right when I gave you the other cassette. He notices she is crying, says, I see this one hits the mark. Si que eres Tejana, ¿eh?

Listen, he says, it's your music, but it's how I feel, and he raises the volume as Flaco sings, Al ver que el cruel destino nos condena . . . Mi bien, de que me olvides tengo miedo . . .

Time to Go Home

*N*ena can't sleep, fearful that they will oversleep. In her mind she goes over the list of things to do before leaving. All done. She's taking with her all her photos, the Xeroxed articles, her notes—all that will be in her carry-on. She'll check a large suitcase with gifts and some clothes. She has already shipped the boxes of books, discarded all her belongings that have served her well but that she cannot take with her. She lovingly packed her coffee pot and coffee grinder, a small clock, the table runner that she had bought the first week she moved into the apartment.

They arrive to find María José waiting at the terminal. Nena checks in, Paco at her side as she lines up and finally reaches the ticket counter. She's ready to go, but not.

Nena walks Paco back to his car. They don't talk. They reach the car, he reaches in and pulls out a small plant out like a trophy. Don't worry, he says, I'll take care of Suzy.

She wants to memorize him, what he looks like, the short-sleeve blue shirt, tan trousers, leather loafers, his smile. What he sounds like, his voice, his laughter. His smell. The spicy mixture of man's cologne, hair product, and his own essence.

There have been fights the last couple of weeks. Paco asks, Why are we fighting?

It's because I am leaving, Nena answers. I've already told you, I read somewhere that it makes it easier to separate, and so couples fight before they go their own way.

But.

He is not convinced. Is perplexed. What's wrong? he asked after their desacuerdo just last week. It had started out as a small trivial misunderstanding as to who was supposed to wait for whom. She thought he was coming to pick her up at the library; he thought she was coming by metro to the restaurant. Both waited interminably until both ended up back at his piso. At another time they would've laughed about it, made a good thing out of a bad one, gone out for Chinese or pizza, but not this time. The trivial minor incident had blown up into a full-fledged fight. Not a screaming, yelling, hair-pulling sort of fight—Nena doesn't do that. She avoids confrontations, can't bear raised voices or displays of anger. Paco can't bear such outbursts either. She has never heard him raise his voice, even when he is cussing under his breath at the driver who cuts in front of him or at the soccer player on TV who is not playing right.

Nena's passive fighting is subtle. Tears. Yes, lots of tears. Lots of tears and recriminations: You don't understand, do you? How can I ever make you understand? I waited for two hours. I thought something had happened to you. I was afraid you'd been in an accident. You know me and catastrophic thinking. An accident. Or worse, that you had forgotten about me.

Y ¿yo? I too waited for almost two hours and couldn't understand why you had not come. I kept thinking you were upset about something, maybe you had gone home or had gone to dinner with others. With someone else. I too was miserable, Paco complains.

That time, as other times, they end up in each other's arms. Her sollozos finally abate, his heart hurting at the prospect of her leaving. That time, as always, the sweet making up comes, and they end up in bed, loving the pain away.

Not often, but often enough, there had been long verbal fights that seemed to go on and on; they would argue, bicker, fight over petty things, but mostly over why she is leaving and why she can't stay, or at least come back next summer after classes end.

No puedo. I can't, she says. Whispers it. Wants to shout it, to yell and scream, when he presses—Why not? But all she can do is cry and turn her back to him. I can't.

Why?

I am going back to Laredo to teach. I can't. That's it. I have my job. My family. My life. My destiny. I can't. I must go back home. It's my home. Please understand.

But. Paco refuses to understand. Perhaps he can't. After all, he's been gone from home for years, and his mother, who swore she would die without him, is still alive and doing well, still mourning his father's death. Paco can't understand Nena's terquedad.

Eres testaruda. He accuses Nena of stubbornness.

Sí, y ¿qué? So what? It is who I am.

Outside the terminal she stands before him. The car is in a no-parking zone, gotta go, he says as he gives her a hug, kisses on both cheeks, and a real kiss before they disembrace.

She's stoic. Won't let him see her cry. She can tell he's holding back tears, too. He walks away. It's not until she's back in the terminal and sits down with María José that it hits her, and she bursts into tears. Nena cries softly. Her friend comforts her. Understands. They hug. As they say good-bye, María José hands her a tote bag. Here, she says, algo para el viaje, some fruit and other things, a couple of books I found en el Rastro. For the trip. She's teary eyed. I'm going to miss our chats, she says.

She takes off her earrings, made of bread dough, delicately hand-painted pink roses, and hands them to Nena. Whispers, Take them so you remember me.

Como golondrina

*O*nce on the plane, there is a delay, and they remain on the runway for two hours. Nena fears she might miss the connecting flight in Houston. She is coming home! But.

Hearing the Texas drawl of the flight attendants, she cringes. That English is not her home. She's become accustomed to the Spanish. She almost gags with the first sip of coffee. Already she's missing the strong café con leche. She imagines what Paco is doing. He was going to the office, and then he had a job to do that night for another new magazine his friend Nico is starting up. He is thinking of her, she feels it. Knows it. Suzy, the philodendron, is on his desk. He promised to take Suzy home and find her a spot next to the jade plant on the window sill. But he couldn't leave her in the car. It's too hot. All day long, every time he sees the plant he thinks of her, remembers her words, Soy como golondrina, flying home.

Rosi comes by. ¿Y eso?

Nena left it with me. She left me all her plants.

Nena settles in her seat and looks in the tote bag María José gave her. Pulls out Mercè Rodoreda's *La plaza del Diamante*. It's perfect. She immerses herself in the beautiful prose. The lyrical narrative tugs at her heart. Colometa, what a character!

She reads a passage:

Y la señora Enriqueta me había dicho que teníamos muchas vidas, entrelazadas unas con otras, pero que una muerte o una boda, a veces, no siempre, las separaba, y la vida de verdad, libre de todos los lazos de vida pequeña que la habían atado, podía vivir como habría tenido que vivir siempre si las vidas pequeñas y malas la hubieran dejado sola. Y decía, las vidas entrelazadas se pelean y nos martirizan y nosotros no sabemos nada como no sabemos del trabajo del corazón ni del desasosiego de los intestinos.

And she burst into tears. True. Her life is like that, entrelazada, entangled, intertwined with all others.

She thinks of Giovanna and Ronnie. Gone back to their lives in the US. They had worried about leaving earlier, leaving Nena to do the last cleaning, but they were reassured when she moved in with Paco. She had bid everyone at the tertulia good-bye on Wednesday. She smiles, thinking of them. Don Luis Cano, salt-and-pepper hair, thin and lively with his raffish ways, a worn leather briefcase under his arm. The poets, and others, Manolo, Antolín, Nelson, María Jesús, and the scholars, Luis, Lorenzo, María José—all smiling, raising their glass filled with the house red at la Labra. Nena remembers them and wonders if she will ever see any of them again: Manolo, long gone to A Coruña; Salvador, the poet who clings to the old forms, writes sonnets and letrillas—his favorite; Ángeles, a white-haired, older scholar visiting from Italy, where her family fled during the Civil War. Every time she returns to Madrid she'll join the tertulia. Tomás and Maru also gone; another expat who is back in Spain from Mexico, where his parents fled during the war, but whose home is Mexico, has gone back after a time in France. And so many others who come and go into her life. Those who were at the tertulia that last Wednesday toasted to her good health and her future. Ciao. Adiós. B'bye. Hasta luego.

She looks at the author's picture on the inside flap and recognizes in Rodoreda a spirit like her own. Wishes she had known about her—she would've sought her out in Barcelona. She and Paco had gone once for a very brief trip, and she had fallen in love with the energy of the city. Had vowed to return some day with enough time to amble down its streets, hang out at a café on the Ramblas, visit Sacre Coeur, learn more about Gaudí. A magical city.

Next time, she thinks. I'll look for her. And in Madrid, I'll look for Nuria Amat. She wonders if Rodoreda has been translated into English. The edition she's reading is in Spanish, 1965. Right then and there she resolves to read it in the original Catalán some day.

Hours into her flight she's almost finished with the book, but she holds off, doesn't want to let go of Colometa, not yet. Yes, definitely would've made a special trip to Barcelona to meet Rodoreda, if Rodoreda lives in Barcelona, that is.

Nena falls asleep. The book rests on her lap like a soft sigh.

Homecoming

*N*ena arrives jet-lagged but excited at the tiny airport in the out-skirts of Laredo—she remembers the old airport out on Mines Road. This one is much better and closer to her home; it's on the grounds of the old Laredo Air Force Base. Seems like the whole family is there to welcome her home. Her parents and siblings and even neph-ews and nieces. She weeps with abandon as she hugs her mother. Papi gives her a bear hug. ¡Ay, m'ija! Is all he can say. Tía Licha has joined the group but stands to the side, waiting for Nena to come to her. She does, and they hug. Al fin, she says. ¡Creí que nunca llegarías! Mami wipes a tear and doesn't say anything, just hugs and hugs.

Nena comes bearing gifts. Embroidered and crocheted doilies for her mother and tías, toys for the young kids, books for her father. A new dress for the newest niece, hand embroidered, and small mementos for everyone. Keychains, flamenco dolls, hairpins. A fancy mantilla for Tía Carmen, who has asked her to bring her a black lace one. Castanets for Xóchitl. Maja soaps for Tía Licha. Somehow it is not enough. Nena wishes she could give them the rest of it, not just the tourist trinkets, but the experience of being there, of smelling the azahares in Granada, watching flamenco in Andalucía, the crisp windy days of A Coruña, the music and vibrant life of Madrid.

Mami can't keep from smiling and beaming with love. Nena senses it. Feels the warm, loving vibes from everyone. We'll have to drive to San Juan on Sunday, Papi says, to give thanks that you are home. Nena has made the pilgrimage to the shrine to la Virgen de San Juan in the Rio Grande Valley several times and smiles and says, Claro que sí. Papi gives her another hug.

That night Martha comes over to welcome her home. They go out for dinner to an Italian restaurant Nena likes, Favarato's. The bad news is that Raúl is sick. He is in hospice in San Antonio. There's not much hope. Yes. AIDS. No idea how long he'll last, Martha says with a somber tone.

I want to see him, Nena says.

No, Martha explains, he doesn't want anyone to see him, and you don't want to. He's emaciated. You wouldn't recognize him, está hecho garras, bien flaco. No es él.

Olivia de la O, her friend from the university, joins them at Denny's for dessert. Chuy, the server, greets Nena like an old friend, welcomes her back with a hug. He was there when she used to come with Cele, short for Celestino; Cele, who came home to die. He had escaped Laredo to San Francisco. But. Eventually he came home, lived with his widowed father, waiting, the AIDS consuming him. He refused medication. He was the first, Nena tells Olivia when they remember Cele. And now Raúl. The sadness consumes Nena, and she fears that the dying will never end.

After this painful reentry, Olivia hesitates to share with her other sad news. Divorces. Separations. Scandals. Honoré is up to no good. Pobre. He means well. But. His poor wife having to put up with his babosadas. En fin, you know this town, Olivia says, there's always some tragedy. So much news, or gossip depending on your perspective. Then they turn to less painful topics. Olivia is hosting a women's conference and wants Nena to help with the arrangements. You, Martha, Rosa, Rose, all the group, las Mujeres, you must help me. Claro, Nena answers. Remember the conference when we had doña Rosario Ibarra, the activist from Mexico, deliver a keynote address, and the place was swarming with men in suits? Remember the time we wanted the state senator to pay registration? Poor Sylvia! She was mortified. They laugh. Nena knows this is home. Feels warm and tingly. She's home. At home, fitting in smoothly and easily with the familiar speech and gestures of her people. With the crazy driving. The web of family and friends that can feel like a trap but is also a cushion and a support. She feels loved. She is loved. Can't wait to get to work. Her classes don't start for another month, so she has time to settle in. She's coming back to the house on campus, old officer's quarters when the campus was an army post. She'll buy some furniture, fix it up.

The only one upset with her is her cat, Maximo, Max for short. He has moved to Peter's house, the psychology professor who lives next door, because Peter has been feeding him wet food instead of the dry food Nena and the house sitter give him. Max won't come back. Nena tries to lure him back with treats and wet food, but Max will eat the food and then rush back to Peter's.

She is quickly engulfed in the trajín of life in Laredo. Sunday carne asadas at her sister Esperanza's or at her Mom's. She relishes the daily needs of her family once again. Mami needs someone to take her to the doctor's, and Papi needs some papers translated. She must take a cat to the vet's and help a neighbor with immigration papers—there's talk that there may be an amnesty. Always so much to do, she complains, but not seriously; she's too happy to mind. Reminds herself, this is home.

Part V   Epilogue

New Orleans, 1981

A year since she came back. Late August. School is about to start. Summer was filled with writing and doing literacy work for the community. One night Nena sits at her desk immersed in her work, trying to finalize her course syllabi, preparing for classes. The princess phone by her bed startles her, rings in a demanding tone until she reaches it. Out of the blue, after months of not knowing whether Paco lived or died, there he is on the line.

Of course, she had not called or written either. Just at the beginning, a letter sent when she got home, telling him of her trip and how her family's homecoming signaled that she had done the right thing coming back to Laredo. She added a PS: this letter is written with special ink, and the letter will self-erase after your eyes have seen it. He swore that in a few days, the ink became so faded it was hard to read the words.

His voice catapults her back to Spain. I'm in Mexico, he says, ¿cómo estás?

Really? ¿En la capital?

Yes, in México City. I'm training the personnel in our Mexico office. I will be going to New York after here to meet with some of the staff there. Let's get together. Why don't you come to see me in Mexico City? O en Veracruz—I want to go see where Agustín Lara was born.

You do know that two towns claim his birthplace, Tlacotalpan y Veracruz.

Yes. I know. What do you think? ¿Vienes?

I think he was born in Veracruz, he practically says so in his song. Pero, mira, I can't go. I have classes beginning next week, and I have to prepare.

How about New York the week after?

Tampoco I can't get away . . . why don't you come see me?

¿A Laredo?

Sure.

I'm not sure. I don't have the time either, and the airport there is too small. I would have to fly to Houston first. Ya lo investigué. Not very feasible.

Well, she says, can you come to Houston? I can drive there.

No, mejor let's compromise. How about if on the way to New York, I stop in New Orleans, and we meet there? Can you get there?

Sí, that's doable. I can drive, it's not that far. Over the weekend?

Right. I leave Friday. And I don't have to be in New York until Sunday night. We have the weekend.

That sounds good. I'll call you back if I can't. Okay. Once you have the flight let me know so I can pick you up at the airport.

Vale.

They talk some more, but not too long; international calls are expensive.

As she hangs up, she panics. There's no money! She has a brand-new car, she can drive, but she has spent her last bit of savings to get by over the summer while she wrote and expanded all that research she collected in Spain a year ago.

She calls Martha, asks for a loan—not much, just to get gas and some food and spending money. I'll pay you back when I get paid in October.

No problem, what are friends for? Hoy por ti, mañana por mí. How much do you need, girlfriend?

And off she goes. She drives carefully, doesn't want to risk a ticket. All in one haul, stopping only to gas up, go to the bathroom, and grab a bite at fast-food restaurants. The entire trip she is thinking of what she will say, what he will look like. Her little Corolla resonates with the music she plays—Flaco Jiménez, Little Joe, Willie Nelson, Linda Ronstadt. She thinks about the year that has come and gone so quickly. All that she's done. All that would not have happened if she'd stayed in Madrid. It was the right choice, she thinks, trying to convince herself.

Nena imagines what it would've been like if she had stayed in Madrid, what would not have happened in Laredo—the refugee work, the literacy project, her classes, her family—she would've missed baptisms, first communions, a cousin's quinceañera in Monterrey, the day-to-day joys of being home. Drives to San Antonio with Martha and Olivia to see films, to an Elton John concert.

She also imagines what she would've been doing in Madrid—going to movies, the opera season, theater, music concerts. And of course, life with Paco. There's a blank. She can't imagine what that would've been like. No political commitment, no Amnesty International campaign, no Chicana feminist conference, nothing that feeds her passion for scholarly work. She might have produced a book of poetry, perhaps she would've already finished the book on fiestas.

What if? That is the big question. What if she had stayed?

As soon as her trip is set, she calls her friend Robin, who had been a VISTA worker in Laredo in the '70s. She welcomes Nena to her antique-filled home with a veranda, a veritable model of New Orleans architecture. She's been renting the upstairs; her good friend—almost like a sister—lives downstairs, so Robin will move downstairs for the weekend. Cool!

Nena and Paco meet in a magical city. Jazz everywhere. The trumpet and the piano music is a fitting backdrop for their reunion. A last time, perhaps. Bourbon Street bars overflowing with music and people.

When he walks through the international arrivals gate at the airport she hardly recognizes him; he's cut his hair!

Later she'll ask, Why? What if I had met you with short hair? It's not you!

I got tired. My mother said I needed to look my age. And to be honest, everyone kept telling me that in the US they don't like hippies, and if I wanted to avoid problems I should cut my hair. She laughs.

But of course, it's still you, and she kisses his earlobe. Absorbs his unique scent.

They hug and kiss right there in public in front of Robin and whoever else is watching. She doesn't care. Feels her body fit into his embrace like wearing a favorite sweater, so comforting. A warm yearning envelops her.

They go straight to a birthday party for one of Robin's friends. TGIF, someone says as they arrive, and he looks at her perplexed. His English is not quite good enough here, he tells her. She translates. But soon he is speaking Spanish to someone, a woman from Spain, an Asturiana, no less. It's no one they know, but she knows Luis; her father was a musician with the National Symphony. What a small world, ¿no? El mundo es un pañuelo.

Sabéis, Luis and Astrid have separated, she tells them. Of course, Paco knows that, but not Nena, who is sad to hear the news of their breakup. She's drinking wine and feels light-headed, won't take a toke from the joints that are going around. Neither will he.

We don't need anything to get high, he jokes with her, we're already there. And she agrees, smiling, squeezing his hand.

It's bittersweet, this reunion. Later that night they go to Restoration Hall, sit on low cushions, listen to the best jazz she's ever heard. The old men, the musicians, are jamming, playing familiar tunes their own way, improvising, just having fun. One thin man with a white mustache winks at her and goes into a solo that moves her to the depths of tears. Her heart throbs, and she feels the music is in her, in every cell of her body.

They've beaten the crowds that will come a bit later, so they get the best seats. She orders a merlot, he asks for tonic water. They take a cab home, and the sweet New Orleans misty night welcomes, engulfs them. They embrace, and it's as if they had never been apart.

They catch up. He got a promotion, which is why he is on this trip abroad to train the staff at the offices in New York and Mexico City. Publishing is going global, he tells her. Pretty soon we won't be printing anything in Europe or the US. India or China will be doing it. It's all about the money. She talks about her classes, her family, her work in the community—the conferences, the literacy classes.

You are happy?

Yes, she answers, simply.

Saturday. It's muggy, and they take the trolley to go to the park, where they walk hand in hand and talk some more; they tour the gardens, and a sudden rain shower leaves them dripping wet, and he kisses the rain from her face. They go back to the house to change, and they go on to dinner at a place where they can sit outside, a little balcony overlooking the hustle and bustle of New Orleans nightlife.

I feel so schmaltzy, he says.

What do you mean? She asks.

Stupidly sentimental and romantic, he answers.

She smiles, remembering that it was she who taught him the word.

He asks, Lobster for dinner? She nods. And we can celebrate with some bananas foster for dessert; it is supposed to be the best, according to my guidebook. Or we can have a crème brulé? he offers, remembering how she loves the sweet dessert.

She coos, Or we can have both. And share them. ¿Sí?

I'll always share my sweetness with you. Todo lo dulce y nada de lo amargo, ¿te parece?

¡Fenomenal! she says. Tomorrow I want some beignets.

After dinner, at around midnight, they go back to hear more jazz at another place where Robin's friend works as a waiter. He's been expecting them, ushers them up the stairs to a choice spot so they have a great view. The place is crowded and smoke-filled, but Nena is so happy that she doesn't notice her itchy eyes and sore throat. Tomorrow he goes on to New York and she back to Laredo. She orders a gin fizz. Enjoys the buzz and floats even higher than their spot above the music. In that state she starts talking, low, almost whispering. Te echo de menos, I miss you. He cups her hands in his, Y yo a ti. Are you ready to come back with me?

When will they meet again? Perhaps never. Perhaps when she goes to Madrid. Or when he returns to the States. But they both have others in their lives now.

I've been seeing someone, he confesses.

She looks away. I figured, she whispers. I didn't expect you to remain alone.

And you? he asks.

Yo también. A colleague. Nothing serious.

Still wanting your freedom, he accuses.

Well, yes, it's just the way I am, she answers. So?

Before boarding the plane, he holds her tight, promises to call from New York.

They will talk every night while he's in New York working, until it's time for him to leave. Small talk. Serious talk. Just as they used to do in Madrid. Going from the ridiculous to the sublime, she observes. From discussion of Reagan's political campaign and whether Felipe González will win in '82 to deep philosophical discussions about paradigm shifts, alternate realities, and the belief that in some alternate state they are together, living the life they imagined, growing old together. But no kids! No. Or maybe yes. ¿Quién sabe?

He promised to call from JFK before leaving on Friday. And he does. But she's not in. The answering machine picks up his voice, crackly with emotion. Professing his love, he calls her the pet name that she has learned to love.

Flaca, he whispers. Te quiero.

She weeps, listening to the message that night. And doesn't erase it, keeps the tiny tape. Plays it back sometimes just to hear his voice. But. With time the tape gets lost, and the machine is replaced with a digital one, no more tapes. His voice fades from her memory, and only a faint hint of it remains and comes to her in dreams.

Madrid, 2000

ena is back in Spain. She's gone back to attend a conference on Chicana and Chicano literature. Decides to stay longer. To enjoy the city, get reacquainted with it. Do some work at the Biblioteca Nacional, attend a play, an opera, a zarzuela. She walks along the Gran Vía, visits her old haunts. Loves the smell of Madrid, the nighttime putrid and smoggy feel of the city, the early-morning, washed-clean smell of the city. It is also the smell of the past. The city welcomes her. Things have changed. But not much. She recognizes the old places. She visits Señora Berreneche, who remembers her and is pleased that Nena has come by. Tells her that growing old is no fun, it is actually pretty awful. Her knees hurt. She can't even go to the nearby Aurrerá for groceries anymore. Can't see well enough to read the paper. But for the slower pace as she walks, to Nena she looks the same, the red hennaed hair, the matronly hand-knit sweater—a rebeca—over a cotton print dress.

Nena invited Martha to join her after the conference. They plan to stay in Madrid then travel to Barcelona, Italy, and France. Martha has never been to Europe and is anxious. She took the job at North Carolina and was not happy. She then went to California to teach at a prestigious university, but that too was not a good fit, so she's back in Texas, but not in Laredo, in San Antonio. Jokes that she just had to come as close to home as possible without actually coming home.

Nena takes the metro and then a train to meet Martha at Barajas airport; she teaches her how to beat the jet lag by not allowing her to sleep until that night. She insists that they get on the red double-decker tourist bus and tour the highlights. They get off at various points where Nena is the tour guide.

Puerta del Sol with the statue of the madroño—the bear and the tree that Nena informs her is the city's logo; el Retiro, with its lake and the exquisite building designed for the world's fair; and yes, she takes her to the small plaza in Lavapiés, with the statue to Agustín Lara. On their tour, they drive by La Castellana, then on Serrano, the exclusive boulevard with all the pricey stores—Gucci, Paco Rabanne, Chanel. Then they go by the Palacio, by Cortes, by Plaza Mayor and Plaza España. Nena has never done this before—been a tourist! Madrid has changed immensely, the population has exploded and everyone seems freer and more European to her eye, and yet it hasn't changed at all. The gypsy is still selling flowers at the corner near las Cortes; the café con leche and a bocadillo de tortilla are just as delicious as she remembers.

They get tickets to the opera for Tuesday night—*Tosca*. Martha has never been to an opera. You'll like it, Nena assures her even as she cringes: a Tuesday night performance. That's Paco's night for going to the opera. She wonders if after all these years he is still attending, still loyal to the seat he first sat at in the early '70s when he first moved to Madrid from Barcelona, anxious about the shift in politics, about the certain demise of Franco and the certain upheaval everyone expected. He had always loved opera. When he lived in Barcelona, he had season tickets for the Liceo. So, in Madrid, he began the Tuesday-night season ritual.

Nena often joined him when he could cajole a friend to switch seats. But that was back in 1980. She relived the experience; what joy to listen to such voices—Caballé, Carreras—Georg Solti conducting. In between acts, crossing the street to have a copita. Paco refused to dress up like the others, wore jeans and cotton shirts, maybe a corduroy jacket when it was chilly. One night he wore a blue chambray shirt she had given him and the khaki chinos that he preferred. The brown corduroy jacket made it passable, but she kept thinking how underdressed he was when all around them there were men in blue and black suits and ties; some even wore tuxedos. He dismissed them as gilipollas who didn't really care about the music, they just want to be seen sitting in what they think are the best seats—orchestra, only because the seats are more expensive. Bah!

He studied the theater acoustics and knew the mezzanine center seats were the best.

As she gets ready for the evening, Nena has an inkling that he will be there. What will I do? Greet him, of course. And introduce Martha. Wonder what he would say to see me now? Probably act nonchalant, like we just saw each other the day before. And that is exactly as it happens. At the end of the first act, she and Martha walk to the lobby for a drink of water, and as she pulls open the heavy red velvet curtain, there he is. They are face to face and can't believe it.

He smiles and looks into her eyes, Vaya, qué sorpresa.

And she too is flustered, light-headed. Hola. How are you? Martha, this is Paco.

They greet, kiss on the cheek, shake hands too.

He turns, and there is a woman with him, petite, perky, with big eyes heavily made up. Y ésta es Alicia. He introduces her.

Everyone says hello. Nena and Alicia also kiss on both cheeks.

Then he says, Venga, let's celebrate old friends. Donde siempre. And they cross the street.

Nena is nervous. Feels woozy. Has a glass of wine to calm her nerves, but it has the opposite effect. She's talking too much and too fast. She and Alicia talk about the opera and how much they like it. It's not Paco's favorite production, but he agrees that it's decent and the tenor is pretty good. Remember the one we saw . . . how many years ago? he asks. Nena says, That was too long ago. I barely remember attending, much less who the tenor was. He seems disappointed.

Tercera llamada. As they return to their seats, Martha can't stand it and is full of comments and questions.

So this is the great mystery man, she says. He is such a wimp. How could you ever be with him? I imagined him tall. I imagined him much more handsome.

It was twenty years ago. He was different. I was different. Y no sé. I was in love. Or in lust . . . no sé. He is short, but not much. I too remember him taller.

They planned to meet between the second and third acts. Martha decides not to go with her. That way you can talk, she says.

Alicia also decides not to come down. Nena and Paco talk and catch up. He leans in close to her to hear what she says, so she can hear what he says, in the tiny café where they stand at the bar. He nods to people he knows. They stare curiously, but he doesn't introduce them. They make small talk.

Yes, I'm still in publishing, still with the same publisher. But it is getting old. I'm still doing freelancing. Maybe I'll retire soon and do that full time.

¿Y el piso? ¿Igual?

Sí, aún sigo ahí. En el piso por Marqués de Zafra.

¿Y Alicia?

My partner—I told you about her in New Orleans.

Nena says, I'm glad you let your hair grow out, te va bien. He's wearing it in a ponytail, not quite salt and pepper since he never had black hair, more the blended colors of caramel and milk, swirls of white chocolate. He comments on her long hair. Still long. Still curly, eh? Yes, she says, and she automatically runs her fingers through her long tresses. She had tried to smooth it out, but the night is humid and it's frizzy again.

He wants to know all about her: Are you still teaching? Are you married? Are you still writing poems? Painting portraits? Tell me everything. Did your book on fiestas get published?

Pues sí, still teaching. I moved to another university, in California, but it was too far from home. So I came back. I'm home. No, I am not married. But I have someone and it's good. And yes, I am writing poems. And I've been painting, too. My book will be out next year. The fiestas book never did get published. I just wrote a few articles instead.

And he holds her hand a bit too long as they say good-bye, wants to know when they can see each other again.

Nena explains that they are leaving to continue their trip—Barcelona, France, then Italy, and then home.

He smiles. Oh, I see. I'll have to wait another twenty years to see you.

Pues sí, Nena teases, unless you come to see me in the States.

In New Orleans, he winks.

As they go back for the last act, they agree to meet back at the door to say good-bye.

Nena can't concentrate. She is feeling sick. Her past has come to haunt her, she thinks, like in one of those strange *Twilight Zone* episodes. I must love him, she tells herself. Why else do I feel this way? She's been with other men. Even women. But it is not the same, she muses. Never the same. No two alike. Love is such a strange malady. So euphoric, so transcending. And also so painful. Forces us to change.

She writes in her journal: I certainly changed when I was with Paco. Although I know he is not my soul mate, he is in my life to teach me about myself. How I can be stubborn and hold fast to my commitments. To my decisions. Like not cutting my hair until the dissertation was done.

She switches to third person as she writes: Silly mandas! No one holds her to them, yet she holds herself to her promises. Her mandas.

It is her choice. She insists on staying in Laredo, refuses job offers from other universities, staying close to home. Her parents now elderly and needing her even more. It's my choice, she tells others who ask why she doesn't leave Laredo, move to San Antonio or even farther. But. She does go away. She goes as a visiting professor to California but is homesick and yearns to get back. It's not home. Then she goes to Washington for a two-year stint, working on folk and traditional arts; she learns that it is not what she wants. It's not home. Maybe that's when she realizes that her love for her land is overpowering. Will not allow her other lovers.

She remembers what her friend, a Chicana writer, once told her when Nena confided in her about her doubts right after she came back from Madrid and was still ruminating and at times regretting her decision, wondering if maybe she should have gone back. Her friend had said, Es el amor de tu vida. Siempre estará contigo. Forever. He will be in your heart. Even if you had gone back, it would not have been the same. He would not be the same. It was so ideal because you knew it would end. Además, she had said, he is Spanish! You must feel some kind of betrayal, no? A Chicana loving a Spaniard! Come on!

Nena agreed; she had considered that but had never quite put it that way. She had to admit that, yes, there was a bit of that. Still. He is a human being, and the conquest was over five hundred years ago! Still. She knows she did the right thing. How long does it linger?

Forever. It's in the DNA and in your memories from lifetime to lifetime. Believe me. It would not have been ideal. You chose your family. Your land. Be happy, her wise friend had advised.

Anxious and feeling nauseous, she applauds as the music fades. There's curtain calls. Martha is beaming. I love opera, she exclaims. Once outside they easily find each other even amid the hustle of the crowd exiting the theater. It's a bit awkward. They say good-night. Nena and Alicia again kiss both cheeks, and Nena turns to Paco. It's been good seeing you, she says. She's thinking that she and Alicia could be good friends. She's kind and honest; her big, brown eyes look at the world with wonder. Nena knows Paco has told her about the time when they were together. Can tell in the way she looks at her. But it is not jealousy or meanness; instead, Nena feels a warmth, a kinship. As if she's saying, It's okay. I take care of him. He's in good hands.

Let's go get a drink, Paco says.

We really do have to go, Nena insists. We're on an early train to Barcelona.

Alicia is distracted, talking to some friends who have approached to greet her, and Paco asks, ¿En serio? You never regret going back to Laredo?

No. But I do wonder what would've happened if I had stayed or come back.

I do, too.

As she says, Bueno, me despido, she fights back tears. Kisses on both cheeks. He hugs her, and her knees weaken; she's afraid they'll buckle. Then a sudden surge of strength emanates from her core, and it's all right. She is at peace. It's a sign that it is as it should be. Her heart is happy. She is glad that they ran into each other, glad that they said good-bye this way. Closure. He deserves to be happy with Alicia, and she is happy with her life. Her work. Her family. Her loves. Happy with the Chicana feminist work she is doing now. Her teaching. Her writing. Her beloved borderlands. Laredo. It's all as it should be. But.